THE

ENGLISHMAN

WHO WENT UP A HILL

BUT CAME DOWN A

MOUNTAIN

THE
ENGLISHMAN
WHO WENT UP A
HILL
BUT CAME DOWN A
MOUNTAIN

a novel by
CHRISTOPHER MONGER

with a foreword by Hugh Grant

MIRAMAX
BOOKS
HYPERION
NEW YORK

I dedicate this book
to Karen Montgomery
without whose help
what the heck
would become-of-me?

FOREWORD

This is a remarkable novel.

It is incredible to think that until a year ago Christopher Monger's only language was Welsh and that he had never spoken, let alone written, any English in his life. To overcome this, his extraordinary looks (Chris may be only 4'3" tall but to me he will always be big), and his overwhelming personality problems is an achievement indeed. Working with him on the film of this story was a rewarding experience in so many ways, but I think the memory I will cherish most is the vision of Chris standing alone every dawn on a hillside, naked except for his beloved Welsh mud, howling to his gods with tears coursing down his bearded cheeks.

I hope you enjoy this book.

Hugh Grant
(*Anson* in the film)

ACKNOWLEDGEMENTS

In the Spring of 1993 work began turning the story of "The Englishman Who Went Up A Hill But Came Down A Mountain" into a feature film. However, after long weeks of casting and location scouting, the process ground to a halt and I returned to Los Angeles with my tail between my legs. The following Autumn and Winter seemed very very long—even in the Californian sunshine—as I waited to see whether I would get a second chance. Usually actors flee when films founder, but in this case several who had already been cast—notably Hugh Grant, Colm Meaney, Ian McNeice, and Kenneth Griffith—stayed committed to the project, thus enabling us to resurrect the film in 1994. I would like to thank them for their loyalty—and especially thank Hugh for becoming an international star over that winter and making it easier for all of us! I must also especially thank the production team—Paul Sarony and Sarah Curtis, and the designer Charles Garrad—who, with a wonderful dogged tenacity, worked throughout those miserable months with unshakeable faith in the project.

Finally I must mention my agents, Jane Villiers and Mic Cheetham, who have steered the novel and the film into the world.

CHAPTER
1

I was born in a small bed, in a small room, in a small house, in a small village set in the south-east corner of a very small country called Wales. Our village, like most Welsh villages, was a tangle of long streets and back lanes crowded between the river and the hillsides on the flat floor of a narrow valley. To the immediate west of the village rose the slopes of Ffynnon Garw mountain, to the east the slopes of Pen-y-Graig hill. Characteristically for a Welsh village of its size, it was a place where everyone knew everyone else, and everyone else's business. Any one of us could have walked through the village and named the occupant of each and every house.

We knew each other's uncles, aunts, cousins and second cousins. We knew family histories and family scandals—who had married whom, and why, and where they moved and how they had fared before they inevitably returned to our clutch of streets in the shadow of the mountain.

On one side of our house was a cobbler, Mr. Evans, on the other a general store owned by Mr. Williams. However, just across the street was a garage run by another Mr. Williams, adjacent to a butcher who was another Mr. Evans. If that wasn't confusing enough, there were two pubs, both with publicans named Mr. Morgan, and everyone else seemed to belong to the Thomas, Jones or Evans families. With a name like Monger we were definitely exotic.

This wasn't a local phenomenon since for some odd reason, lost in the mists of time, there is an extraordinary shortage of Welsh family names: open any Welsh telephone directory and you'll find pages and pages of Davies, Evans, Jones, Morgans, Thomas and Williams. To add to the confusion there are few popular first names. It's true that there was a Cheyenne Jones in my village whose father liked Westerns and a Groucho Evans whose father had been expelled from the local Communist party and took revenge when naming his son, but one is much more likely to find locals named David, Evan, John, Morgan or Thomas. In any Welsh pub there is, inevitably, a David Davies, an Evan Evans, a John Jones, a Morgan Morgan and a William Williams. Not to mention the Evan Morgan, the Morgan Evans, the William Davies and the David Williams.

Welsh people cope with this confusion of similarity by adding a person's occupation or idiosyncrasy to their name. In my village, for example, there was Evans The Bottle, who was an infamous drunk, and Evans The End Of The World who believed in an ever-imminent apocalypse and wore a sign to that effect. There was Williams the Petroleum, who owned the garage; and Williams The Telephone Box who lived in an isolated farm, though people chose to remember him by where he had been born on a bitter, snowy night.

There was Evans the Boots, Evans the Butcher—and Evans the Prize Cabbage, which described his hobby and his personality. There was Jones The Coal and Jones The Dole, and even a Mrs. Jones More Welsh, who came from West Wales, and to our ears had a stronger Welsh accent.

There was Williams The Bucket, the local undertaker, who was not to be mistaken with Williams The Death—the latter having earned his name from a perpetual, sickly, ashen appearance. I remember hearing two men talking when he passed away.

"Williams The Death is dead, then," said Evan.

"No, get away with you," replied Morgan.

Evan shook his head, "Serious, not joking, he's gone."

There was a pause while Morgan took this in, and then with the wryest of smiles he observed, "Well, fair play, it's about time and it probably suits him."

As a child I was puzzled by two men's names. One was Tommy Evans' dad, who was known as Evans Come To Me Go From Me. I thought that he was a sailor, a wanderer, perhaps a philanderer. It was years before I saw him playing in the local silver band and suddenly his name made sense: he was a *trombone* player; yes, Evans Come To Me Go From Me.

But the other man's name was a bigger puzzle since he was English and had an uncommon name to start with. Considering there were probably no other Ansons this side of the Welsh border, it would have been easy to simply call him Mr. Anson. If one insisted on giving him a title it would have been logical to call him Anson The Teacher, or Anson The School, but no, my teacher had the longest and most enigmatic name of all.

I was probably ten years old when I first asked my grandfather why Mr. Anson was referred to as The Englishman Who Went Up A Hill, But Came Down A Mountain. I expected a short answer but my grandfather paused and looked at his watch.

"Hmmm. That's a long story . . ."

"Go on, tell me," I begged.

He thought for a moment and pulled a long face, "It's not just a long story, it's a *very* long story." Though he was trying to dissuade me, his vacillation had the opposite effect, my curiosity was now piqued and piece by piece over the following days I wrung most of the story from him.

Most of the story? Well, yes. My grandfather's discomfort was caused by his not knowing what was suitable for a child's ears. Should he tell me of Morgan The Goat and his pack of illegitimate children? Of Betty from Cardiff and her purple past? Of the decimation of the village by the First World War and its effect on Johnny Shellshocked? Of mining disasters that left streets of widows? He wanted to tell me the story, but he didn't want to catch hell from my mother.

The version he related was therefore censored, as many stories were. There were versions of stories for every stage of one's life: Versions for children, versions for adolescents, versions for adults—and especially versions for strangers. It was only as I grew older that all the details were slowly revealed. The story that I will relate has been gradually gathered from conversations with my grandfather, my parents, aunts and uncles. And while I may claim to be the author, it is really their story, and the story of a Welsh village—and two Englishmen, one of whom became not just an Englishman, but The Englishman Who Went Up A Hill, But Came Down A Mountain.

CHAPTER 2.

George Henry Garrad and Reginald Arthur Anson first crossed the border on a hot summer's Sunday in 1917. Ahead of them lay the daunting task of updating large areas of Wales on His Majesty's Ordnance Survey Map. Ostensibly, it was an important job—"One must know one's own terrain in time of war," explained Garrad's superior as he ushered him from Whitehall with a sheaf of maps and a carload of instruments—but in essence it was created to keep two semi-retired soldiers out of harm's way, or in George Garrad's case, out of London, where he had managed to bore the whole city rigid.

They cut an odd sight as their open-topped, equipment-filled vehicle lumbered up a hill at ten miles an hour with Garrad's gloved hands gripping the wheel as though he were dicing with death on the race track at Le Mans.

Garrad, though not tall, was a large man with cheeks purpled by a lifetime's indulgence in strong liquors and rich foods. As a man who had lived his life in the far corners of the British Empire, at variance with all around him, and imagining treachery at every turn, his features had set in the deep creases of lifelong suspicion. Folds of skin fell from the corners of his eyes and mouth. His pupils lurked under hooded, unhappy lids. He looked the wrong side of fifty, but he was possibly nearer forty.

Anson, in stark comparison, was in his thirties but looked younger. Tall, with the lithe figure of an adolescent athlete, he had the open features of a youth. His skin was pale, almost opalescent. His eyes had the healthy sparkle of the naturally curious. Whereas Garrad had spent his life trying to close himself down to all around him, Anson had spent his recent life trying to wake up.

Through thick motor-goggles Garrad glared at the road ahead and saw the sign he had been dreading, "Welcome To Wales."

He grunted and muttered something under his breath which was swallowed by the roar of the struggling engine.

"Are you sure you wouldn't like me to take over the driving?" asked Anson. Compared to Garrad, he looked utterly relaxed, taking in his surroundings with the simple enjoyment of a man who had lived too close to death, and had assumed that he would not live to enjoy such idyllic scenes as surrounded him today: the hedgerows were filled with flowers, a swift took a fly on the wing, a cow bellowed, and the landscape stretched out endlessly before them . . .

"No thank you, I'm absolutely fine." Garrad resented Anson's offer. As the senior officer Garrad felt that the car was his and moreover that he, and only he, was qualified to drive it.

"I just thought you might be tired," continued Anson blithely.

"Do I look tired?" snarled Garrad. Was Anson implying that he was old? Perhaps he was a little older, but for God's sake!."

"No, not at all, I was just being polite," smiled Anson.

Garrad testily chewed his moustache, "Besides," he barked "I thought we'd stop soon. Can you find that first blasted village on the map?"

That was the other reason why Garrad insisted on doing the driving. Even after twenty years of surveying for the British Empire, he was still absolutely hopeless at reading the simplest map.

While Anson had seen the horrors of battle and won almost every decoration available to a British soldier, Garrad had advanced up the ranks through a spectacular series of failures, aided and abetted by his singularly irksome personality. Commanding officers never failed to recommend him for other "most suitable" posts far, far away from them. He was too inefficient to follow orders and thus had been promoted to those higher ranks where he could do less harm, since he was now below the men who made real decisions, and above those men who actually had to carry them out.

He was much too boring to have in one post for long, and had thus been transferred up and down the length and breadth of the British Empire, and back. After India, Africa, the Middle East and the Far East, there was only one place left where he hadn't served: Wales.

Wales! The very mention of the place made Garrad's bile rise. An insignificant region full of ragamuffins and gypsies, miners and reprobates. The roads were rutted, the houses substandard, and the hills ran amuck with bleating, filthy sheep. The Welsh were scoundrels who were renowned for letting their gardens and their children run wild. It was even said that they scoffed at the English Crown. One could barely put up with these things in the far-flung areas of the Empire, but, damn it, this was right smack on England's front door. The area was, frankly, an embarrassment.

The inhabitants made it worse by pretending to have a language of their own which was, Garrad suspected, a type of German dialect. Thus he was unsure where their sympathies lay in the Great War currently being waged. Garrad felt that he was entering a very menacing land, full of people who could not, and should not, be trusted.

The car crested a hill, affording them, momentarily, a spectacular view of rising ridges before it quickly started to descend and gather speed. Garrad gripped the wheel and tried to downshift. The gear box screamed.

Anson merely glanced at the map before announcing, "I think the village should be visible very soon." As soon as he said it, Ffynnon Garw appeared before them.

Damn Anson, thought Garrad, does he have to be right all the time?

Morgan The Goat, a ginger-haired reprobate of unquenchable thirst and lust, was lying in bed on this particular Sunday morning watching with great sadness as a beauty known as Betty From Cardiff gathered yet another layer of petticoats around her luscious frame. He hated seeing her cover her body with clothes: it was like using a perfectly ripe, juicy peach to make jam—a complete waste. If Morgan had his way, Betty would never wear a stitch of clothing ever again, or leave his bedroom for that matter.

"I'm not coming again," announced Betty.

"Don't say that," said Morgan and tried to pull what he thought was an angelic expression, "you know my heart would break."

"Your what?"

"My heart!"

"Ha."

"But Betty, my love," crooned Morgan.

"Your love? If I was your love you'd want me here as your wife—and your partner—fifty-fifty."

That was the least of what Morgan had promised when he first seduced and borrowed money from her months ago, but lately he seemed to have forgotten. It was money she had earned the hard way, and she was damned if Morgan was going to walk off with it.

"You're a tough woman," sighed Morgan. Over the years he'd made many rash promises to many gullible women. Why did Betty take it so personally?

She was about to reply when her attention was disturbed by an approaching car which she assumed was coming for her. "He's early," she said, and Morgan was suddenly glad that she was leaving. One can, after all, have too much of a good thing.

It wasn't however, a car for Betty, but Garrad and Anson pulling up outside. If the village had a centre, they had stopped in it. There was a small square bounded by a chapel, a miner's institute hall, an inn, several houses, and a police station. In the centre of the square was a flagpole, flying the Union Jack. That flag—(the King's flag, the Empire's flag, *his* flag)—and the police station, made Garrad feel slightly more comfortable.

He stayed in the car and waited as Anson walked towards the inn. Garrad wasn't moving from his comfortable driver's seat until he was certain that the place was open for business. He liked to pretend that his war wounds played up in warm weather, but the only wound he had suffered in his entire career was when he had impaled himself on his own dress sword, stumbling down the steps of a restaurant in Bombay after a night of gin and gambling.

Anson paused to gaze at the hill which rose behind the pub. He fancied that this would be the first hill which they would survey. He couldn't wait to get out into the country and stretch his legs.

The sounds of a choir filtered down the street from the chapel. Garrad shuddered. They were singing in Welsh and it sounded deeply mournful and horribly foreign.

"Come on Anson! Haven't got all day!"

Anson came out of his reverie—the hill looked so pretty in the morning light with the sun playing on the heather—and rapped at the pub door.

Garrad frowned at the sign, "Yr Ffynnon," more Welsh! "Proprietor M. Morgan, licensed to sell Wine, Spirits and Tobacco." Well, at least the important part was in English. Anson knocked again.

Upstairs, Betty tidied her hair quickly as Anson's insistent knocking continued. "Tell him I'm coming as fast as I can!"

Morgan pushed back the sheets, moved lazily to the window, and shoved it open to find two unfamiliar faces staring up at him. Without thinking, he spoke in Welsh and cursed the strangers for waking him on a Sunday morning when, unlike him, any respectable, God-fearing person should be in chapel.

Reginald Anson stared at him blankly. For a moment he didn't even recognize Morgan's words as language, but then he replied very slowly and clearly, "Excuse–me–but–does–anyone–here–speak–English?"

Bloody English! cursed Morgan in Welsh before pasting a smile across his face and switching to English.

"Oh, English are you? Well that would explain every-thing—they're all in chapel, it's Sunday."

"Yes," said Anson, "we know it's Sunday but what we were wondering was . . ." His voice petered out because Mor-gan The Goat had disappeared from view, slamming the win-dow shut behind him.

Morgan had confirmed all of George Garrad's preju-dices: a bare-chested, ginger-mopped, German-speaking moron with the manners of a pagan ape. "Charming," he said, "I think we'll press on, don't you agree Anson?"

Anson was just getting back into the car when the door to the pub opened and Morgan lumbered out, pulling on a shirt which had seen better days, and swigging a pint of beer.

"Well?" said Morgan, "Do you want to come in or don't you?"

Garrad saw the alcoholic beverage in Morgan The Goat's hand, and deciding that he'd done quite enough driv-ing for one day, was out of the car and limping into the inn as fast as his gouty legs would carry him.

How extraordinary, thought Anson, as he incredulously watched Morgan and Garrad disappear together. Only mo-ments before they had eyed each other with suspicion, but now they were joined in the international brotherhood of al-

cohol. Anson shook his head and started to unload their
mountain of luggage.

—ɯ—

As Morgan had said, all the God-fearing members of the village were in chapel—which included everyone except Morgan The Goat, and the village police sergeant whose job it
was to protect the district from invasion while all were at
their prayers.

The air was thick with singing, and the smell of mothballs which all used liberally to protect their Sunday best. As
the hymn finished the congregation sat carefully—trying to
avoid creases—and prepared themselves for the worst as Reverend Jones entered the pulpit and opened the mighty Bible to
find his text. Before he began, he stared hard at the assembled
throng as if he knew their each and every sin.

Though he was an elderly man with watery eyes, he cut
a terrifying figure. From his frail body he could produce the
roar of a tiger. From his ancient mind he could conjure sermons to make even the most pious quake. If the village had a
leader it was the Reverend. During the week he was never
very far away as he traversed the length and breadth of his
parish dispensing moral guidance, and nothing escaped his
eagle eye. And while he visited the villagers on six days of the
week, on the seventh it was their turn to come and pay their
respects to him, both in the morning and in the evening.

"Oh the arms of the wicked shall be broken!" started
Reverend Jones quoting from the Old Testament. He liked the
Old Testament, it had so much more vigour than the newer
stuff which tended to creak with love and forgiveness. Just in
case any of his congregation had missed his text, he repeated

it, and punctuated the sentence by slapping the Bible with a blow worthy of a lumberjack half his age. That made his audience pay attention.

He gazed out at them again, and did not like what he saw. Since most of the young men had gone to war there seemed to be a profusion of unmarried mothers with ginger-haired babies. There was no doubt in Reverend Jones' mind as to who was the father of this illegitimate crowd, and every week he preached against Morgan The Goat—and the war in Germany—though he never mentioned Morgan by name, of course.

"Well, well, well, the arms of the wicked shall be broken," he lowered his forehead and stared through his bushy eyebrows, knowing that this was his most frightening expression. Grown men in the congregation quaked. Children sank deeper into their mothers' arms. The very pews seemed to step a foot back from his glare. It was a look to stop a charging bull at ten paces.

"Wouldn't it be nice if all the Germans were on the battlefields of France, easy to spot, easy to break, wouldn't it, eh?" For a moment his face softened, he broke out into a gentle smile, and caught his audience fully off their guard as he once again bellowed and slapped his pulpit, "But! They are not! Some of them are here, in this very village!"

He pointed an arthritic finger to a window in the south wall of the chapel, through which all could see Morgan's pub. As far as the Reverend was concerned all pubs—and Morgan's in particular—were the work of Satan. If pressed (and there were few who dared) he would admit that alcohol seemed to appear in the Bible and that St. Paul even appeared to put in a good word for it. However, the Reverend would vehemently argue that he had seen too many men ruined by the drink for it to be a good thing. Worse, in his opinion, were the families who starved because the household wage had been spent in the pub. And worst of all was the licence that people gave themselves when drunk. If the Reverend could have had a prayer come true it would have been for Morgan and his pub to be struck by a thunderbolt.

—⁕—

Anson fought through the low-beamed door with armfuls of luggage and found that Garrad was already propped up at the bar swigging a gin and tonic.

"What's yours?" asked Morgan.

"Excuse me?"

Morgan spelled it out, "What do you want to drink?" It wasn't a difficult question. This Englishman seemed a bit slow.

"Oh," Anson struggled to set down several heavy items, Garrad didn't come to help him, "I didn't know one could drink in Wales on a Sunday."

Morgan rolled his eyes, and parodied Anson's posh grammar, "Well *one* can't, but you're my guest, so what do you fancy?"

Anson wiped the sweat from his brow, the surveying equipment was heavy, "Well in that case, I'll have a pint of bitter."

"A pint of bitter coming up," said Morgan and was pulling the pint when Betty's voice boomed from above them.

"Morgan!"

Morgan stopped in mid-action, and without a word of explanation, ran from the dim bar and up a rickety flight of spiralling stairs.

Anson stared forlornly at the half-pulled pint. Then, as his eyes became accustomed to the gloom, he looked around. Low oak beams supported an uneven smoke-coloured ceiling. The flagstone floor was not clean, but then again it wasn't filthy. There were sturdy tables and benches, most of which bore the detritus of the previous night's drinking. Three steps led from the main body of the bar into another smaller room with a large fireplace and comfortable chairs. Two windows looked out onto the village square while a third revealed a large garden overgrown with wild flowers. Anson thought it was peaceful and quite charming. "Pleasant enough sort of place," he remarked.

"I suppose so," said Garrad, as he swilled down his gin, "considering it's Wales."

Morgan reappeared, at speed, and Anson again anticipated his pint of cool beer. However Morgan rushed to his money box and grabbed some notes, explaining that upstairs he had "A valued guest, a regular, and very particular." And without another word, he disappeared from view again. Anson was beginning to feel very, very thirsty.

Upstairs Betty was livid. Right in the middle of their argument about the money that he owed her, Morgan had disappeared to open his doors to a pair of strangers, and promptly settled down to drink with them. She'd had to yell like a common trollop to get his attention and now, after a good haranguing, he had returned with just a few measly notes.

"A little something to tide you over," he winked and fondled her bottom, "You were worth every penny, my lovely!"

What was Morgan insinuating? "You bugger!" she started, and decided right then and there that the best way to knock some sense into him was with a warming pan. She grabbed it from the bed and swung it at Morgan. He ducked and Betty smashed a vase of flowers.

"Now, now, lovely," said Morgan, "you might do yourself an injury."

"Do myself an injury?" snarled Betty, "I'm going to do you a bloody mischief!" and swung again, this time raking a picture from the wall.

Downstairs Anson and Garrad waited in silence, listening with some embarrassment to the fight raging upstairs in Welsh. They were far too polite and English to discuss what they could hear. Instead they both searched the room, looking for an alternative topic of conversation. It was very difficult, since the voices upstairs continued to rise and the crashes became more frequent.

The tension was broken by the arrival of a motor car which pulled up outside and honked its horn. Anson was glad to have something to talk about, "This is turning out to be quite a busy spot," he observed.

"That's one way of putting it," said Garrad and slyly poured himself another gin before Morgan returned.

Morgan limped down the stairs, nursing a bump on his forehead. "Now where was I?" he asked before noticing the half-pulled pint. "Ah, that's right." He grasped the glass and with two sharp tugs on the pump, filled it to the brim. Anson had been contemplating this pint of beer for some time. He'd been thirsty when he had arrived, and had had some time to anticipate its flavour and coolness. His thirst, one could say, was now more than ready to be quenched . . . However, Morgan—parched from his fight with Betty—proceeded to drink the pint himself. Anson watched in horror as Morgan swallowed it down in a few, fast gulps.

"Excuse me!" exclaimed Anson, but he was interrupted again by Betty flouncing down the stairs and slapping Morgan's money on the bar.

For a moment Anson was going to introduce himself to this very attractive lady, but on consideration this didn't seem the right moment. Her eyes were fixed on Morgan with a look that could roast sweetmeats.

"You can keep your . . ." she hissed, and stopped herself just before she let loose an unladylike obscenity. She gave Morgan one last venomous look before turning on her heel, storming from the room and slamming the door behind her.

Outside in the square a chauffeur driven car was waiting.

"Did you have good weekend?" asked the chauffeur.

"That bloody Morgan!" replied Betty and urged him to drive off quickly before she was tempted to go back into the pub and sever Morgan's head from his body.

Anson and Garrad, English to the core, avoided looking at each other, or Morgan. They couldn't abide intimate, emotional scenes of any sort. They both felt that if they just ignored and failed to mention the incident with Betty, then it would not have occurred.

Morgan could shrug it off easily—but then he saw the averted, embarrassed eyes of his English guests.

"She comes every weekend, all the way from Cardiff, just for the good mountain air, terrible trouble with her chest." He was improvising wildly, but it came easily.

"All the way from Cardiff? Just for the weekend? Ex-

traordinary." Said Garrad, which was his way of politely calling Morgan a liar.

The subtlety was lost on Morgan, "Well," he grinned
and pocketed the money she had refused as part payment of
his debt, "when money's no object . . ."

This was all very interesting, but Anson was now thirst-
ier than ever, and becoming quite irritable, "Look, I really
would like a pint of beer!" It came out rather stronger than
he meant, a tendency which had developed since he was in-
valided out of the war.

"Now, now," said Morgan, hurt by the tone of his voice,
"no need to get all English about it!" He immediately started
to pull another pint for Anson.

No need to get all English about it! Garrad was about to
respond to that defamation of character when the door
opened and in walked the local police sergeant. Garrad, only
too aware that he was technically breaking the law by drinking on Sunday, coughed up some gin. He was a terrible coward. He composed himself and put on what he thought was
his most authoritative face before smiling at the policeman
who had, until that moment, failed to even notice him.

The burly sergeant slumped onto a stool. He had
traipsed down to the allotments and back along the river,
looking for a stray dog that was reportedly harrying sheep.
Twice he thought he'd seen something, but it was too quick
for him. It was too hot a morning to be running around. He
removed his sweaty helmet to reveal a red welt running right
across his forehead.

He sighed "God I hate the summer." And only then did
he register the strangers.

Garrad, who felt compelled to introduce them formally
and explain his drinking, announced grandly "Morning;

George Garrad, and this is my assistant, Reginald Anson. I think the innkeeper will confirm that we are his guests."

Sergeant Thomas couldn't have cared less. As far as he was concerned the English laws dealing with the selling of alcohol were invented solely for England and the English. They were the ones who seemed to be harmed by alcohol, whereas the Welsh, Scots and Irish could drink it all day, every day, and suffer no ill effects whatsoever. He noted Garrad's accent and his rather silly clothes. "English are you?" he asked with the slyest of grins.

Anson returned the smile, "Yes, actually." The smile disappeared from his face when he saw Morgan hand the beer to the sergeant. Surely that was *his* beer! Would he never get a drink?

The Sergeant looked at their mound of luggage and noticed two striped poles sticking out of the sea of cases, "Surveyors are you?"

"No," replied Garrad grandly, "cartographers actually."

Garrad could call himself what he liked, but the sergeant had only known this type of Englishman to be after one thing, "Looking for more coal I suppose," he guessed.

Garrad corrected him, "No, we're map-makers."

Anson wanted to ask Morgan where the hell his beer was, but Morgan had wandered off, collecting dirty glasses from the night before, and it was difficult to interrupt the Sergeant and Garrad.

"Map-makers?" The Sergeant was genuinely surprised. Who needed a map of this village? There were only a handful of streets, why, he could have drawn up a map in ten minutes.

But Garrad continued, "We've come to measure the mountains."

The police Sergeant smirked. "Very useful I'm sure," he said and took another swig of his pint.

Garrad did not like this policeman's tone and was damned if some village bobby was going to patronize him and the work of the British Empire. "I'll have you know," he sat erect on his stool and puffed out his chest, "that it's an important part of the war effort." He repeated the lie that his commanding officer had fed him, "One must know one's own terrain."

"Well," interrupted Morgan, "you've come to the right place, because that there is some terrain." He pointed out of the pub's back window, up to the hill that Anson had noticed earlier. "That," said Morgan proudly, "is the first mountain in Wales."

They all moved closer to the window to get a better look.

"Whatever do you mean," asked Garrad, "the first mountain in Wales?"

"Well if you come from England, as you did . . ." started Morgan.

"Or up from the coast . . ." continued the sergeant.

"That's the first mountain you encounter," concluded Morgan, "and when you see that you know you're in Wales."

How absurd, thought Garrad, it's nothing more than a little hill.

"What's it called?" asked Anson who also thought it was rather small, but nevertheless quite pretty.

"Ffynnon Garw," the sergeant and Morgan spoke as one.

"Good God!" exclaimed Garrad, "these Welsh names! Could you repeat that?" He was sure they'd made it up as a joke.

"Ffyn-non Gar-w," said the sergeant. "Look, I'll write it down for you so's you'll get it right on your map doings."

Garrad snorted, "Of course it will only appear if it's over a thousand feet."

Morgan looked at him as if he were mad, "Don't be *twp*," he said, "that's well over a thousand."

Anson and Garrad exchanged glances—they very much doubted it. Still, they didn't have to say so, yet.

Morgan returned to the bar and noticing the Sergeant's empty beer glass, forgot that he had never served Anson. "Another for you Mr. Anson?"

—⁂—

From within the pub Sergeant Thomas could hear the rousing harmonies of the Sunday service's final hymn echoing from the chapel, which gave him just enough time to finish off another pint before resuming his job and giving the villagers the appearance that he had been hard at work all morning, patrolling the village. He was keen to be at the chapel's front door when the congregation left so as to share his news.

"The English are in the pub, they say they've come to measure the mountain!" he told Megan Evans.

"Seen them with my very eyes, two of them, with measuring equipment," he told Davies The School.

"Measuring it for the war, they say," he told Thomas The Trains.

And Megan Evans told Blodwyn Davies, who told Branwen Jones, while Davies The School told Reverend Jones, who told Jones The Post, while Thomas The Trains told Williams The Petroleum, who told Thomas Twp who went home to tell his brother.

In less than an hour, every man, woman and child within five miles of the village had a detailed description of the two Englishmen, the car they had arrived in and the equipment they had brought with them. Moreover, they knew that Garrad liked gin, but Anson preferred beer, and that while both men were somehow attached to the army, they didn't wear uniforms.

But most of the gossip concerned the reason for their visit: they had come to measure their mountain, the first mountain in Wales.

The first mountain in Wales? Garrad had asked, and well he might, but it was something the villagers had claimed since time immemorial. They couldn't claim to live among the biggest mountains of the north, nor the beautiful mountains of mid-Wales, but they could claim to live in the shadow of the first mountain inside the Welsh border. And while they had defined it, it had come to define them.

Not many centuries ago Anson and Garrad would have been greeted by a Morgan The Goat who would have offered them a whack from the better side of his sword. In these more civilized times he had used beer to bring them crashing to their knees. His line of attack may have differed, but the underlying sentiment was unchanged.

The ancient country of Wales was now a Principality of England and the historical battle-fronts had been reduced to a bureaucrat's simple line on a map. And while the border was no longer a political divide, it nevertheless described a place of great and deep transition. To this very day one can drive the road that Anson and Garrad drove and find, as they did, that people speak English until the hills start, and then, with the hills, the language returns to the tongue of the ancient Britons: Welsh.

Within the space of a few miles the colouring of the inhabitants is noticeably different, as the flaxen-haired Saxons are replaced by dark and red-haired Celts. The vegetation changes as the oaks and sycamores give way to birch and mountain ash. The lush meadow grass of the English border counties are succeeded by the tough crouch that covers the Welsh hills. Neat fences are exchanged for drystone walls.

One cannot live in such a border area and be neutral: one belongs to one tribe or the other, in this case English or Welsh. The mountain that Garrad viewed with his jaundiced eye is either an aberrant mountain at the edge of lowland England or the first of many in the country called Wales. The people of Ffynnon Garw had made their decision centuries ago and stuck to it: they were Welsh, this was Wales, and this would be known forever as the first mountain in Wales.

CHAPTER
3

While the vast majority of locals lived on the floor of the valley, some braved the slopes of the surrounding hills and mountains. There were perhaps a half-dozen farms in the immediate area, clinging like aged, yellowed teeth on ridges of inhospitable gums. The farms were, consequently, sturdy, no-nonsense buildings, constructed to weather the worst of the winter storms which whistle through from the stark Atlantic ocean.

In such a farmhouse above the village two elderly brothers stared out at the mountain. They were the twins of the late Mavis and Thomas Jones, a sweet couple who had been daft, simple people, or as the Welsh say, *twp*.

With little imagination these parents would have found it hard enough to come up with a name for one child, and were absolutely stumped when they were blessed with two.

With a perfect lack of inspiration they had named one son David Thomas, and the other Thomas David, and promptly mixed them up. On some days they would both be David, on others they would both be Thomas. Finally the parents decided that they preferred the name Thomas to David and both boys, now elderly, had thus come to be known throughout the area as Thomas Twp and Thomas Twp Too.

The brothers had only a few crops and a small herd of cows, since their principal business was sheep. They would not be able to tell you the acreage of their farm but nevertheless knew every step of it. They walked Ffynnon Garw by day and by night, in summer and in winter, tending their flock.

Thomas Twp sat near the log fire and stared out through the door where his brother Thomas Twp Too was standing. Though the cows needed milking, neither brother moved. They were paralysed with questions and worries all brought on by the arrival of the English.

"I don't see that it's possible," said Thomas Twp. "How will they measure it?"

"And what would they be doing with the measurement once they've got it?" asked Thomas Twp Too.

"By God, that's the worry of it," replied Thomas Twp.

They both continued to stare at the mountain, deep in thought. Finally Thomas Twp broke the silence.

"The English only come when they want something."

It was a sentiment shared by Reverend Jones as he walked home to his small, spartan cottage. Over the long span of his life he had seen the English come when they wanted Welsh iron, the English had come when they wanted Welsh coal, the English had come when they wanted Welsh taxes, and the

English had come when they wanted Welsh soldiers to fight their war with the Germans. He had little time for the English and the war they were waging with their European cousins. As far as he was concerned the English *were* Germans. After all, isn't that where the Saxons came from when they invaded the British Isles?

And now these barbarians had come to measure the mountain, the village's mountain, *his* mountain, and while the Twps were concerned with the simple question of "How?" Reverend Jones was more concerned with the bigger question of "Why?"

He considered the philosophy and practice of map making. The most innocent maps were concerned with helping one from place to place. The English already had those— they'd found the way here, hadn't they? No, they didn't need new maps for that. The more the Reverend pondered the subject the more he concluded that maps, by and large, were made for less than altruistic purposes: maps were made to define the borders of property, more for reasons of exclusion than inclusion, it seemed to the Reverend. Maps were made to measure properties for taxation. Maps were made to define borders and thus became more and more important in times of war.

Moreover, he had heard that these men, these Englishmen, were from His Majesty's Ordnance Survey. Apart from "His Majesty" there was another term in that title that the Reverend didn't like: ordnance. Wasn't that a synonym for bombs and ammunition? The more the Reverend thought about it the more suspicious he became.

Anson and Garrad, blithely unaware of the controversy they had engendered, were dozing in the pub garden. Morgan had served them a frugal lunch of bread and cheese with some fresh lettuce he'd filched from a neighbor's garden. While lunch may have been meagre, Morgan had filled them up with glass upon glass of his strongest beer. Garrad was snoring in the hammock, Anson was asleep in an old wicker chair.

"Can I get you gentlemen anything else?" asked Morgan as he woke them and offered yet another jug of dark, murky ale.

Garrad woke with a start, for a moment he thought he was back in India, "Good God, no!" It was the first time he'd turned down a drink in many years, but the Welsh beer, and the summer sun, had disturbed his equilibrium.

Anson woke slowly, feeling that he'd been hit on the head by a largish oak tree, before sliding down a rocky ravine and lying in the path of a herd of galloping elephants, "Very kind of you," he managed, "but absolutely no thank you."

Morgan left the beer with them anyway. "Well I'll be off then," he said, "have to take the dog for a walk, help yourself to anything you fancy, and don't wait up, so if there's nothing else . . ."

He started to leave at speed but Garrad had remembered something.

"There is one thing, Mr. Morgan, I know it's hard to find able-bodied men in these times of war, but we will require the services of a porter."

"To carry our equipment," Anson elaborated, "and he'll have to be quite strong."

Garrad continued, "His Majesty's Ordnance Survey will provide some remuneration."

Morgan stared at him blankly. "Remuneration?" He'd never heard of such a thing.

Anson explained, "They'll pay—but I'm afraid it's not very much."

"Oh," said Morgan and racked his brains. "Those that aren't in France are down the mines. Of course there's Johnny Shellshocked."

Anson's face clouded, he knew only too well the state in which some men had left the front. He had seen dozens reduced to gibbering fools, their minds destroyed by months of continuous explosions from heavy armaments.

"Johnny Who-the-heck?" asked Garrad.

"Johnny Shellshocked," repeated Morgan, "back from the war, gone a little doodle-alley-tap, poor thing. Lives with his sister."

"Hmmm," said Garrad.

"Oh," said Anson.

"But he's strong," continued Morgan, "and fine as long as you don't need him to talk—or think."

"Perhaps we could meet him tomorrow?" suggested Anson.

"Absolutely." said Morgan, "So, if there's nothing else?" He didn't give them time for another question before hurrying on his way.

Garrad watched his hasty retreat. "He seems to have rather an impatient dog, wouldn't you say, Anson?"

Anson hadn't really noticed, he was thinking about Johnny Shellshocked.

Meanwhile Morgan was thinking about Johnny Shellshocked's lovely sister Blod, whom he was rushing to see. For some months now he'd been managing affairs with both Blod and Betty. Blod, like all the women in the village, would not set foot in a male enclave like the pub, whereas Betty came to stay at the pub on Saturday nights, and Morgan saw to it that she never made an appearance in the village. On Saturdays, Betty arrived when Blod was at the market in Pontypridd, and on Sundays Betty left when Blod was in chapel. It seemed to Morgan that he had come up with the most perfect arrangement.

It was however, well nigh impossible to keep secrets in Ffynnon Garw and it hadn't been long before Blod learned of the posh lady from Cardiff who visited each weekend "for her health." She had been seen arriving in a chauffeur driven car. Her clothes, it was said, were very fine, very Cardiff. These facts made Blod less suspicious: what would a woman like that be wanting with Morgan The Goat? However, she knew exactly what Morgan would be wanting from a woman like that . . . Increasingly Blod was asking questions, and Morgan knew that it was only a matter of time before one or both caught him out.

Morgan's excuses for not seeing Blod on a Saturday night were getting thinner and thinner and, knowing Morgan as she did, Blod couldn't imagine Morgan putting up with a customer who was "so demanding as to keep him up all night."

This evening, however, he was lucky for he could distract Blod with the news of the English. Apart from the Sergeant, he was the only villager to have actually met them and Morgan was making the most of his privileged information. He described their arrival with embellished detail, making it sound like the entrance of the Queen of Sheba.

Mr. Garrad, in Morgan's theatrical re-telling, was a very important, but, nevertheless, pompous oaf, who had travelled the world and found Morgan's inn fit to compare with some of the most salubrious places he had visited.

Anson, on the other hand, had made far less of an impression. Morgan described him as a bookish type who had probably been breast-fed into his twenties and was suffering homesickness after a single day away from home. So much for Morgan as a judge of character.

"How long will they be staying?" asked Blod.

"Well as long as it takes," replied Morgan who hadn't the faintest idea.

"But how long will that be?"

"Days," replied Morgan, and then in a fit of optimism added, "perhaps weeks."

He had no idea how they would measure the mountain and naively thought that since it was such a large object it would obviously take a long time. Morgan was looking forward to a very lucrative summer. He was hoping to make some good money off these Englishmen, and with the way Garrad drank gin . . . Morgan was already calculating a healthy profit.

"Weeks?" Blod didn't know anything about measuring mountains either, but common sense told her that if it took weeks to measure one mountain, they wouldn't yet have maps of the whole country.

Morgan evaded her question, he liked to appear knowledgeable, especially since she was a woman. He changed the subject, "And I think I've managed to get Johnny a job with them."

"Johnny? A job?" Blod wasn't pleased. Johnny wasn't ready yet.

"All he'll have to do . . ." started Morgan, but Blod interrupted.

"We'll talk about it in the morning."

—〰—

At dawn Anson was woken by the familiar sound of men in hobnailed boots tramping through the streets. But when he rose and looked out of his bedroom window he saw not soldiers but miners, returning from the night shift. They were uniformly covered in matt, black dust. Their eyes shone out of their faces like the eyes of concert hall minstrels. Only their lips were clean, and appeared oddly feminine, as if painted with glossy rouge.

He tried to go back to sleep, but a cacophony of scrubbing began, as every housewife attacked her doorstep with vigour. Next came the sounds of horses and carts as each village shop took their morning deliveries from the local farms. In no time at all, children were playing in the street. Anson decided to shave and made his way down to the kitchen to see if Morgan had any hot water.

Morgan's kitchen was an unpleasant, though predictable, mess. Morgan was not yet home, and the place was in utter disarray. The ashes from the winter's fires spread out from the grate. Unpaid bills spilled from a large bowl. Crates of unwashed beer bottles, awaiting return to the brewery, filled the room with a sweet, nauseating smell and took up most of the space. The only domestic article was a large, low armchair, but unfortunately its seat had collapsed some years ago. As an improvised solution Morgan had wedged a sack of flour under the chair, and there it had stayed for many years. Anson's first job of the day was to lay a fire and work through a sink of dirty mugs and plates.

After almost an hour and a half of hard, continuous drudge work, he had the place approaching respectability. He was just sitting down to pour himself a cup of tea when Garrad entered.

"Lazing around in the kitchen, Anson?" observed Garrad, "Won't do, won't do at all."

"You don't fancy a cup of tea, George?" asked Anson who knew each and every one of Garrad's weak spots.

"Tea wouldn't go amiss," replied Garrad, "but I think it's breakfast on the move. Now," he sank into the chair, "I've given this a lot of thought and I'm recommending a foot reconnoitre of the hill this morning . . ."

"With pedometer?" asked Anson who had suggested this exact course of action yesterday. For some reason Garrad had to make these simple ideas his own.

"Exactly," said Garrad, "and then barometers this afternoon. Is there any sugar?"

Reverend Jones left his house, as usual, on the dot of nine o'clock. He was a man of fastidious habits. He had risen at six-thirty and washed and shaved before saying his prayers at seven. He had then allowed himself a full forty-five minutes with the newspaper before writing in his journal for another forty-five minutes. Now it was the time to take his walk through and around the village. In this way he kept in contact with his parishioners, but more importantly it was his time to reflect, for he found that there was nothing like the rhythm of a brisk stride to free his mind.

This morning he had much to reflect upon. He had woken with many of the thoughts with which he had gone to bed. One thought above all others was nagging him badly, like an unoiled gate banging in the wind: the English had apparently doubted that Ffynnon Garw was a thousand feet, and—here was the rub—had said that it had to be over a thousand feet to appear on their map as a mountain. Sergeant Thomas had relayed this information quite casually, and only this morning had Reverend Jones grasped its full import: their mountain might not be a mountain. Even worse, it might not appear on the map!

The village of Ffynnon Garw was far too small to appear on many maps, but the mountain had appeared on all maps of Wales. In the villagers' minds the places were inextricably linked. For them Ffynnon Garw was an area where there happened to be a village and a mountain. To lose the mountain would mean losing their foothold, losing their tiny appearance on the pages of history.

With a heavy heart the Reverend set off on his walk. He felt lonely and isolated, wishing that there were someone with whom he could discuss these problems. Were these questions of geography, of natural law or the political sciences? Did precedent have any bearing? After all Ffynnon Garw had always been *called* a mountain—did that mean nothing? Suddenly seized with inspiration he turned out of the lane and into the meadow, taking the short cut to the village school. This was a problem which needed to be discussed with an educated man, and if there wasn't one around then Davies The School was the next best thing.

Morgan was still in bed when Blod opened her kitchen door to find her neighbour Megan The Mouth. Megan was the sort of good neighbour who only arrived when there was gossip to be spread.

"Megan," said Blod warily.

"Morning, Blod," said Megan with a wicked smile, "can't stop, but I thought you ought to know that Betty From Cardiff was at the pub again on Saturday, stayed the night she did."

"And why are you telling me then?" asked Blod.

"No reason. Morgan here, is he?"

"Why would you think Morgan was here?" said Blod haughtily.

"I know how he likes to come and see Johnny," said Megan with as much innocence as she could muster. "He's very affectionate like that, don't you find?"

"Oh, very affectionate," said Blod.

"I mean, whenever there's someone in need of attention, you're likely to find Morgan, I always say," continued Megan.

"Well, you've come to the wrong place this morning," snapped Blod and prayed to God that Morgan wasn't about to stumble into the kitchen in his underwear.

"And how is Johnny?" asked Megan.

"See for yourself," said Blod, "he's in the garden some-where, perhaps you'll find Morgan with him." And with that she slammed the door in Megan's face.

Though Megan wasn't the least bit interested in Johnny she couldn't resist walking around to the side of the house on the off-chance that she'd catch a glimpse of Morgan through a downstairs window.

Her walk was not rewarded, and instead she found her-self face to face with Johnny, who was standing stock-still in the garden, staring at a tortoise.

The door slamming woke Morgan, but he suspected nothing as he ambled downstairs, pulling on his shirt.

"So, Blod," he yawned, "what do you think about Johnny working for the English then?"

Blod was fuming, but Morgan was too sleepy to notice, "He's not ready," she hissed.

"C'mon, Blod," pleaded Morgan, "it would be good for Johnny. All he has to do is hold a pole straight."

"No-one gets paid for just holding a pole," replied Blod, "unless you're Betty From Cardiff."

Aha! There it was! Blod couldn't help herself!

Morgan held up his hands in a motion of surrender, "Now Blod, don't start that again."

"Megan said she saw her at the pub again on Saturday, all tarted up." She added that bit herself, she was sure that she had been.

"So?" said Morgan, trying the innocent approach approved by so many men.

"Oh, it's just something you failed to mention," said Blod.

"Did I?" said Morgan, "It slipped my mind, what with all the excitement of the English."

"So the English are more exciting than Betty From Cardiff are they?" retorted Blod, "If they're so exciting I'd better come and have a look for myself."

"Anyway . . ." Morgan attempted to segue to safer ground.

"Anyway my arse!" said Blod who could match language with Morgan on any morning of the week, thank you very much. "So what was she doing there—again?"

Morgan tried to look serious and grand, he thought it helped whenever he tried to lie. "With her refined and superior tastes she has been advising me on the refurbishment of my establishment."

Blod let out a roar of angry laughter, "Refurbishing your establishment? Well, I've never heard it called that before!" She flounced out of the room and Morgan made his exit while he still had a chance.

* * *

Outside in the garden the gaunt figure of Johnny was still standing next to his pet tortoise. Johnny was just nineteen but the war had put years on him. He had left Ffynnon Garw with the baby fat still on his cheeks, only to return a year later with sunken eyes and thinning hair. His limbs, previously so vital, now hung from his frame like withered branches, half-broken from a tree. In one short year he had seen and heard more pain than most would see in a lifetime. It was only natural that the war had aged him.

Johnny watched patiently, and ever so gently the tortoise's head emerged. Suddenly, Johnny clapped his hands and the tortoise's head quickly retracted. Johnny watched as the head reappeared, and again Johnny clapped. Again the head sunk back into the shell.

"Morning Johnny," said Morgan.

Johnny didn't reply. Morgan dutifully watched for a couple of minutes as Johnny clapped and the tortoise's head crept out and in, before continuing the one-sided conversation.

"I got some English staying at the pub, making maps, come to measure the mountain, daft buggers." He paused, Johnny clapped again.

"Anyway, they're looking for someone to help, to carry what they can't—or won't." Again he paused. There was no reaction from Johnny who continued to stare and clap at the tortoise.

"There's renumbered-rations—that's money to you," continued Morgan, completely hashing what Garrad had told him, "and it can't involve much now can it?" There was no reaction from Johnny and the tortoise's head stayed in its shell.

"So, shall I tell them you're interested?" Johnny didn't

say yes, but then again, he didn't say no. That was as much of an answer as Morgan expected. "So," he concluded, "come along to the pub later, all right?"

Only after he'd left did Johnny softly reply, "All right."

As Morgan descended from Blod's garden to the stepping-stones that crossed the stream, he bumped straight into Reverend Jones.

"Morning, Reverend Jones," said Morgan cheerfully. He looked around at the beautiful summer's morning, "I see God's in his heaven and all's well with the world."

The Reverend took a deep breath and was composing himself for a suitable riposte when he noticed Blod waving at Morgan from her window; Morgan had forgotten his scarf. Another woman to add to Morgan's list?

The Reverend turned purple with rage, "Have you no shame?" he demanded.

Morgan just laughed, "No," he replied and pretended to search his pockets, "And I can't think where I left it!"

Morgan swaggered away, leaving the Reverend to wonder whether God had sent him Morgan to test his faith or his temper.

In the village square outside Morgan's pub, the Thomas Twp twins were sitting on the bench around the police station's flagpole. After a restless night of worry, they had descended from their farm to see the English for themselves. But now that they were here, they were unsure as to how to proceed. They'd never met any English people before, and while they could speak their language, they weren't sure whether their English was the same English as was spoken across the border in England.

"Perhaps we should go in," said Thomas Twp.

"No, we'll wait for the English to come out," said Thomas Twp Too.

"You're right," replied Thomas Twp, "best wait for them to come out."

"But then again," said Thomas Twp Too, "perhaps we should go in."

And so they sat, unsure about how to approach the strangers who were coming to measure their mountain.

In the garden of the inn George Garrad was surrounded by maps, planning the day's work as if he were the general he thought he deserved to be, mounting a military campaign. He intended to return from Wales with such definitive measurements that the next edition of charts would have to bear his name. For years, nay decades, to come, people would quote "Garrad's Wales." This meant that in the weeks ahead Reginald Anson would have to work very hard indeed.

Garrad had fully intended to make an early start but Anson's cup of tea had led to a piece of toast, and then another cup of tea, followed by a second piece of toast. It was ten o'clock before he moved to the garden for a better look at the mountain—and another cup of tea. With that finished he was getting dangerously close to actually making a move. Still, it had all been planning, and planning was the key to any campaign's success.

"So, Anson, ready to calibrate the pedometer?"

Anson looked up from the barometer he was cleaning, the plane table he was repairing, and the transit he was recalibrating. "Absolutely!" he replied with vigour. He had been ready at eight o'clock this morning and was ready to do some decent walking.

Walking? Well, you may not have realized, but until very

recently one of the primary methods of measurement was the simple walking pace: men walked and counted their paces. Actually their paces were counted for them by a simple device, which to the untrained eye, looked rather like a pocket watch. The instrument, or to give it its proper name—the pedometer—clicked forward one calibration each time a person's body moved upward to take a pace. However, for this method to have any accuracy, a man must have a good, steady, regular pace. Each and every morning, Reginald Anson measured his pace against a set distance which they carried with them in the form of a chain, sixty-six feet long.

Of course, none of the villagers knew this, so you can imagine the confusion when Anson and Garrad emerged from the inn carrying a very heavy canvas bag. The Twp Twins and several other villagers followed at a distance and watched with some amusement as they selected a flat section of street and laid down their sixty-six foot length of chain. Why were they measuring the distance from the baker's shop to the Post Office, everyone wondered?

More confusion followed when Anson set his pedometer to zero and paced the chain's length with the concentration of a monk at prayer. A soft click came from the pedometer with each step.

Click, click, click, click . . .

"One, two, three, four," he counted quietly to himself.

Garrad limped slowly behind, watching Anson's action as zealously as any trainer watches his prize racehorse.

Anson stopped at the end of the chain and checked his count with the pedometer reading.

"Yes, Anson?" Inquired Garrad.

Anson smiled, "Twenty-one paces, dead." It was always twenty-one paces. Anson's pace was remarkably regular.

Garrad scratched this in his notebook, "Quite consistent Anson, you're improving." No matter how perfect Anson might be, it was never enough for Garrad. Anson didn't mind, he was his own judge, and he was suitably pleased with himself.

When they both turned to retrieve their chain they found that half the village was standing and staring at them and their curious antics. The Twp Twins were even fingering the chain, as if it possessed magical properties. They quickly dropped it and the crowd dispersed, leaving Anson and Garrad alone in the square.

Garrad felt uneasy—he didn't like crowds of foreigners.

"Well, best get up that hill, I'd say."

There was that word again—*hill*.

Garrad waited while Anson returned the chain to the pub. Then, from a seemingly arbitrary spot in the village, they set off with Anson walking at a steady pace, while Garrad limped behind, and the pedometer did its stuff, clicking with every pace.

The Twp Twins followed at a reasonable distance, unsure as to whether they were watching the scientific marvels of the future, or a pair of madmen.

Reverend Jones waited for the morning break in the school hallway. He felt odd, strangely large, perched on the child-size bench, among dozens of children's coats. He should have felt like a giant, but instead he had the awful feeling that he was about to shrink and that soon these coats and bench would fit him. He hadn't felt like this before the arrival of the English.

*   *   *

Inside the classroom, and blissfully unaware of Reverend Jones' presence, Davies The School droned on to a group of ten year olds who were quietly falling asleep. Davies was a character sorely lacking in humour and charisma. He was a man who believed that he had been destined for better things, but who had, through a nasty trick of fate, ended up here, in Ffynnon Garw, hectoring children.

He wasn't from the village, having been born on the North Wales coast. He had studied at a minor English University and had hoped to lecture. However, on leaving University, some twenty-five years ago, he had taken this post imagining that it would quickly lead to better things. It had turned out to be a trap—no-one was interested in a teacher whose only experience was as headmaster of an obscure school in an unpronounceably obscure village. It had been an easy job to get, but an impossible one to leave.

For some years he had been bitter, but these days he didn't even have the energy for such a strong emotion. He had fallen into a dull, slumbering torpor and consequently made the worst kind of teacher. His history lessons were completely without interest, since he managed to strip historical figures of their character and wars of their passion. Indeed Morgan had once observed that if Davies The School had taught the world how to reproduce, the race would be extinct within a generation. Of course, those aren't the words Morgan used—his language was rather more colourful—but it renders the essence.

"And so," droned Davies, "finally in 1283, after another heroic battle, Llywelyn ap Gruffydd was killed."

He looked around his class. He had just described a crucial moment in the history of their country and they were bored and listless. Tommy Owen was carving his name in the desk top. Marged Jones was re-plaiting her hair. Morgan Evans, was, as always, picking his nose.

He tried to regain their attention, "And what do you think the English did with his body?" A few of them had the decency to look up at him, but only momentarily before their eyes strayed to the clock: they were moments away from play-time. Davies raised his voice, "They cut off his head and took it decorate the Tower of London!"

The children recognizing that they were being cued to do something, let out a collective "Oooh!" before slumping back into the one thing that Davies had taught them—apathy.

Davies let out a quiet sigh, stared at the ceiling and fin-ished his lesson, "And with the death of Llywelyn The Last, the era of the Welsh princes ended."

A bell rang in the playground and the children were out of their seats before he could even say "Class dismissed."

Davies moved to his private cupboard which contained his framed degree and all that he needed to make a cup of tea. He was putting his key in the lock when he was disturbed by an intruder.

"May I come in?" asked Reverend Jones.

"Reverend Jones!" Davies was pleased to see an adult, "Will you join me, I'm about to make a cup of tea."

"Thank you, thank you very much!" It was a Reverend's job to drink tea whenever and wherever he could.

Reverend Jones took a seat at a desk near the front and watched transfixed as Davies carefully measured two cupfuls of water into the kettle, and added two absolutely level tea-spoonfuls of tea into the pot. Davies performed this act with such care that Reverend Jones didn't dare interrupt. It was this kind of precision that kept Davies sane.

With his preparations completed, and while waiting for

the kettle to boil, Davies turned his full attention to the Reverend.

"So, Reverend, to what do I owe the honour of this visit?"

"I don't know if you've heard," started Reverend Jones, "but we have some visitors in the village. And they are English."

Reverend Jones wasn't strictly accurate, since at this very moment Anson and Garrad were halfway up Ffynnon Garw. Having reached a point where the angle of the incline noticeably changed, Anson stopped to take a reading from his pedometer. He had just walked three hundred and eight paces at an angle of twelve degrees. He made a note of this in his book and then with a clinometer he calculated the slope of the next stretch. As the angle of an incline becomes steeper, so a man's pace becomes shorter. His Majesty's Ordnance Survey had comparison charts which he would use later to calculate just how far forward, and upward, he had walked.

But now he paused and turned to see that George, having just done battle with a muddy path and a large thistle, had decided that it was time for a breather. Anson strolled back to chat with him.

Garrad was breathing heavily. It was a long time since he'd done any physical exercise beyond bending his elbow, but on seeing Anson's approach, he busied himself with the map.

"I'd say we must be about here," he said, pointing almost at random.

"Well almost," replied Anson guardedly, "but I think you'll find that's a different hill and we're actually closer to there." Anson pointed to a spot several inches away.

"Of course, that's what I mean, just a slip of the hand," said Garrad, and quickly folded the map to avoid further embarrassment. "And how does the next stretch look?"

"An angle of almost twenty degrees, I'm afraid," said Anson.

"Indeed," Garrad consulted the table of slope and stride-lengths, "that'll almost halve the length of your perfect stride." He couldn't avoid the malicious tone which crept into his voice.

"Yes, I think you're right." There was nothing more to add. Anson fiddled in his pocket, "So, pedometer back to zero and onward and upward . . ."

And with a click, click, click emanating from his pocket, he continued up the mountain with Garrad wheezing behind.

At a safe distance, and hidden by a large tree, the Twp Twins watched them with bemused interest.

"He clicks," said Thomas Twp.

"And then he writes," said Thomas Twp Too.

Was this how mountains were measured?

I'm afraid," said Davies The School, "that geography is not my specialty."

"But you do see my point?" asked Reverend Jones, "when does a hill become a mountain?"

"Oh, indeed, indeed," replied Davies The School, "but I think it must be a comparative term. Take the Himalayas of the Indian sub-continent for example; there they have mountains of ten thousand feet which are referred to, I believe as *foothills*."

"But take our mountain," Reverend Jones' voice quavered, "that isn't a foothill!"

Davies The School turned and gestured to a framed en-

graving of the Swiss Alps, "Well, again, if placed in the Alps,
Ffynnon Garw wouldn't even be considered a hillock."

Reverend Jones was now becoming angry. Davies The
School's insensitivity was beyond belief.

"But it isn't in the Alps!" exclaimed Reverend Jones,
"It's here, here in Wales!"

"Quite."

Reverend Jones tried to calm himself, "So who decides
for British maps?"

Davies shrugged, he had no idea. Reverend Jones came
closer, taking Davies' shoulder and sharing a confidence,
"Look, they're saying . . ."

Davies interrupted, "Who is saying?"

Reverend Jones exploded, "The English!" He tried to
calm himself before he continued, "The English are saying
that it has to, be over a thousand feet to appear on the map
as a mountain."

"Really?" Davies pondered that, "I always imagined the
standard would be five thousand."

Reverend Jones was now severely irritated, Davies
seemed to be continually missing the point! "One thousand,
five thousand whatever!" Reverend Jones moved to the nub
of the problem, "How high is Ffynnon Garw?" he asked, "A
thousand, two thousand? More?"

Davies The School scoffed and looked over his spectacles, out at Ffynnon Garw, "Oh dear me no, I always imagined it was just a few hundred."

Reverend Jones wavered on his feet, *a few hundred*? For
a moment he thought he would faint with rage.

He fixed Davies with his beadiest eye, his heart brimming with disgust and pulled himself together. He snarled,
"And I always thought you were an educated man."

As Reverend Jones left the school he noticed three children standing apart from the general mêlée. They were staring at the mountain. He followed their gaze and could just make out the silhouettes of Anson and Garrad as they reached the summit.

CHAPTER

4

Reginald Anson crested the ridge, walked to the cairn that marked the summit, duly noted his pedometer reading and then relaxed to look out at the spectacular view. To the east he could see the plains of England checker-boarded with crops. Turning to the west the landscape changed dramatically as range after range of hills rose, rising higher as if the country of Wales had been lifted by the vast waves of a stormy subterranean ocean. The country looked timeless, ancient. While the landscape seemed to hold the memory of past battles and bitter days, it now had the quiet dignity of a place at peace with itself. Had France looked this way before the war? It was hard to imagine that the seas of mud and craters through which he had waded had ever looked like this.

To his left the hill sheared away precipitously and a large bird was hovering in the updraft. Its wings fluttered just below him. It looked so close as to appear available to his touch if he just reached out his arm. Was it an eagle? A hawk? There was a flash of red feathers on its back and he wondered whether it was a Red Kite. The bird veered away with a "mew" that sounded almost like a cat. He was trying to remember the classifications of hawks when his reverie was broken by a dull thud. He turned to find that George Garrad had arrived, collapsed in a heap and was wheezing like a broken accordion.

"By God those last stretches are steeper than they look," groaned Garrad as he reached for his hip flask. "I don't know that your pedometer will be much use at all."

"No," Anson agreed, "but nevertheless . . ." He settled down with a slide rule to make his calculations.

Garrad stared up at the clouds that seemed to rush past like the smoke from a train. They made him feel worse. "Can you see either of our trig points?" he asked.

He was referring to two hills which had been previously mapped and would form triangulation points for a more accurate measurement. Anson stared into the distance. He wasn't sure, there was a heat haze forming to the South.

"No," he replied, "but I can see those two men again."

Garrad rose to a sitting position. Yes, there they were, the Thomas Twp Twins, who had been following them at a distance since they had left the village. They stood furtively watching from among the ferns on the lower part of the final slope. They had kept a good distance but it was inevitable that they would be spotted on the higher, bare slopes of the mountain.

Garrad didn't like it one bit, "Hmmm," he mused, "rather ominous, reminds me of surveying Abyssinia in "eighty-eight."

Anson quietly grinned and continued with his calculations. He'd be very surprised if Garrad had been anywhere near Abyssinia in "eighty-eight."

Johnny Shellshocked entered the pub to find Morgan organizing a pool. On a small blackboard he was writing the names of all his patrons and their guesses for the height of the mountain.

"So, Clem," he asked a regular, "a penny for the kitty, winner takes all, how high do you reckon the mountain is?" So far the bets ranged between fifteen hundred and three thousand six hundred feet, the latter being Morgan's hope. As Clem went into a deep think, Morgan spotted Johnny.

"You missed the English, you daft bugger! They left hours ago."

Johnny shrugged, and took his usual place at the bar where he was duly served his usual half pint of dark.

The descent was, if anything, more strenuous and difficult than the ascent. Anson, and particularly Garrad, lost their footing regularly. Garrad regarded each slip as a personal affront, a blow to his pride inflicted by a malevolent hillock. Their return was consequently punctuated by much swearing. Most humbling of all it had taken the better part of the day to make their initial recce. Garrad had hoped to do this, and then remeasure with barometers, before teatime. It was already nearing suppertime, and while there was no doubt in Garrad's mind that Ffynnon Garw was still a hill, it was a larger, steeper hill than he had imagined.

Before entering the village Garrad paused to readjust his clothing. It would not do for him to present himself to the villagers in such a state. As he pulled swatches of ferns and clumps of heather from his person, he casually asked Anson, "And what did you calculate?"

Anson referred to his notebook, "Nine hundred and thirty-two feet. But as you say, possibly useless."

"Probably," said Garrad, "probably."

Pedometers were notoriously inaccurate for measuring changing inclines. From the valley Ffynnon Garw had appeared to present a constant, gradual pitch. The view from the valley had been deceiving.

Having arrived at the inn on a Sunday when the place was closed to villagers, Anson and Garrad were quite unprepared for the crush that greeted them on their return. The bar was full of smoke and men, all of whom were anxious to see these strangers for themselves, and to hear the result of their measurings. Anson and Garrad hadn't realized there were so many men in the village, and it was a shock to find that they were the object of their attention.

"Aha!" said Morgan, "The very men we need. Mr. Garrad sir, settle our bet, how high is Ffynnon Garw?"

The pub fell quiet. Garrad's calculations had never been the subject of a wager before. He vacillated, "Oh, come come, much too early to say, just done a preliminary reconnoitre." He looked to Anson to see if he would give them his calculation.

Anson stammered, he wasn't much for public speaking, "Nothing accurate yet, I'm afraid," as he quickly headed upstairs.

Garrad followed, but couldn't help himself, for he knew that Anson was never very far off: the man had never been wrong by more than fifty feet. After only a couple of steps he turned to face the crowd and with his most pompous delivery announced, "Of course, I might be wrong, but after twenty-five years of doing this I doubt it: I would say that Ffynnon Garw will turn out to be about nine hundred and thirty feet." And with that he turned on his heel and continued upstairs leaving Morgan and the villagers in a state of complete and utter shock.

Morgan slapped himself around the ears. Had he heard that correctly? Nine hundred and thirty?

All eyes turned to Morgan expecting him to do something. After all, the English were under his roof. It was Morgan who had been boasting about them, Morgan who had organized the betting around their measurings. Morgan thought for a moment. He turned to Williams The Petroleum, "Look after the bar," and he sped upstairs.

By the time Morgan arrived at Garrad's door, George was already fast asleep and Morgan could hear his snoring from the corridor. He quickly moved to Anson's room and rapped loudly.

"Come in," said Anson as he stared out of the window. There were the Twp Twins again, in the village square, approaching the inn.

Morgan crashed into the room, "Mr. Anson," he started but Anson stopped him before he got any farther.

"Ah, Mr. Morgan, perhaps you can help me? Who are those two gentlemen?"

Morgan only had to glance out of the window, "Oh that's Thomas Twp and his brother, Thomas Twp Too. Hill farmers, not quite with it, they're daft, stupid, a bit touched, *twp*." He thought about it before continuing, "That's Thomas Twp on the left and Thomas Twp Too on the right, or the other way around, not that it matters."

Anson tried to take that in, "It's just that they've been following us all day."

"Nothing to worry about, now," Morgan puffed out his chest and pulled himself to his full height, "I have to say that your Mr. Garrad has done a pretty shoddy job measuring our Ffynnon Garw, which is, to any trained eye *a mountain*."

"Excuse me?" said Anson, who was genuinely confused.

This "excuse me" duly confused Morgan, who thought it was an apology. "Thank you," replied Morgan.

"No, that's not what I meant," continued Anson, "I'm sorry but I don't quite follow . . ."

"Nine hundred and thirty feet?" roared Morgan, "I hope he doesn't intend sticking with this obviously euphonious measurement." He meant to say erroneous but he was apt to get these things mixed up when his temper was roused.

Anson rolled his eyes, why had George chosen to give them that figure, the fool! He slowly sat down and tried to placate the raging Morgan, "Firstly Mr. Morgan we haven't measured your "mountain" yet; we've just done a preliminary reconnoitre which yielded a *very* approximate figure."

Downstairs in the bar the Twp Twins were telling their side of the story. Thomas Twp walked the length of the bar, "Click, click, click," he said with each and every pace.

"And then he wrote in a book," added Thomas Twp Too.

"That's it?" asked a bemused Williams The Petroleum.

"That was it," said Thomas Twp, "they clicked and then they wrote and then they clicked and then they wrote again."

"All the way to the top," added Thomas Twp Too.

"Well no wonder they got it wrong!" said Williams and the pub broke into laughter.

*   *   *

Upstairs Anson began to outline their working procedures to Morgan The Goat.

"Tomorrow we will make readings using barometers," Anson picked up a barometer and handed it to Morgan. Morgan held it gingerly, as if it might go off in his hand. "They're quite accurate if the weather is good, but climatic changes render them almost inoperable."

"Inoperable," repeated Morgan. That was a word he'd like to use again, if only he knew what it meant.

"And finally," said Anson, "if the weather is changeable and the barometers don't work, we'll make measurements using this." With a flourish he removed a dust cloth to reveal a beautiful brass instrument standing on a tripod. It looked rather like a small, very complicated telescope, which in fact it was. "But to use this transit, as we call it," continued Anson, "we must be able to see the summits of Newport Beacon and Whitchurch Hill clearly."

"But they're not mountains," complained Morgan who was following, but only just.

"No, they're not mountains," Anson agreed, "but the survey of eighteen-ninety-seven established their heights, and the distance between them and Ffynnon Garw, and given those measurements we will, with some great degree of accuracy, be able to calculate the height of Ffynnon Garw." Each time he pronounced Ffynnon Garw he made it sound like the mating call of a wild animal in Brazil, but Morgan didn't mind. This was music to his ears.

"So!" beamed Morgan, "What you are saying is that it probably isn't nine hundred and thirty feet!"

Anson smiled, "Correct. I would be *very* surprised if today's reading were accurate."

Morgan slapped him on the back and made for the door, "See you in the bar then."

However, there was one point that Anson had to make before Morgan left.

"Ah, Mr. Morgan," Anson didn't really know how to put this. He would have to be direct.

"Yes?" smiled Morgan.

"While your mountain might well be more than nine hundred and thirty feet . . ." Anson paused, took a deep breath and continued, "you should also consider the fact that it could also be less."

Less?!

Morgan composed himself on the pub landing before returning to the bar. Less? The word resounded in his ears, and bounced around his skull like a dried pea in a biscuit tin, making a very large rattle for such a small word. Less! He pulled himself together, he must concentrate on the other things Anson said: this was just a rough measurement and was probably wrong; They would be measuring it again, and again; Anson had said "It could be more", yes he had said that. He took a deep breath, pasted a smile across his face and returned to the bar.

"So?" asked Williams The Petroleum. His voice was followed by a half dozen others, "So?" "So?" "So?"

"Bloody hell," said Morgan, "there's an awful echo in here. Now listen, it's just a rough first guess, they haven't measured it properly, they're going to do that tomorrow, and the day after." He hoped that would stop the questions.

"But he said . . ." Williams The Petroleum started again.

Morgan stopped him, "I didn't talk to him, I talked to

the younger one and he told me all about it. He reckons it's probably more."

"Well, that's stating the obvious!" said Williams and there was a general laugh.

Morgan spoke again, hoping that his words would be lost under the laughter," He said it might also be less."

The laughter stopped like a frozen stream. Williams looked around, "Less?!" he said incredulously. He looked from face to face, had they heard that word too?

Then his features spread and his chest filled and out came a roar of laughter!

"Less!" He'd never heard anything so funny in his life. The others joined in, "Less!" Oh, those mad, insane, stupid English! How could it be less! They laughed and laughed and laughed but no matter how Morgan tried, he found he couldn't quite join in.

—⁓—

Now for those of my readers who are not Welsh, I feel I should pause and explain something: why all this fuss? Why should it matter if Ffynnon Garw is a hill or a mountain? Perhaps it wouldn't matter anywhere else, but this is Wales. The Egyptians built pyramids, the Greeks built temples, but we Welsh didn't feel that any of that was necessary, because we had *mountains*.

The Welsh mountains are a hostile place, difficult enough to climb, and harder yet to farm, but these rocky slopes saved the ancient Britons and their language. This is where the Britons fled when they were invaded by the Romans, the Angles, the Saxons, the Vikings, the Normans. Wave upon wave of European tribes invaded Britain, and while they took the rich lowland farming, and the pretty hills and dales, looting the centres of learning, and desecrating the old religious sites, they never took the mountains.

It was here that the Britons were forced to live, losing everything, even their name, to be renamed "weallas"— Welsh—by the invaders. You know what Welsh means, don't you? It means *strangers*. Imagine that! Being called a stranger in your own land, in someone else's language.

It is in these ancient mountains that our ancestors practised their religions and met their gods. Yes, the mountains are regarded as sacred places and Cader Idris in central Wales is the most sacred of all. On this mountain brave men went to spend a night, for it was known that anyone who dared to spend a night on the Holy Mountain would return a madman, a poet, or very, very wise.

So the Welsh were saved—or you could even say created—by mountains. Where the mountains start, there starts Wales. So if Ffynnon Garw isn't a mountain?

Well, as far as the village was concerned, if Ffynnon Garw wasn't a mountain then Anson and Garrad might as well redraw the border and put them all in England!

And that, to a Welsh person, is frankly a fate worse than death.

—◊◊◊—

Sergeant Thomas' heart sank as he approached the police station in the early morning light, since he could plainly see the figure of Hughes The Stamps waiting for him. The postman had a large cylindrical package under his arm and Sergeant Thomas knew that it was a new list of war dead for him to pin to the village notice-board.

He just nodded to Hughes The Stamps and Hughes The Stamps just nodded back. There was nothing to say and both men silently prayed that the fresh lists would not contain the names of relatives or friends. War had dragged on now for three long years. No-one had imagined that a single war could take so many lives. Any grand purpose had long been forgotten. Few villagers even read the war news in the daily papers. They were only interested in two things: when it would be over, and whether their loved ones would survive.

Sergeant Thomas entered the police station, laid the package down on his desk and stared at it. No, he would light the coal fire first, and have a cup of tea. Only then would he face the contents and brace himself for the task of publicising them for the village to see. It was the part of his job that he hated most.

Up at the pit the night shift were coming off. As they stepped out of the trams their places were immediately taken by the day shift.

"You missed a good night in the pub last night," said Jones The Front, who hadn't been to war but lived in one of two adjoining cottages running up a hill.

"I miss a good night in the pub every bloody night," said Evans The Scowl.

"The English made a right balls-up—nine hundred feet they reckoned!"

The night shift laughed, all except Jones The Scowl. "Very bloody funny, I don't think," he spat, "while we're hacking coal, they're gallivanting over the mountain . . ."

But no-one was listening to him. They were all too busy going home to bed.

*   *   *

Mrs. Jones The Scowl was washing her front steps when the horse and cart, filled with filthy miners stopped at her door to deposit her moody husband.

"Bloody English," he muttered, as he left a filthy boot print on her clean front doorstep.

"Well there's no need taking it out on me!" she said but he was already asleep at the kitchen table.

Sergeant Thomas could see the last of the miners dropped off in the village square. Ivor The Grocer was already out, brushing the pavement outside his shop. Soon the children would be on the way to school. Sergeant Thomas couldn't put off his unpleasant job any longer. He had looked at the lists and there was one local fatality. Another widow in the village, three more children without a father. Another elderly couple without a son.

With a sour stomach he walked out into the square and lowered the flag to half mast. He avoided Ivor The Grocer's eyes, strode back to the notice-board and pinned up the list as quickly as he decently could. Ivor removed his hat and stood silently in deference to the dead.

Over his shoulder Sergeant Thomas could see a group of young women approaching. Please don't let Enid Jones be among them, he thought, and scuttled back into the station before he had to look directly into their eyes.

Enid Jones was not among them, but her sister and best friend were. Ivor watched as they wept, and hurried away with the tragic news that no-one knew how to break. There were parents to tell, aunts, uncles, cousins—and the wife and children.

Within moments the square was empty. Up and down the village people were drawing their curtains. Bright flowers were removed from vases. Another day of mourning had begun. Ivor looked around—only moments before he had been enjoying a lovely summer morning. Now the very sunshine seemed to have lost its sheen.

Reverend Jones approached him, and seeing the flag at half mast his face turned into a scowl. That bloody, insane, futile, *English* war!

"Good morning, Reverend," said Ivor.

"Ivor . . ." replied the Reverend.

They stared at the flag for some moments. Eventually Ivor broke the silence, "I am tired of widow's weeds." He was referring to the black lace which seemed to cover more and more women in this small community. The whole village was losing its balance. There were old men, middle-aged men, and boys. A whole generation had all but disappeared. Only the miners were left to represent the young.

Reverend Jones nodded, and took a deep breath. If he started on the subject of the war he would be here all day. "Well," he forced a smile, "at least the good Lord has sent us the English to provide some amusement."

Ivor tried not to grin on this day of mourning, but he couldn't help himself, "Did you hear?" he whispered, "They calculated nine hundred and thirty feet!"

"Ha!" exploded Reverend Jones, "A mistake of biblical proportions! Still what can you expect?"

Ivor looked at him questioningly, the Reverend continued, "They were both educated in London!" He emphasized "London" as if it were a shabby market town in a neglected backward country, which was exactly what he thought of it.

"They're going to try again today," said Ivor.

"Well you have to give that to the English," said Reverend Jones, "never happy to make one mistake when there's a chance to make two!"

"Morgan's taking bets on the height. Would you like me to place one for you, under another name of course," asked Ivor, fully aware that he was on precarious ground.

"I'm shocked that you should suggest such a thing," said Reverend Jones, "but, now that you mention it there is an elderly parishioner, a man who cannot get to the pub you understand . . ."

"Infirm?" asked Ivor, knowing full well that they were talking about the Reverend himself.

"Yes, that's it, quite infirm."

"And do you know what height he might be guessing?" asked Ivor.

"I think," the Reverend feigned trying to remember what his "infirm parishioner" had guessed, "that he mentioned three thousand six hundred feet."

"Three thousand six hundred it is then," said Ivor, "and I'll put it under my cousin's name."

"Very good, excellent," said the Reverend. "And how much should I be asking my friend to wager?"

"A penny," said Ivor.

"Yes, I think he can afford that," said the Reverend, "I'll see you get it later today."

As he walked off Ivor had to laugh: Reverend Jones and Morgan The Goat had bet the same height.

In the garden of the pub Morgan watched with interest as Anson and Garrad fiddled with some gadgets that looked like small, brass clocks, but with only one hand on the face.

Anson noticed Morgan watching, "Barometers," he explained.

"Absolutely," replied Morgan as if barometers were a part of his everyday life. Anson was absorbed with trying to get the two instruments to display the same reading. Garrad was preoccupied with the more difficult job of spreading gloom.

"I thought you knew how to do this, Anson!" growled Garrad who hadn't a clue.

"Well, I do," replied Anson. "It's just that it takes rather a lot of patience and shouldn't really be done in the early morning when the pressure is still stabilizing. If we could just wait an hour or two . . ."

"Haven't got an hour, Anson," said Garrad. He was keen to make up for lost time. Now that he thought about it he realized that it was Anson who had slowed them up yesterday: he did insist on that cup of tea, remembered Garrad and wondered whether that was too petty to include in his report. Now Anson was shilly-shallying with these barometers, as if they were delicate scientific instruments.

"We may not have an hour," said Anson, "but we will have to wait five minutes for them both to calm down."

"Five minutes here, five minutes there," moaned Garrad, "and the whole day will be gone."

"You're absolutely right," replied Anson, "but in this case we daren't actually move until we know that these are in agreement."

They both hunched over the barometers and stared at them, willing them to display the same figures. However their concentration was broken by the arrival of the Twp Twins who shuffled in through the gate which opened from the pub garden into a meadow.

"Morning, Thomas, and Thomas," said Morgan.

"Good Morning," replied the Twps in perfect unison.

"And what can I do you for?" asked Morgan.

"We have come to see the men who are measuring the mountain," said Thomas Twp.

George Garrad looked at them as if they were trained monkeys, juggling bananas in the bazaar in Cairo. "George Garrad," he barked, "and this is my assistant, Reginald Anson, and—as I'm sure you can see—we are *terribly* busy." He'd used his strongest voice, usually reserved for small boys and rabid dogs. It was meant to send them running.

However neither Twp moved a muscle and Thomas Twp Too had the temerity to continue, "This is my brother Thomas Twp and I am Thomas Twp Too."

"We've no learning," added Thomas Twp, "and most people say we're *twp*, but we're not so *twp* as to not know that we're *twp*."

There was a stunned silence as Anson and Garrad took this in.

Eventually Garrad gathered his wits and once again tried to end the encounter, "How novel. Well it was very nice to meet you, but please don't let us detain you any longer."

Again neither Twp moved. They were quite used to short conversations which lasted all day, and since they'd walked all the way from their farm, they were unlikely to leave until they'd had their say.

"We would like to know how you are going to measure the mountain," said Thomas Twp Too.

"We would like to watch—and we'd be happy to carry your rule," added Thomas Twp who was sure that the English would be taking a very large measuring stick.

Anson had been keenly watching the two farmers. He admired the fact that George Garrad had failed to intimidate them. Even more he liked the way they just stood there, stock-still, speaking with a heartfelt, unadorned sincerity. They might well be twp, but they nevertheless exhibited a solidity which was rare in more "sophisticated" individuals. Anson had decided that he liked them.

"It's a splendid offer to carry our equipment," he said, "but actually we don't have very much to carry today."

"Yes," added Garrad, "only Mr. Anson is ascending today, I'll be staying here."

"You'll measure from here?!" asked Thomas Twp. He was amazed that Garrad could do such a thing.

Garrad rolled his eyes and kicked Anson under the table, "Anson!" He was not going to waste his time explaining the ins and outs of barometer measurements to two Welsh hill-farmers—especially since he'd never quite grasped the principle himself.

"Well," started Anson, "we don't really measure from here, we make comparisons: I will ascend the er . . ."—he didn't know what to call it—"er *mountain*, with one barometer . . ."

Mountain? Garrad shot him a dirty look.

Anson continued, "and Mr. Garrad will stay here with another, and we'll make readings at twenty minute intervals. Mr. Garrad's barometer will be the control, but my barometer will show a change in barometric pressure, and the degree of change will tell us the height, since barometric pressure lessens with altitude."

Morgan The Goat smiled at the Twps as he pretended to have followed what Anson had said, "Got that then boys?" he asked.

The Twps smiled back in complete silence.

Anson tried again, "Just imagine all the air around us, and on top of us, stretching right out to the edges of the atmosphere. We don't feel it but it does have weight, not much, but enough to measure. Now when I climb the mountain there will be less air pressing down on me. I'll measure how much is pressing down on me up there, and Mr. Garrad will measure how much is pressing down on him, here. And the difference will tell us how high the er—*mountain*—is."

Again the Twp's just smiled.

"So," Garrad made a sweeping gesture with his arms which was his way of pretending that the British Empire was eager for them to get on with things, when really he just wanted them all to leave so he could have a good lie down in the hammock, "are the barometers matched?"

Anson looked at them. They were in perfect accordance, "Yes, I think we can start."

"Good," said Garrad, "shall we synchronize watches, Mr. Anson?"

Anson and Garrad compared watches.

"Seven minutes past nine," said Garrad.

"I have five past," replied Anson.

"Seven," repeated Garrad, and Anson deferred, re-setting his watch to match Garrad's. The Twps and Morgan watched with more confusion: were they measuring with barometers or watches? How did they know that Garrad's watch was right, and that Anson's was wrong? It was very puzzling.

"Reading at twenty past, twenty to, and the hour," said Garrad.

"Right. Well, I'll be off then," said Anson, and taking one barometer, he left the garden. Thomas Twp followed him, Morgan disappeared to get a drink and Garrad found himself alone in the garden with Thomas Twp Too.

"Yes?" he asked.

"Yes, what?" asked Thomas Twp Too as he settled into a chair to watch the barometer.

"You're going to watch the barometer?" asked Garrad incredulously.

"Why yes, aren't you?" replied Thomas Twp Too.

"Well, yes, and no," said Garrad. "I will take measurements every twenty minutes—I don't actually watch it continuously."

"But what if it moves when you're not watching?" asked Thomas Twp Too.

"That's extremely unlikely," said Garrad.

"So it only moves when you watch it?" asked Thomas Twp Too.

Garrad did not want to continue this absurd conversation, "Yes, all right, you could say that yes."

"Good," said Thomas Twp Too, "I'll watch it all the time then, to make sure that it moves for you."

Garrad didn't have an answer for that and instead settled down in the hammock to read a book about Gordon of Khartoum.

Outside the pub, Thomas Twp noticed that Anson had paused: he had just noticed the list of war dead and was staring, as if he'd been transported to another world, which, in fact, he had. Hundreds dead, announced the sign, many more injured. "Injured?" The word tried to suggest something slight, a scratch, a graze, at worst a flesh wound, but Anson had seen injured men, men who would have been better off dead, men with their skin stripped by phosphorous, their lungs collapsed by gas, their limbs lost to shellfire. The dead, Anson knew only too well, were the lucky ones.

Thomas Twp took off his cap and waited beside him.

After a few moments Anson let out a deep sigh, and seemed to come back to earth. Thomas Twp said nothing, but gave a small smile, and tugged Anson's arm, rather like a dog tugging on a lead. It was a very simple gesture but it struck Anson as intimate and comforting. Together they walked through the village in silence.

As they approached the outskirts Thomas Twp took a turn off the road, onto a steep path through woodland. "This way's the prettiest," he said, "in fact, my brother says it's as pretty as Betty From Cardiff." He blushed a deep red as he said it. Anson found it amusing that an elderly man should blush in such a way, and wondered whether "Betty From Cardiff" was a girl from their youth.

He didn't have long to ponder the question since he was surprised to find himself in a glade, bristling with wild flowers. The sunlight slanted through the first, mint-green leaves of summer. The soft rustle sounded like a length of silk unraveling in the wind. It was indeed very, very pretty.

In the garden Thomas Twp Too stared at the barometer. In fact his eyes were starting to get sore from staring. There were moments when he began to imagine that it had moved, and even more moments when he hoped it would. Meanwhile Garrad continued to sway in the hammock, lighting cigarette after cigarette, and dreamily wishing that he had actually been the great General Gordon.

Anson and Thomas Twp left the woods and started across a steep field. Anson glanced at his watch—twenty past nine. He stopped. "Time for our first reading!" he said, and passed Thomas Twp the barometer while he fumbled for his notebook and pencil.

"Has it moved?" asked Thomas Twp.

"Yes, look, just the tiniest amount."

"And that's because we're higher?" said Thomas Twp.

"That's right, you've got the hang of it."

"And who discovered this?" asked Thomas Twp who was fascinated by the modern world and its marvellous inventions.

"That's a very good question," said Anson, "and I'm embarrassed to say that I don't know. I'll look it up for you later if you like."

"Thank you," said Thomas Twp, and they continued up the hill.

Garrad, who had also noticed that it was twenty past the hour, struggled out of the hammock and made his way to the table where Thomas Twp Too was resolutely staring at the barometer. Garrad noted the reading.

"It hasn't moved," said Thomas Twp Too who was disappointed that all his work had come to nothing.

Garrad stared at him long and hard, "No, it hasn't moved, but nevertheless we must note the fact that it hasn't moved." As Garrad limped back to the hammock he cursed under his breath, "A country of imbeciles!"

Luckily, Thomas Twp Too didn't know what an imbecile was, and anyway he was distracted by the arrival of Johnny Shellshocked, who had come to see if the English had a job for him.

"Hello Johnny," said Thomas Twp Too, "come and join me. I'm watching the barometer."

Johnny came and sat beside him and stared at the barometer's face. Then he stared at Thomas Twp Too.

"No," said Thomas Twp Too, "it doesn't move, but we

watch it anyway. And that's how they measure mountains." He noticed Johnny's stare turn to Garrad in the hammock and added in a whisper, "No, he doesn't move much either—he's a lazy old bugger."

Up on Ffynnon Garw, Anson and Thomas Twp were being anything but lazy. While Thomas Twp had started them out on the pretty way, Anson now found that he was being led up a rather precipitous slope. What was really embarrassing was the fact that the old Welsh hill farmer moved on upwards, from turf to rock, from rock to crag, with the ease and agility of the sheep he farmed. In comparison Anson found himself slipping and sliding and it was quite difficult to keep up. In his sweating lather Anson didn't notice the clouds which were gathering to the West.

Down in the garden Thomas Twp Too shook with a start. The barometer needle had moved! He was sure, but then again, he had been staring at it for so long that he was frightened to say so just in case his eyes had betrayed him. He looked quickly to Johnny, and Johnny nodded in agreement—yes, he had seen it move too.

"It moved!" Thomas Twp Too called to Garrad.

"Don't be silly," replied Garrad and turned another page—he had reached a good bit, Gordon was giving restless natives hell in foreign climes.

"By God, it did!" said Thomas Twp Too, who, while he was used to being called stupid, was not used to being called a liar.

Garrad let out a long, withering sigh, and dragged his bulbous frame from the hammock. He stretched, wiped his spectacles, and eventually deigned to take those few steps to the table which were necessary for him to view the barometer properly.

To his chagrin he found that the needle had moved.

"Hmmm," he said, "falling, weather's changing."

Thomas Twp Too didn't know anything about falling barometers. Instead he used the method his father had taught him—he stared out along the meadow. Then he licked a finger and felt the gathering breeze. The air that was coming was hotter, heavier. Thunder.

"It's going to rain," he said, "and heavy too."

"Pshah!" said Garrad more through his nose than his mouth, "No, I don't think so."

"It's going to rain cats and dogs," continued Thomas Twp Too.

Johnny Shellshocked knew that Thomas Twp Too was never wrong about the weather. He didn't want to be caught in a storm. Ever since the war he hated thunder, "I'll be off then," he almost whispered, and sidled from the garden.

Garrad looked at the barometer again. "Definitely not enough for rain," he announced as a roll of thunder broke over the garden and the rain came down in sheets.

Up on the mountain Anson and Thomas Twp huddled under an umbrella while Anson took his final reading.

"Useless really," said Anson, "but since we're here . . ."

Thomas Twp looked around nervously. He'd lost several sheep to lightning on the mountain peak in a summer storm the previous year.

Anson saw his anxious look, and thought that Thomas was worried about the measurement, "I'm just doing it for academic interest," he explained, "won't take a minute."

"We should get down," said Thomas Twp, "it can crack here in the summer."

Anson was distracted with his figures, "Crack?" he asked nonchalantly.

"Lightning," replied Thomas Twp, "like you wouldn't believe."

Anson looked around. They were standing on the highest spot for miles, in a thunderstorm—with an umbrella. Not very clever. "Right!" said Anson. He quickly collapsed his umbrella and finished his reading as they rushed from the peak.

The march back to the inn was a struggle. The couch grass turned to glass, every path to mud, every little stream into a raging torrent. By the time Anson and Thomas Twp reached the inn, they were muddy and sopping. Anson's best leather boots were heavy with water. Even his notebook was wringing wet.

He found Garrad sitting by a roaring fire nursing a very large scotch.

"Bugger of a day," nodded Garrad, "we were fairly pissed on in the garden." He didn't seem to notice the fact that Anson had suffered rather more. Anson smiled weakly, and propping his notebook next to the fire to dry, he retired upstairs to change.

When he returned to the bar he was surprised to find the Twp's, Morgan The Goat and a half a dozen strangers waiting for him. Garrad took him aside. He looked a little pale. He whispered nervously to Anson, "They seem very keen to get a result."

"A result?" Anson was dismayed, "Didn't you explain to them? I think you should."

He said it loud enough for the assembled group to hear and all eyes turned to Garrad. Garrad stammered, "Well, not very good I'm afraid . . ."

"Not very good?" thundered Morgan who was fearing the worst after Anson's less-than-nine-hundred-and-thirty warning.

Anson looked from face to face—they were all expecting a better explanation than that. Wearily he took Garrad's page of figures and laid them on a table. Above them he set his own notebook. All gathered around.

Anson pointed to Garrad's figures, "These should have been consistent, a constant, something to measure against mine, but as you can see they started to fluctuate quite erratically as the weather changed."

"Very erotic," observed Morgan.

"Didn't have any of these problems when I was surveying East Anglia," interceded Garrad, "no need for damned barometers there, wonderful county, quite flat, and lovely weather—did the whole area in a matter of hours."

Morgan wasn't interested in East Anglia, wherever that might be, "So is it useless?" he asked.

"We-ell, not useless, but probably inaccurate" Anson took up his slide rule and started to make some calculations, "we might get something out of it."

The room fell silent as he concentrated. From time to time he wrote down a figure, occasionally he voiced an equation to himself, "Dh equals delta dz . . ." He might have been practising alchemy as far as the villagers were concerned.

Eventually he put down his pen and cleared his throat, "As I thought, the varying baseline gives a variety of figures, thus forcing me to average a result . . ."

"Yes?" All eyes were on him.

". . . Of nine hundred and seventy-five feet."

"What!" exploded Morgan.

"But!" continued Anson, "By no means accurate, given the problems with the weather. It's quite obvious that we will only get an accurate height by using the transit." He turned to Garrad, "I'm afraid we'll need another day here, George."

Garrad looked like a man who had been sentenced to five years. "Damn," he muttered.

The pub fell quiet.

Thomas Twp broke the silence. "It's grown almost forty feet," he said with a smile.

"Quite," replied Garrad with a patronizing scowl, "but still not a mountain by our standards."

"But if it keeps growing at this rate, it will be a mountain tomorrow," added Thomas Twp Too.

CHAPTER

5

For those of my readers who have never lived in a small Welsh village, I should explain certain realities that are as true today as they were in 1917.

Firstly, not much happens in a small village. The birth of a child, the death of an elder, events like these that go unnoticed among people who live cheek by jowl in a large city are scrutinized, disseminated and commented upon in a small village. But it's not just these important events that lubricate the conversation of village life; A new hat, a pruned tree, a different hairstyle, a hacking cough—all these minute modulations, and more, stand out as significant changes to be pondered and discussed.

Secondly—and logically, given that every little difference is noticed—strangers and their actions stick out like the proverbial sore thumb. If you live in an urban conurbation you probably pass several hundred, even thousands of people a day and take it for granted that your world is thus populated by strangers. In a village however, the assumption is reversed and one expects to know each and every face. You may not like your fellow villagers, you might not want to talk to them, but, nevertheless, you know them, their clothes, their habits and their allegiances. A stranger can be spotted—almost intuitively—at a distance, in the shadows, on a very dark night. His or her movements, no matter how innocent they might be, become the stuff of melodrama.

Given these facts, and the added feelings with which the villagers of Ffynnon Garw regarded their mountain—the first mountain in Wales, remember—it was only to be expected that by the third morning of Anson and Garrad's stay, the village was rising to something of a fever pitch regarding the measuring of the much-loved peak.

Both Morgan The Goat and Reverend Jones woke with deep feelings of foreboding. While the rest of the village still assumed that Ffynnon Garw was a mountain, and were mainly interested in just how high a mountain it was, Morgan and Reverend Jones had had their faith shaken to some large degree. It must be said that it was only the second time in their lives that they had ever shared a feeling or instinct about anything. The first had been days before when they had both imagined the mountain to be over three thousand feet.

Now both of them were obsessed with the Englishmen's two preliminary measurements. Both measurements, they had been assured by Anson, were wrong. However, that did not change the fact that both measurements fell short of a thousand feet. It had been easy to dismiss the pedometer-based calculation of nine hundred and thirty feet, but less easy when a second reading had also fallen short. A pattern was emerging which both men could read, and which neither man liked.

Reverend Jones sat at his kitchen table, nursing a tepid cup of weak tea, and decided that he could not sit here all day in the grip of fear. He would climb Ffynnon Garw and watch the measuring procedure. At the very least he could keep an eye on these English outsiders and make sure that they were conducting themselves properly. With that decision made, he roused himself, washed out his cup and changed into his sturdiest walking shoes.

Morgan gazed out of the pub window and discovered that Reverend Jones wasn't the only villager who was intending to be at the summit for the measurement. Ivor The Grocer was closing his shop for the day, Davies The School was taking his whole class and many other villagers were also trekking past the pub, on their way to the mountain.

Fools, thought Morgan, as if the measuring was a circus act. He'd seen the English with their barometers and guessed that today's proceedings would be as interesting as watching a sheep moult. Moreover there was something superstitious about these people going up the mountain today, as if, in solidarity with the mountain, their presence would add extra feet.

What a crowd, thought Morgan, and immediately came out of his trance. The thunderstorm had cleared the air and it was shaping up to be a scorcher of a day. They would all be walking up a steep mountain in this heat, and waiting while the English did their work. In a flash Morgan saw his opportunity, and very quickly started to calculate how much beer, lemonade and saspirilla, bread, pies and sandwiches, he could sell on the mountain today. He had only one problem—who would carry it up there for him?

Up in his room Anson was packing the last part of the transit. It was a cumbersome piece of equipment. The transit itself was housed in a hefty baize-lined wooden box. There was also a sturdy tripod, and a plumb line, not to mention the calibrated brass plates which encircled the base of the telescopic sights. It was a lot for one man to lug up a mountain.

There was a knock at his door. It was Garrad.

"Ready Anson?"

"Yes, I believe so . . ."

"Good," said Garrad, "I'll be glad to get this measurement established and on to the next. Spent far too much time here."

Garrad made no move to lift a single item of equipment.

Anson tried to be tactful, "Rather a lot here for one man, George."

"Yes," agreed Garrad and looked at his watch, "I wonder where those damn coolies are?"

"Coolies?" said Anson, wondering where on earth Garrad had managed to find some coolies in a small Welsh village.

"The Twerps," he mispronounced, "those idiot twins, I told them to be here on the stroke of nine."

"Nine . . ." said Anson.

"Yes," replied Garrad, "do you foresee a problem?"

"I was just wondering if they have watches," said Anson. It was a reasonable worry.

"I doubt it," replied Garrad, "but let's face it, that's hardly an excuse for tardiness."

Anson glanced out of the window and saw that the Twps

were sitting on the bench around the flagpole, staring at the inn. They'd been there for an hour.

"Actually, George," said Anson, "I take it back: they are waiting outside."

When Anson and Garrad left the inn—with the Twps carrying their equipment—they discovered that the Twps' place at the flagpole had been taken by several old-age pensioners and widows. The small crowd of villagers rose and followed them at a distance.

Garrad didn't like it. He stopped and the elderly villagers stopped, maintaining their distance. Garrad started again, and the villagers followed.

"I haven't encountered this sort of interference since I surveyed the Great Pyramids," he huffed.

"Not to worry," chirped Anson with a grin, "I don't think they're carrying guns."

As with Anson's ascent the previous day, the Twps set the pace and Anson and Garrad were ashamed to find that they could barely keep up. George Garrad was having an especially hard time. He paused at the halfway mark and made a general pronouncement, intended for all. "Ten minute rest, I think," he said grandly, like a Colonial Governor granting a public holiday.

The Twps just nodded, and kept on walking.

"See you up there," said Thomas Twp Too.

Worse, the elderly villagers kept walking too, following the Twps example.

Much as Garrad needed a rest, he could not let these people shame him. He looked at Anson as if Anson were the cause of their stopping, "Come on Anson," he said loudly, "can't loll about here!" And with a huff and a puff he continued up the mountain, desperately attempting to catch up with the locals.

Garrad may have found their elderly entourage unnerving but even they couldn't have prepared him for the view that met him when he crested the ridge of Ffynnon Garw and discovered that the summit was crowded—schoolchildren were playing in the heather, groups of villagers were dotted about, chatting, and the crow-like figure of Reverend Robert Jones stood at the cairn, dominating it all, like the very guardian of the mountain.

All turned and watched Anson and Garrad's approach, and as they neared the cairn the villagers gathered around them, since everyone wanted to hear what Reverend Jones might say.

Ivor The Grocer, with a decidedly mischievous twinkle, introduced the English to Reverend Jones, "Have you met our Reverend Jones?" he smiled.

Reverend Jones glowered from under the brim of his funereally black hat, "You'll do your best now, I'm sure . . ." he said with as much sarcasm as he could muster on a weekday.

Anson and Garrad shook his hand, and were both taken aback by the firmness of the old man's grip.

"Well," said Garrad, looking about, "we will, but—and it's a big but—we won't be able to do a thing until the mist lifts from Newton Beacon and Whitchurch Hill."

All eyes turned to the east, towards England, towards the two hills which would form the triangle of Anson's calculation. They were quite obscured by the morning haze.

Reverend Jones smiled like a bottle of sulphuric acid which had just been unstopped, "We're in no hurry—this *mountain* has been here since before you Saxons came, and will still be here after you leave."

There was an uncomfortable silence and all shuffled to find comfortable places to sit while they waited for the mist to burn off.

Thomas Twp looked to his brother. Thomas Twp Too squinted into the haze, then noted the way the crows were circling. "It will clear up, this afternoon, about teatime," was his prediction.

Garrad snorted, "A definitive forecast!"

"My brother is never wrong about the weather," said Thomas Twp, and the villagers who all knew that this was true, settled down for a long wait.

Down in the village things were very quiet. Morgan, without a single customer, was using the mirror behind the bar to shave when Johnny Shellshocked arrived looking for the English.

"You missed them again, you daft bugger," said Morgan, as he cut himself, "but never mind, I'll find something for you to do." He pointed to a small barrel looped with rope for carrying. "See if that fits around your shoulders."

Within minutes he had Johnny loaded down like a pack horse. He had the small beer barrel strapped to his shoulders, bottles of saspirilla hanging from his belt, and a basket of sandwiches filling his arms.

Morgan, for his part, volunteered to carry a box of not-very-heavy tin cups, since he had to lead the way. "C'mon Johnny," he said, "It's a fine thing you're doing, they're going to appreciate this."

Morgan's timing couldn't have been better, for the villagers were just starting to feel the first pangs of hunger when he and Johnny came into view.

"Lunch, anyone?" he called out with a large smile, and all rushed to greet him as if he were Santa Claus.

"I've got sandwiches and meat pies; saspirilla for the women and children—and beer for the gentlemen."

Reverend Jones scowled and distanced himself from the mob. No matter how hungry or thirsty he was, he would never buy from Morgan.

"A beer for you, Reverend?" taunted Morgan and Reverend Jones shot him a look that could have felled a weaker creature at twenty paces.

"He's teetotal," Morgan explained to Anson, "thinks I'm one of Satan's envoys." He groped in his waistcoat pocket for a scrap of paper, "Now where did I put my price list?"

As Morgan did a roaring trade, Davies The School insinuated himself alongside George Garrad. Garrad, he assumed, was a man of education, possibly erudition. This in Davies' mind, gave them much in common. It fell to Davies, as an act of common courtesy, formally to welcome Garrad to the village intelligentsia, of which he was the sole representative.

"Sir," said Mr. Davies, "May I introduce myself? Edward Davies, Headmaster of this parish, Bachelor of Science, second class honours."

George Garrad was a little disconcerted, partly because he hadn't managed to get a drink yet, partly because he was very uncomfortable around men of learning—which he himself wasn't—but mostly because, as in the adage "it takes one to know one," he had a great instinct for recognizing boors.

"Charming," said Garrad, attempting to cut the introduction and any consequent conversation short. He tried to get closer to Morgan and a good healthy draught of alcohol.

"I was wondering," Davies pressed through the crowd

on his coat tails, "whether you might talk to my pupils about cartography."

Garrad turned and gave him a brief attempt at a smile, "Of course, delighted, but you know how it is—so busy." Garrad hoped that would end it but Davies continued.

"I myself find it an endlessly fascinating subject, and since we seem to be at something of an impasse with the weather, I wondered whether you might give them your attention," he noticed Garrad pressing closer to Morgan, "after you've had something to eat of course."

Garrad now had both a beer and a sandwich in his grasp. Nothing would induce him to talk to a group of brats when he could be enjoying lunch, "Actually, the man to talk to is my assistant, Anson. Excellent with children. Anson!" he called out.

Anson stepped up, "George?"

"This is the local teacher . . ." said Garrad.

God how Davies hated that term! "Local teacher" Ugh, it made him sound as lowly as a veterinarian.

"Mr. Davies," repeated Davies, since it was obvious that George had forgotten his name.

"Yes, quite," continued Garrad, "now have a word with his pupils, would you Anson? Apparently they are fascinated by maps. Can't think why, odd thing for children to be interested in."

With that Garrad made his escape, settling down on a comfortable tuft of heather, at a noticeable remove from the villagers.

Davies was slighted—he did not want his pupils to be lectured by a lowly assistant. Thus, unwittingly, George Garrad lost his only potential ally in the whole of Ffynnon Garw.

"Well," said Anson, all too aware that yet again he

would have to make up for Garrad's *faux pas*, "do you think they'd like to look through the transit?"

As the village ate and drank Anson lifted up each child in turn and showed them a view through the transit and patiently drew simple diagrams explaining their procedures. By the end of lunch most of the children in Ffynnon Garw had a more comprehensive understanding of map-making than George Garrad.

It was a wonderful improvised picnic which lasted, for some odd reason, as long as Morgan's beer supply. Gradually the group of adults became quieter, and slowly but surely they sank down into the heather for an afternoon nap.

It was some hours later, almost teatime in fact, as most of the village still lay there, sleeping off the effects of Morgan's beer, when Thomas Twp and Thomas Twp Too stared off into the distance and saw that—as predicted—the mists were burning away from Newport Beacon and Whitchurch Hill. They were now clearly visible.

Thomas Twp and Thomas Twp Too looked at each other, and then at the transit which Anson had set up on a tripod. They weren't sure whether the transit could do the job by itself, or if Anson needed to operate it in some way.

"Do you think it's working yet?" asked Thomas Twp.

"I don't know," replied his brother.

"Well do you think we should wake them?" asked Thomas Twp.

They thought about this for a few minutes. They looked at the sea of sleeping figures. Anson looked very peaceful, lying flat on his back with his hat pulled over his features and Garrad was snoring heavily. They were loathe to disturb them, but then again they had come up here to work.

"I think we should wake them, if only to tell them," said Thomas Twp Too.

Together they rose and walked among the villagers. "It's almost teatime," said Thomas Twp as he walked among the dozing villagers, "and we can see."

"Wake up," said Thomas Twp Too, "we can see."

Anson was on his feet in no time and moments later he was surrounded by villagers, craning to watch him at work. Only Garrad had a hard time waking and rising to his feet. He had been dreaming that he was back in India, commanding the empire from a mosquito-netted padded sofa.

"Excuse me," said Anson, with a winning smile, as he moved a half dozen villagers who had been blocking his view. Having checked that his transit was levelled, he focused the cross-hairs of his telescope on the peak of Newport Beacon. He carefully noted the latitude, longitude and the angle of deflection before swinging towards Whitchurch Hill.

"Good," he said, as he noted the second angle of deflection, and the angle of incidence between the two sites.

"So?" said Morgan The Goat, impatiently.

"A result?" asked Reverend Jones, at the exact same moment, and with an equal urgency.

"You must understand," said Garrad, reverting to his tone reserved for speaking to the uncivilized, and uneducated, "that we have hours of calculations to do."

Anson grinned. Garrad was using the royal "we" since Anson, and Anson alone, would be sweating over the slide rule.

"But we will know later this evening," said Anson, and immediately regretted that he'd spoken so hastily. Now all knew when to expect a result, and he had a horrible feeling that he knew who would be delegated to tell them.

Johnny Shellshocked, finally seizing his chance to work for the English, stepped forward and grabbed the transit.

"Thank you very much," said Garrad, and then hastily followed him, like a maiden aunt watching a youth walk off with her prize aspidistra, "but do be careful with it."

Anson was making a few general notes about the weather and visibility for his journal, when one of the Twp's quietly asked, "But how will you know later?"

"Well," said Anson, determined to try and explain as much as possible, "we've made comparison with those other hills."

"But how were they measured?" asked another Twp.

"The same way," said Anson, "by comparing them to other hills." He smiled and left to follow Garrad.

The villagers were still confused, but as always it was one of the Twps who dared to voice the confusion, "But who measured the first hill?" he wondered.

"God, my boy! God!" said Reverend Jones, and Morgan The Goat rolled his eyes.

"But when was that?" asked Thomas Twp Too.

"On a Sunday," laughed Morgan, "when no-one was sinning and he had nothing better to do." And with a big smile to the scowling Reverend, Morgan swaggered away.

That night Morgan's pub did big business as all gathered to hear the result—all except Reverend Jones of course, who wouldn't step into such a den of iniquity. He sat on the bench around the flagpole, wringing his hands. Unlike most of the men in the village the Reverend wasn't the least bit interested in the wager he had made through Ivor. He was consumed with the status of their landmark.

It was standing room only as every male of drinking age,

and many younger, were packed into Morgan's parlour. The blackboard was now white with bets. Apart from Morgan and "Ivor's Cousin" two other men had chosen the same height—this time, three thousand feet—but it was all right because they were Thomas Twp and Thomas Twp Too.

Morgan's beer pumps were working like a steam engine. Morgan hadn't pulled this much beer since his last child had been born. Davies The School pushed his way through the crowd to the bar.

"Another for you?" asked Morgan.

"No," said Davies The School, "I want to change my bet."

Morgan thought for a split second—this could lead to anarchy, he'd have the whole pub changing their bets! "No," said Morgan firmly, "you can't do that. A bet's a bet."

"Well," said Davies, "I wish to make another one." The pub fell silent.

"Another one?" said Williams The Petroleum.

"That's allowed isn't it?" said Williams, "If I pay another penny?"

Upstairs in Anson's room both Englishmen were horribly aware of the seething mass of villagers who, under their very feet, were awaiting their result. One moment they would hear them erupt into laughter, or, as now, fall into disquieting silences.

Garrad broke the silence, "I have a terrible headache," he feigned, "and I should really lie down."

Anson had seen this ruse coming, "So would you like me to tell them?" he asked.

"No, no," pretended Garrad, "but then again, it would

give you some practice talking to the natives—and you never know when that might come in handy."

"Quite," replied Anson drily. He hated speaking in public but knew that there was little chance that he was going to escape this particular ordeal. Still he wasn't going to let Garrad off easily. "You know, they're not going to like this much," he said.

"No," replied Garrad, never one to be easily guilt-stricken, "but nevertheless these figures are Science. And what is Science, Mr. Anson?"

This was one of Garrad's favourite aphorisms, and Anson knew it well, but delighted in pretending that he'd forgotten it, "Yes, um, that one always slips my mind."

"Oh come on," said Garrad testily, "science is *dispassionate*."

"Of course!" grinned Anson, "Dispassionate! I wonder why I can never remember that, it's so simple: dispassionate!"

Downstairs in the bar Davies The School dug deep in his pockets and found a coin which he dropped into Morgan's jar for wagers and announced his new bet. "Nine hundred and eighty feet."

For a moment the pub fell silent, and then many voices were raised in protest.

"That's not fair!" exclaimed Williams The Petroleum, "he's an educated man, he watched them measuring, he might know something!"

It was a chilling thought—if Williams was right then the whole pub was wrong—and Ffynnon Garw wasn't a mountain.

Morgan fished Davies' money out of the jar and returned

it to Davies palm with a slap, "Objection substained. Besides, I'm not taking any bets under a thousand feet—traitor!"

"Judas!" hissed Williams The Petroleum and Davies The School walked out of the pub, through a scrum of scowling men.

Morgan shouted after him, "Are you sure you haven't got any English blood?" and the pub erupted into laughter.

Outside Reverend Jones heard the roar and saw Davies storming out, "Tell me," he pleaded, "a result? Do they have a result?"

"No!" said Davies curtly, and marched off into the night.

No need to be like that, thought Reverend Jones, but remembered that he'd never liked the man anyway.

Anson paused at the top of the stairs and took a series of deep breaths, too many in fact, for he had to catch the banister to stop himself from falling. Right, he thought, best do this quickly and efficiently, just like a raid, and with that he proceeded down the stairs. He'd only taken a few firm steps however, and he heard the bar quieten—the drinkers had frozen in anticipation, listening to his approach. Anson's last steps, as he came into full view of the assembled throng, were among the slowest he'd ever taken, but suddenly, there he was, with a sea of villagers' faces staring at him.

He cleared his throat, and tried to force a smile, "Mr. Morgan, with your permission?" Morgan made a magnanimous gesture—the floor is yours—and Anson swallowed hard. His mouth had become as dry as old paper, his throat seemed as constricted as Garrad's arteries.

"Well, gentlemen," he started, and hardly recognized his own voice, it sounded higher, and horribly reedy, "we have completed our survey of Ffynnon Garw," again he made the Welsh name sound like a monster from another universe, "and I have to inform you that it is nine hundred . . ."—a collective sigh filled the room—"and eighty-four feet."

The sigh burst into explosions of anger. Everywhere he looked men were scowling, growling, spitting, gesticulating. Anson held up his hand to restore order, it almost worked, "I know," he continued, "that this is a great disappointment, but it's just a measurement . . ." The pub fell utterly silent again, "and this measurement should in no way detract from the beauty of, or your affection for this . . ."

Anson dried . . . The word he had to say to complete his sentence was *hill* . . . He shifted his gaze, only to find another group of faces staring at him, his eyes skipped from them quickly only to find more glares. He looked at the ceiling and said it: "and this measurement should in no way detract from the beauty of, or your affection for this . . . *hill*." As soon as he said it he dashed back up the stairs.

There was utter, sepulchral silence. Morgan slumped, onto the bar, with the breath knocked out of him. "*Hill?!*" he said softly.

Men put down half finished pints and started to leave immediately. In the face of such a disappointment—such an *insult*—they didn't know how to look one another in the eye. Reverend Jones sat up as the pub started to empty. He feared the worst from their faces, the sad slouch of their shoulders, "Please tell me!" he asked Williams.

"It's a . . . hill." said Williams, and walked away with his head bowed.

"*A hill . . .*" sighed Reverend Jones and collapsed into an attitude of mourning.

The men of the village trudged slowly home to break the

news to their waiting wives and children. All through the village curtains were drawn, lamps were dimmed, candles were extinguished and conversation stopped.

A deathly hush fell over the valley and the only sound to be heard was of Reverend Jones, slowly rocking himself like a baby, on the bench around the flagpole. With each rock he let out a deep sigh, as if his very soul were leaving his body in pieces.

—᳁—

Perhaps it would have been different if there hadn't been a war, but this was 1917, and people were exhausted by loss. The young men left, and the young men returned, dead—or ruined like Johnny.

The few young men who were allowed to stay manned the pits, digging the coal which would fuel the ships. The shifts were long, twelve hours on and twelve hours off, a day shift and a night shift. The machinery never stopped. Men took up pick-axes whose handles were warm from the previous man's labour. Corners were cut, coal was hacked hastily, and safety precautions were loosened—and those who survived the Germans died for the coal.

It was a sad time. Friends had been taken, sons, husbands, fathers, lovers . . . And now here were the English, taking the mountain, removing a beloved spot from the map. At first the strangers had been a welcome distraction, a topic of gossip which lightened the long dark days. But their purpose had taken a darker turn. They had come to erase the mountain, erase the village's name, the village's pride.

How could the villagers face those who survived the war and would return to find no mountain? While they had fought the Germans their families had lost the mountain to the English? It was unthinkable. How could the village let the English take our mountain, take our very Welshness?

—∽—

Reverend Jones was filled with such thoughts. His mournful mood swung from despair to anger, from grief to fury. Suddenly, as the spiritual leader of the village, he felt very isolated, and very lonely. While he was trying to suppress his anger, he found that it could not be held back. It was bursting the banks of his reason. Well, let it come he thought! And as it raced through his body he had a moment of utter, blinding clarity: he would not stand for it!

He knew that the village felt as he did, and he knew that he could mobilize their opinions behind his. He—they—would not give in so easily, not without a fight.

With that, he jumped up from the bench and raced into the police station.

Sergeant Thomas and Jones The Constable were silently staring at the fire when the Reverend crashed through the door.

"Up off your fat arses!" He cried, shocking them to the core, "I want all the village, in the hall, now!"

"In the hall?" said the Sergeant.

"Now?" said the Constable.

"Now!" said the Reverend, "Or are you just going to sit there and accept what these barbarians have done to our mountain?"

The policemen fairly exploded out of the station, "Meeting in the village hall!" they cried, "Meeting in the village hall!"

William Jones, Justice Of The Peace, educated at a minor Oxford College, master of a minor stately home on the outskirts of Ffynnon Garw, and owner of a fatter arse than either of the village policemen, was a man of very few actual functions, but who, nevertheless, through his title, liked to imagine that in every way, shape and form, he managed the affairs of the village.

His work consisted largely of living in a manner which exemplified a standard to which the villagers should strive, though never attain. His table was set with the sorts of foods which, if they were available to them, the villagers should have enjoyed. His library housed the sorts of books the villagers should have read. His house was decorated in a manner which the villagers should have emulated if they'd ever been allowed over his doorstep to see it. While his children studied Latin in English schools, and his wife played Mozart, very badly, on an untuned French piano, his major contribution to the well-being of the community was his annual lumber, on the back of a sturdy horse, across the Welsh fields, chasing timid, hungry foxes.

He kept his distance from the village over whose Peace he was Justice, preferring his influence to happen by some magical distant osmosis, rather than any direct contact or intervention. He was consequently surprised when, as he was relaxing, listening to the sonorous sound of his footman cleaning boots and his maid scrubbing pots, his front door was hammered with some force, followed by Sergeant Thomas's booming voice. Had they been invaded by the Germans, he feared as he rose from his chair?

Sergeant Thomas was wheezing in the porch, there was

sweat streaming from under his helmet, the ride from the village had been hard after four pints of beer.

"The Reverend Jones," he panted, "has called a meeting," he broke for breath again, "at the village hall . . ." another breath, this was like weekly installments at the moving pictures, "now! And he wants you to come!" Another sharp intake of air, "He says you must come, it's a matter of great import."

"A meeting? Now? Was it scheduled Why wasn't I told?"

The Sergeant was shaking his head, "No, it's just come up, it's urgent, it's about the English."

Bit by bit it spilled out of the Sergeant and with each new detail the emerging picture filled Jones The JP with rage. A meeting at the village hall because Ffynnon Garw was *a hill*? Had they all gone mad?

He would liked to have said no, in fact he was on the verge of saying no, but one thing, or rather one person, stopped him. Reverend Jones . . .

He had never crossed swords with Reverend Jones and wasn't likely to start now. Though Jones The JP was a fool, and a lazy fool, he was wise enough to know that the real political power in the village lay with the chapel. To break with the Reverend would be suicidal. Jones The JP sucked in his belly, ordered his horse and trap, and prepared for a bumpy ride.

Anson was packing when he noticed the growing commotion outside his window and looked down into the square to find the whole village massing. For a moment he thought they were coming to the pub, and some of George Garrad's more lurid tales of native uprisings in faraway places sent a chill up his spine. He was relieved to see that they were pouring into the village hall.

He laughed to himself, what a vain, conceited idea, he thought, to imagine that all those people were gathering because of me! And he returned to his packing.

People were thronging into the village hall when Williams The Petroleum burst back into the pub. Only a couple of regulars were left drinking with Morgan who was ranting and raving, largely for his own benefit. "We'll be off the map!" he moaned, "Off the bloody map!" He went to the base of the stairs and yelled up towards the Englishmen's rooms, "Under my own roof, foreign meddlers!"

"Reverend Jones is holding a meeting at the village hall, now!" panted Williams.

Morgan's mouth curled down, his eyebrows up, "What's the old coot think he's going to do, raise the mountain?"

"He's going to organize a petition," replied Williams. Morgan didn't move. "Are you coming?" asked Williams.

The drinkers rose to leave. Morgan stayed put, "A petition?" he said, contemptuously.

With the village assembled and Jones The JP adorning the stage beside him, Reverend Jones brought the room to order. "Thank you all for coming," he started, which was something he never said in chapel, "and firstly I call upon Jones The JP to say a few words and give us his insight."

Jones The JP's heart sank. He'd been briefed in the most desultory way. Everyone assumed that he had been following the saga of the English and their measurings, whereas he had been, up until this evening, oblivious to their presence. Moreover he couldn't have cared less about Ffynnon Garw's status; hill or mountain, on or off the map. So in a time honoured tradition which extends to politicians today, he started to speak about something of which he knew nothing, but in a tone of voice which suggested authority. And more precisely, he started to string together many phrases and platitudes which all seemed to hold the promise of something, but which in fact amounted to nothing more than decorative vacillation.

"Well, thank you Reverend Jones," he paused before shifting into politician gobbledygook, "this is obviously a complicated matter . . ."

"Why?" called Thomas Twp from the audience.

Jones The JP's monocle fell out, he wasn't used to being heckled, he hurried on, "and one of great import, significance even, but at this present moment in time I'm afraid I don't have all the evidence," the audience began to stir. He wasn't prepared for this, most audiences could usually be worn into submission with this verbiage. He struggled on, "and I will have to ascertain, collect and collate all the facts . . ."

"Facts?!" This from Reverend Jones who had leapt to his feet like a Jack-in-the-box. He couldn't believe what Jones The JP was saying! "Facts?!" he repeated, "What facts do you need? Yesterday it was a mountain, today it's a hill!"

"Yes, I quite see that, but . . ."

Again Reverend Jones cut him off, "But nothing! Look, I propose a petition demanding the inclusion of Ffynnon Garw on all His Majesty's maps as the first mountain in Wales!"

The audience roared its approval and burst into a bout of prolonged applause. Jones The JP nodded and quietly sat down, leaving the floor to Reverend Jones.

However, before the Reverend could continue, a voice

boomed from the back. "And who's going to read this petition?" It was Morgan The Goat. He was standing just inside the door, with his hands placed firmly on his hips.

"I don't think we need any advice from you, Mister Morgan . . ." began Reverend Jones, but Morgan drowned him out with his beery bass voice.

"I haven't finished yet!" roared Morgan. The room turned to listen to him. Begrudgingly Reverend Jones gave him the floor.

"I don't want Ffynnon Garw on the map because we begged for it," continued Morgan, "because we pleaded. If Ffynnon Garw has to be a thousand feet then let it be one thousand feet!"

There was a moment of confused silence. No-one had yet caught up with Morgan's idea which had come to him after his offhand remark to Williams. "What does the old coot think he's going to do?" Morgan had said, and answered himself cynically, "Raise the mountain?"

After Williams had left that phrase had resonated in Morgan's mind and he had had a vision: all they had to do was to drag some soil from the top of Ffynnon Garw into a heap and then it would classify as a mountain.

The audience stared at Morgan, still not understanding. He explained, "A twenty foot tump, that's all we need!" In Morgan's mind it was very simple, firstly because he had no idea how big a twenty foot tump would be, and secondly because he had little or no intention of getting involved in the manual labour himself. Morgan saw himself on the inspirational end of things, rather than the perspirational.

Villagers in the hall suddenly caught on, a ripple went around the hall. Jones The JP didn't like it one bit. It smelt like conspiracy, or larceny.

"I'm not sure how legal that is," he said in his best judging voice.

"Or ethical!" added Reverend Jones.

"Legal?" retorted Morgan, "Ethical? How legal is it to decide one thousand feet is a mountain but nine hundred and eighty-four isn't?" Villagers were nodding in agreement. The Reverend would find this hard to argue, for he felt much the same.

Morgan continued, working the hall, "Do we call a short man a boy? Do we call a small dog a cat?" There was much laughter, now he had the village behind him. This was the Morgan they knew, and they were laughing with him.

Morgan puffed up his chest to bring them all to his cause, "No! This is a mountain, *our mountain*, and if it needs to be a thousand feet then by God let's make it a thousand feet!"

The applause started but quickly stopped as Reverend Jones thundered back, "I would prefer if you did not take the Lord's name in vain, Mr. Morgan!"

The hall quietened out of respect for the Reverend's views and in the silence Ivor The Grocer rose to speak. The Reverend considered him a good, God-fearing ally, and so gave him the floor, "Yes, Ivor."

Ivor smiled at the Reverend sheepishly, knowing that the Reverend was not going to like what he had to contribute, "Morgan The Goat," began Ivor and the hall burst into laughter, for while everyone called Morgan, Morgan The Goat behind his back, no-one ever said it to his face.

Morgan gave a yes-have-a-good-laugh-at-me nod and Ivor apologized before continuing, "Sorry Morgan," he turned back to the Reverend, "Morgan has a point: I've seen mountains topped by burial chambers, and the chamber's height is included as part of the mountain."

Reverend Jones was appalled! Ivor was siding with the reprobate Morgan?

To make things worse, a small, wiry miner, Billy, rose to announce that at Rhondda Fach there was a huge coal tip which appeared on maps.

A swell of conversation started to sweep the hall as all discussed Morgan's proposal. Was it possible? How could it be achieved. Reverend Jones looked around and saw that he had lost the crowd. He had to stop the rot now.

He rose to his feet, "Am I the only one," he glowered, "who thinks this smacks of sharp practice? Of cheating?!" The hall fell silent with embarrassment "What do we do? Lower one part of our beloved mountain to raise another? If I know Mr. Morgan, I'm sure that will be his plan!"

"Take it from your garden if it will make you feel better!" countered Morgan and all had a good laugh imagining the Reverend's garden perched up on Ffynnon Garw.

But the Reverend was ready with a reply. He knew how to freeze the laugh in people's cheeks. "Yes! It would make me feel better!" he shouted in fury, "I would be happier if the mountain were raised by toil, by sweat, by work, by sacrifice!"

The audience was deathly quiet now. He had imposed his spiritual leadership on them, he had made this hall his chapel. He looked around them, from face to face as he continued, "Take it from our gardens, take it from the river bank, take it from the valley floor! That would make me feel better!"

"You're just making it impossible!" moaned Morgan.

"No, Mr. Morgan, I am not!" said the Reverend and

had to pause to catch his breath, "For perhaps the first time in my life I agree with you on one point and on one point only: I too would rather not beg, plead, petition . . ."

"So?" interrupted Morgan.

"Or cheat!" thundered the Reverend, "If we are going to have this mountain, then we must earn it!"

Morgan thought the Reverend's proposal was mad, why did it matter where the extra soil came from? The height was the thing. Surely the English didn't care where the extra feet came from.

"So how, exactly are you going to make this mountain?" he countered, "By hauling your compost heap up Ffynnon Garw?"

That got a titter from the audience and again the Reverend found that he had reached a stalemate. He paused to re-group his thoughts and was surprised to see the figure of Johnny Shellshocked slowly rise in the middle of the audience. Would Johnny speak in public? The room fell silent for Johnny, and Jones The JP, who wanted to get home, took this as an opportunity to re-establish his prominence and bring the tedious meeting to a halt.

"Well this has been . . ." he began but was stopped by the Reverend who was still staring at Johnny.

"Johnny . . . ?" the Reverend coaxed him.

Still Johnny said nothing. His breathing was shallow, his voice pale, he stared at the floor. His sister, Blod, gripped his hand. The audience was beginning to turn away, it was upsetting to watch.

"In France," said Johnny so quietly that only the people next to him could hear. Blod squeezed his hand harder. He swallowed and started again, marginally louder, "In France we dug trenches ten miles long . . . We took earth from here and built hills there, we moved fields, you wouldn't believe what we did . . ." He paused. To speak he had to bring the words to mind. With the words came the images, with the images came the memories, with the memories came a wave of feeling that was so intense that it crushed him back to silence. "It's possible. It's just hard work," he concluded, "I'll help," and sat quickly down.

There was a moment of total silence, and then as one the audience started to speak, to organize, to plan.

And that's how it all started: Reverend Jones had an idea, but Morgan had a better one, which the Reverend further amended, and Johnny believed it was possible.

However, it didn't change the fact that Morgan The Goat wouldn't speak to Reverend Jones, and Reverend Jones wouldn't speak to Morgan The Goat, and Johnny would rarely speak to anyone.

CHAPTER 6

Morgan The Goat, Ivor The Grocer and Sergeant Thomas, being three men who considered themselves village leaders if not elders, returned to the pub for a quiet, private drink and to discuss one nagging problem: the English were planning to leave in the morning.

"They've got to stay and measure it again," said Morgan, "that's all there is to it."

"But what if they won't?" asked Sergeant Thomas.

"Well you order them to stay!" said Morgan.

"Don't be twp!" said Sergeant Thomas, "What am I going to do? Arrest them?"

Morgan thought about that for a minute, it obviously wouldn't work. "Well, you'll just have to be firm with them."

"Me?" said the sergeant. "It was your idea!"

"Ivor?" said Morgan, thinking that he would be a good persuader.

"Don't look at me," said Ivor.

"Bloody hell!" moaned Morgan, "Do I have to do everything myself?" He started to go upstairs. The sergeant and Ivor stayed at the bar. "Come on!" said Morgan, "Back me up! We're an official delegation from the village council."

"We are?" said the sergeant and Ivor.

Morgan, the sergeant and Ivor stood on the landing and listened carefully at Garrad's door. There was the sound of loud snoring.

Without a word of discussion they moved to Anson's and seeing that his lamp was still lit, Morgan knocked gently.

Anson was a little surprised by the sight that met him: the three men fairly filled the doorway, "Mr. Morgan? Sergeant?" He wondered if something was wrong.

"Mr. Anson," Morgan took the lead, "on behalf of the village we would like you to convince your Mr. Garrad to stay and measure the mountain again."

"Again?" said Anson and shook his head, "Look, I'm very sorry, but today's reading was accurate . . ."

"We're going to add twenty feet," interrupted Ivor.

Morgan wasn't absolutely sure if Ivor should have said that, still, the deed was done, there was no going back now.

Anson's jaw dropped, "What do you mean, add twenty feet?"

"It is legal isn't it?" asked Sergeant Thomas.

Before Anson even had time to think about it, Ivor and Morgan gave him the correct answer, "Heights of other mountains contain burial mounds," said Ivor, "Even coal tips," added Morgan.

"That's true," stammered Anson, "permanent additions to the landscape are included, but twenty feet? How . . . ?"

"Good!" said Sergeant Thomas, "Twenty feet it is!"

"We can't possibly hang about waiting while you add twenty feet . . ." Anson petered out as the enormity of what they were proposing hit him, "How are you going to add twenty feet?" he wondered.

"Never you mind," said Morgan, who wasn't keen for Anson to find a loophole, "you just convince your Mr. Garrad to stay."

That really was asking too much! In their schedule for measuring Ffynnon Garw, Garrad had allowed one day and it had already taken three. He was desperate to get on. They would be off first thing in the morning, and nothing, but nothing, would make Mr. Garrad stay.

Anson started to close his door, this conversation was utterly absurd, "I'm sorry gentlemen," he pushed the door in their faces, "but it is very late, and I am very tired, and we will be leaving in the morning."

Morgan showed Ivor and the sergeant out of the pub.

"It's a damned shame," said Sergeant Thomas.

"Oh don't worry about them," said Morgan, "they aren't going anywhere."

Sergeant Thomas was pleased with that, but in his official capacity as officer of the law, did not really want to know what Morgan was up to next, "I'm sorry Morgan," he said, "I missed that, I think I'm going deaf in this ear."

Morgan laughed, "I said 'Goodnight Sergeant.' "

"Goodnight!" grinned the sergeant, and cycled unsteadily away.

Morgan pulled Ivor into the shadows, "I need two pounds of sugar."

"But Morgan, it's rationed!"

"I know it's rationed," said Morgan, "but this is a national emergency."

"But two *pounds*?" said Ivor. A family's weekly allowance was four ounces. Morgan could have been asking for a handful of diamonds. "I don't think . . ."

Morgan cut him short. He fixed him with a beady stare, "I don't want to be telling people that it failed because of you," whispered Morgan darkly.

Ivor sighed, "Come on." He started down the side lane.

"Where are you going?" asked Morgan. Ivor's shop was cheek by jowl with the pub.

"I can't go in the front way!" said Ivor, "Not at this time of night, people will know that I'm up to no good."

"It's your bloody shop," said Morgan.

"We go round the back or we don't go at all," said Ivor.

"Fair's fair," said Morgan and followed him into the gloom.

By the light of a match Ivor crept around his storeroom, "I feel like a thief in my own shop," he moaned.

"Cheer up, Ivor," said Morgan, "It's for a good cause, and after the war I'll be able to tell people and you'll be a hero."

"If I'm out of jail," replied Ivor dourly. He pointed to a sack of sugar, "There you are."

"Just the job," said Morgan and started to fill a bag.

"But this," said Ivor, "is the problem." He was holding

his book in which he had to record, for inspection, the dispensation of rations.

"Well just fill in a few names," said Morgan.

"A few names? That amount of sugar would fill half a page and, what's worse, they sometimes check them against people's ration books."

"Bloody hell, it's bureaucracy gone bananas," said Morgan as he realized the scale of the problem. "Can't you say the sack was two pounds short?"

"You don't think every bugger has tried that one?"

They both sat in the gloom, thinking about the problem.

"I've got it," said Morgan, "give me a pen and ink."

"Morgan . . . ?"

It was too late, Morgan had the book from Ivor's hands and seizing a bottle of ink, Morgan poured its contents into the book, completely obliterating a couple of pages.

"Dear me!" said Morgan, "What a clumsy devil you are Ivor, and all those names, lost under the ink."

Ivor was speechless.

"And if they give you trouble tell them to call on me—I was here when you spilled the bottle, couldn't help it could you? Simple mistake."

Moments later Ivor and Morgan stole quietly around Anson and Garrad's car, searching for the petrol tank.

"Are you sure this will work?" hissed Ivor.

"It will work if we can find the bloody tank," replied Morgan.

Twice they circled the car in vain, but on the third inspection they discovered a chromed cap, hidden behind the spare wheel.

"There you are," said Morgan, intimating that it was Ivor's job to complete the dirty deed.

"I don't know what I'm doing!" complained Ivor and wondered for the umteenth time why he had allowed himself to get caught up in this absurd piece of larceny.

"There's nothing to it," whispered Morgan, "you pour it in, I'll keep a look-out."

Ivor slowly unscrewed the cap. It seemed to creak louder with each turn, but eventually it came free. He gently set it on the ground and then taking the bag he slowly poured in the whole bag of sugar. To Ivor's nervous ears, it sounded like a cart unloading a load of sand, and it seemed to go on for ever.

Morgan casually leaned against the pub wall and lit a cigarette, "Finished?" he asked.

"There's just a couple of teaspoonfuls caught in the folds at the bottom."

"Good," said Morgan, whisking the bag from his hands, "Blod will be glad of those."

When Morgan arrived at Blod's that night she greeted him with a question, "So? Are the English staying?"

Morgan smiled a wicked smile, "Oh I think I won them over my love, I think I won them over!" and Blod gave him a great big kiss, and much much more.

—ⅲ—

There are days which are different. Take Christmas Day, or any national holiday: It may fall on a Tuesday, a Thursday or a Saturday, but whatever the calendar may say, the day takes on a character of its own. Familiar places seem to change subtly, the quality of sunlight appears special, the event that all are celebrating seems palpable in the very air.

The day that dawned after the village hall meeting was

like that: the whole village awoke with purpose, all ready to work, all ready to co-operate, all knowing that there was a job to be done, and that if the job was completed, their honour would be restored. When they looked out of their windows that morning they looked at the fields and saw poetry; they looked at the landscape and saw sculpture; they looked into their souls and saw hope.

Johnny Shellshocked was the first up. By the light of dawn he was pacing the meadow that sloped down to the river. It was too damp for grazing and too shaded for crops, but might make good material for a mountain. He sunk his heel into the sod and ran it along scoring the earth. No pebbles, no stones, that was a good sign. As he paced he imagined a tump twenty feet high. How wide would the base be? How steep the slope? He looked over to one of the houses that ran down to the river. Twenty feet must be to the top of an upstairs bedroom window, if not the eaves. He imagined something roughly pyramidical in his mind, and then worked in reverse, imagining that volume of soil spread out over this meadow. This rough imaginary calculation told him that they might have to dig a couple of feet of top soil from the whole area. It would be a huge mass of earth. The plan was ambitious, foolhardy even. And while getting the soil up there would be a huge undertaking there was yet another problem to solve—how would they measure their own addition?

The very same question was occupying Sergeant Thomas as he walked past the flagpole on his way to work. He looked up at the pole, how high was that? He remembered replacing it four or five years ago and a figure of twenty-four feet stuck in his mind. As he drank his tea he stared out at it. How would the villagers know when they had assembled twenty feet of earth? It would be a terrible thing to lug all that soil up there, have it measured again and still be a few feet short. They'd need some sort of measure. He looked back at the flagpole. In a flash he knew the answer, and rummaged in the *cwch* under the stairs, looking for his saw.

Up at the Twp Farm the brothers had perfunctorily rushed through their morning's work. The cows had been milked, the chickens and geese had been fed. Luckily, it was summer and the sheep could look after themselves. Now they set to the real work at hand. They harnessed their best pair of ploughing horses, selected their heaviest, deep-cutting plough and set off for the village.

Bright and early, Ivor was back in his store-room rummaging around for old sacks, half barrels, anything that would hold soil.

At the allotments old men greased their wheelbarrows and cleaned their spades. In kitchens, women emptied buckets and tin baths. Bedpans came out of cupboards, old sheets from closets.

And at the inn Anson and Garrad still slept, dreaming their last dreams before waking up in a village which had been transformed overnight.

Reverend Jones sat at his desk and planned the day ahead. He doubted that Morgan would play any great role in the work and toil—if he knew Morgan the man would stay in bed—and thus it fell to the Reverend to act as inspirational leader and tactical organizer. All hands would be needed, and the Reverend's first job lay at the village school. Putting on his best Sunday clothes, combined strangely with his sturdiest weekday boots, he strode from his house with the vigour of a younger man.

By the time most of the villagers assembled at the meadow they found that the Twps and Johnny had been hard at work. A large swathe of meadow had been freshly ploughed revealing rich, loamy soil. Having ploughed it in one direction, Johnny had turned the Twps' plough through ninety degrees, and they were now set to plough the same patch again. The first time had been to expose the soil, the second pass would break the tightly knotted turf. It was not a technique that any farmer would have used, instead it was the product of Johnny's unique and horrific experiences in France. With the turf cut away the soft soil lay ready for the eager villagers and their army of buckets, handcarts and wheelbarrows.

Davies The School was practicing the morning hymn on the piano when there was a knock at the door. "It is not nine o'clock!" he yelled, assuming that it was a pupil.

However the door opened anyway and there appeared the smiling face of Reverend Jones. "I'm not disturbing you am I?"

Davies The School was surprised, and suspicious. Why had Reverend Jones chosen to pay him a call at this busy time of day? Nevertheless Davies forced his features into a smile, "No, no, not at all, Reverend, do come in."

Reverend Jones made his way across the room in a swaying, jolly, obsequious manner. Davies became more wary. "I thought you were one of the children," explained Davies.

"Ah!" sighed the Reverend with significant emphasis, "Just what we need to talk about . . ."

"Pardon me?" Davies was confused.

"The children, your pupils, the children of this village . . ."

Where is the Reverend leading with all this, wondered Davies. "Ye-es," was all he managed in reply.

Reverend Jones put down his hat and came eye to eye with Davies, "Today is an historic day!" said the Reverend, "Historic! A day generations will talk about for years to come!"

"Is there news from the Front?" asked Davies, hoping that the stalemate had been broken in the war to end all wars.

"No," smiled the Reverend, "the news is here," he pointed through the classroom window at the mountain, "the news is up there! Today we are building a mountain, and I want your pupils to help."

"Building a mountain," said Davies drily. He had attended the town hall meeting and had left believing that they were all indulging in a childish hysteria.

"We are adding twenty feet to Ffynnon Garw," said Reverend Jones, just in case Davies hadn't understood their true intent, "this morning a hill, this afternoon a mountain, and that, my dear friend, is surely an education!"

Davies rose from the piano, "It is quite beyond my power," he pontificated, "to release my pupils to anyone but their parents or legal guardians."

"*Your* pupils?" chided the Reverend. He wanted to add "*my* children" but stopped himself, "These are the children of the village."

"*My* pupils!" repeated Davies and started to walk away,

"My pupils, to help you labour? To help you falsify the height . . ."

He had used the wrong word, and Reverend Jones was on him like a panther, grabbing him by the shoulders. He spun him round and almost pressed his nose against Davies's face. The Reverend's eyes shone with fire, spittle curdled at the edges of his mouth, his voice rose like a banshee, "Falsify!" He thundered, "Mr. Davies! Both your sense of community and your vocabulary leave much to be desired!" And with that he thrust Davies back into his chair, leaving him, much as one would leave a discarded article of soiled clothing.

Reginald Anson laboured out of the pub with the last load of their luggage to find a very exasperated Garrad.

"Come on, Anson!" he moaned, as if he had carried his fair share, "Give me a hand here with the crank."

Anson tried to smile, and having placed the cases and measuring poles in the back of the car he took up the handle and applied himself to cranking the motorcar into life.

The car gave a wheeze, a clutter, a fart, and stopped. Anson tried again. This time there was a series of burps and hiccups.

"Hmmm," said Garrad and Anson tried again. This time the car did nothing. Garrad climbed down out of the driver's seat and opened the large gleaming bonnet to reveal a large oily engine. "Hmmm," he repeated, staring at the engine. He had no mechanical expertise, and no idea of what he should be looking for—he might just as well have been studying the score for a Chinese Opera.

Anson joined him. Together they gawped at a large block of steel from which emanated a series of dull pipes, brass tubes and electrical wires. "Could it be damp?" asked Anson who knew as little as Garrad.

"Perhaps, perhaps," muttered Garrad and, feeling that his mere look at the engine must have done some good, he returned to his favourite spot behind the wheel, "Right Anson, once more."

Anson gave the crank a vicious jerk, but again nothing happened. Not even a wheeze. The effort almost put Anson's arm out of its shoulder socket.

"Crank harder!" barked Garrad.

"I *am* cranking harder," said Anson, who was rapidly losing his patience, "perhaps you'd like to have a try." He couldn't resist adding, under his breath, "Though I'd hate you to have to exert yourself . . ."

Garrad heard him, this was insubordination, "What was that?" he demanded.

Luckily for Anson, Garrad was distracted by Morgan The Goat who had just arrived home from Blod's.

"Trouble gentlemen?" Morgan couldn't help grinning.

"Yes, I'm afraid so," huffed Garrad.

"Oh dear, oh dear, oh dear," sighed Morgan.

He was about to enter the pub when Anson stopped him.

"Mr. Morgan," he inquired, "I was wondering if you knew what happened to the flagpole." It was the first thing Anson and Garrad had noticed that morning: the flagpole—and Garrad's beloved Union Jack—had disappeared. All that remained was a sawn-off stump.

Morgan didn't know for sure, but he had a pretty good idea. He thought quickly, "Dry rot," he smiled.

Garrad's brows furrowed deeper than the meadow, "Dry rot? In Wales?"

"Amazing isn't it?" said Morgan and disappeared into the pub.

Anson stopped in his tracks and for the first time the possibility of sabotage entered his mind. Earlier that morning he'd been intent on sharing with Garrad his experience the previous evening when Morgan and the delegation had arrived at his bedroom door. However, Garrad had been in such a foul mood that Anson had kept his distance and busied himself with loading the car. Now he wondered whether he should mention it, since their car wouldn't start and the flagpole had disappeared. Were these things coincidental? Were they victims of a plot?

"Anson," snapped Garrad, "you're day-dreaming again."

Bugger Garrad, thought Anson, I'm damned if I'm sharing my insights with him . . . "No, not day-dreaming," said Anson, "but thinking. I find it helps sometimes, when one is in a predicament."

"We are not," said Garrad, "in a predicament. We merely have a small problem in that our motor car won't start—and I suggest *you* find someone to help us."

"And *who* might that someone be?" asked Anson. He was genuinely mystified since they were, after all, in a small, rural, Welsh village, and some distance from the kind of size-able town which might be expected to boast a mechanic schooled in the complexities of an automobile engine.

"Well, for a start, you could try that fellow down the road with the petrol pump."

Down near the river the meadow had been transformed from a quiet sloping pasture into an assembly line for building a mountain. Rows of elderly men shovelled soil into buckets which was then piled onto carts by the women. There was only one thing missing—as yet no-one had actually carried any earth up Ffynnon Garw.

The flagpole, however, had been lugged up the mountain by the sergeant, the constable and Billy. With a couple of joists they nailed it upright and then stared at its height. It towered over them.

"That looks a hell of a lot more than twenty feet," said the constable.

"It's twenty," said Billy, "I measured it." And he started to mark each foot as far as he could reach.

Sergeant Thomas shook his head, "Jesus, boys, we're going to need a lot of soil to cover that."

He and the constable exchanged worried looks. For the first time they doubted the feasibility of this venture. It was all very well for Morgan, the Reverend, and Johnny to stand in the village hall and blithely talk about "just twenty feet." It was quite another when one faced the reality.

Williams The Petroleum—whose modern enamel sign advertised farm machinery, grease and petroleum—had installed a petrol pump the previous year. Something of a visionary, he had seen the future and knew that the motor car was coming. However, the future had resolutely failed to reach Ffynnon Garw. There were a handful of motor cycles in the vicinity, but as yet no-one, not even the wealthy Jones The JP, owned a car of their own. Williams' underused petrol-pump had become something of a local joke, and his new nickname, Williams The Petroleum, had a very sarcastic ring to it.

Williams had been down at the meadow, labouring with the rest of the village, and had only returned to his workshop to collect more buckets when he was stopped by the smiling Anson.

"Morning," said Reginald, "we seem to have a little bit of a problem with our car. Do you think you might be able to help?"

Well you would have a problem, thought Williams, with two pounds of sugar in your petrol tank. He coughed, "Well . . ."

"We really would appreciate your help," continued Anson, and Williams didn't know how to say no without arousing suspicion.

"What kind of engine have you got?" he asked, thinking that this was the sort of question that a real mechanic might ask.

"To tell you the truth, I have no idea," replied Anson, "as far as I'm concerned an engine is an engine."

"Well, you're right, up to a point," said Williams who felt much the same.

While Garrad waited for Anson and Williams at the front of the inn, Morgan laboured in the rear, loading his horse and cart with beer, lemonade, saspirilla and pies. Since his success feeding the measuring party, he was confident that he could sell a whole cartload at lunch-time. He intended to be the first up Ffynnon Garw, ready to feed and water the thirsty throng. Considering how hard they were going to work, it was the least he could do.

Anson returned to the car with Williams in tow. "George," he said, "meet Mr. Williams, he knows all about motor cars."

Garrad looked him up and down and decided that Williams's clothing was suitably greasy for a bona fide engineer.

He opened the long bonnet for him and waited as Williams scrutinized the huge engine block.

Williams had never seen anything like it and quickly improvised in a manner that has since become a tradition for all mechanics: he wiped an oily rag along an engine part, fiddled with a wire and poked at a tube. He had no idea what he was doing, "Now try it again," he said.

Anson cranked again. Nothing.

Williams wiped a different part, poked at another tube and played with an alternative wire, "And again . . ."

Anson cranked again. Less than nothing.

"So?" snapped Garrad. He was sitting on the running-board, kicking petulantly at the gravel. He had somehow imagined that their problem was simple. A mere glance under the bonnet, a little tweak, and he hoped to be on his way.

"Well . . ." demurred Williams.

"Well what?" demanded Garrad, who was quickly losing his patience with this man.

"Well, whatever it is, you've probably flooded it by now, so I think it's best if we just leave it for ten minutes." Then, since they were standing outside the pub, he added the *coup de grâce*, "Fancy a drink?"

Garrad brightened immediately, "Well, I suppose it is almost lunch-time," he noted, and limped into the bar with Williams.

Anson watched them in amazement. It was nowhere near lunch-time! One minute Garrad was desperate to get away, the next he was desperate to get help, but at the first mention of alcohol he was prepared to drop everything. Anson put down the crank, closed the bonnet and reluctantly followed them.

No sooner had they left the car than the wraith-like figure of Reverend Jones emerged around the corner and stopped in his tracks—the English were still in the village! Here was their car, loaded, and apparently ready to leave.

The Reverend, who was still steaming from his encounter with Davies The School, looked around to make sure that no one was watching as he took a small penknife from his pocket. Fumbling with terror he opened the blade and looked skyward to God.

"Forgive me Lord," he whispered, "but they know not what they do." He plunged the blade into the tyre, quickly returned it to his pocket and left the scene of the crime singing to cover the sound of the escaping air.

"Bread of heaven, bread of heaven, feed me 'til I want no more . . ."

"Morgan?" Williams called at the empty bar. There was no reply. Garrad settled himself on a bar stool that he was rapidly making his own and stared hopefully at a bottle of gin. Anson collapsed in the corner, thoroughly bored by the proceedings.

Williams called for Morgan again, but was again met by silence. "Hold onto your horses," he said, "I'll have a look for him, he's never far."

"If only we did have horses," mused Garrad and turned to Anson. "Did I ever tell you about the time in the Sudan when all our horses were rustled and we had to use camels."

"No, George, you didn't," replied Anson and tried to imagine Garrad's bulk perched upon a dromedary.

It was as he was poking around the upstairs bedrooms that Williams heard a clink of bottles in the garden and looked out to see Morgan still loading his cart. Williams went down the back stairs and confronted him.

"Morgan! I've been standing at that bar like a lemon!"

"Help yourself, but write it on the slate," said Morgan who had bigger fish to fry.

"But I've got the English with me," now he had Morgan's attention, "they want me to repair their car."

"So?" asked Morgan, and realizing that he had a spare pair of hands available, motioned for Williams to help loading the heavier items.

"Well, what shall I do?" asked Williams.

"Take it down to the garage and take the engine apart," replied Morgan. It all seemed very logical to him.

"But I've never taken one of these apart," said Williams, whose experience was limited to a couple of motor cycles, "it isn't a simple two-stroke."

"Doesn't matter," said Morgan, "it can't be that different."

"You don't know what you're talking about," said Williams, "you should see the size of that thing! It's as big as Tommy Twostroke's motor cycle!"

"But the principle's the same," said Morgan blithely, "I'm sure there's nuts and bolts and screws and things."

"Of course there are."

"Well then?" Morgan really couldn't see the problem.

"But what if I take it apart and can't put it back together?" asked Williams. He didn't want to incur the wrath of George Garrad.

Morgan thought for a split second, and in that moment had a wonderful vision of Garrad's car, lying in pieces, "Well," he smiled, "if you can't put it back together you'll have done us all a great service and we will all be eternally grateful."

—m—

Down at the meadow Reverend Jones was delighted with what he found. The adult population of the village was here, digging for all they were worth. He walked around dispensing congratulations, "Well done, well done," he glowed, "there's more than one way to beat those Saxons, eh!"

At the centre of the work he found Johnny shovelling hell-for-leather. He shook Johnny's hand warmly, "You know you're the inspiration for all this," he smiled, and Johnny blushed.

He moved on to Ivor and his wife Rachel, "Where are those strapping lads of yours" he asked, "We could use them on a day like this!"

"They're in school," said Rachel.

"A chronic waste of a youth's time!" said Reverend Jones, "Don't you want them involved on this day of days? Shame on you, letting them idle away indoors when here we are, engaged in lifelong struggle with the invading English!"

Rachel didn't have to be told twice. Within moments she and a phlanx of other mothers were marching on the school.

Two gins later George Garrad, followed by Reginald Anson and Williams The Petroleum, left the pub to resume work on the car. They were immediately faced with a new problem: the front tyres were flat.

"Bloody hell!" exclaimed Williams.

"Quite," agreed Anson.

Garrad snapped and glared at Williams, "Do you know who is behind this?"

"I don't know what you are suggesting!" said Williams defensively.

"What I am suggesting, Mr. Williams," Garrad spelled

it out, "is that our problems seem highly coincidental with my qualification of your mountain as a hill. I am beginning to suspect bad sportsmanship, childish revenge and . . ."

"Stop!" said Williams, "Stop before you say something that you will regret! Yes, it's true that many people are upset, but to suggest . . . !" He pulled himself to his full height, inflated his chest and stuck out his chin, "Mr. Garrad, sir, we are an honourable people."

He said it with such force and commitment that Garrad felt moved to back down. "I'm sorry," he said, "but it just seemed very, very odd . . ."

"Well, that's as maybe," said Williams, "but let's get on with the job in hand. Let's get this down to the garage."

Anson, who was now absolutely sure that he was at the centre of a mounting conspiracy, asked with a twinkle in his eye, "And how long do you think these repairs might take?"

"Oh, I'll have you on your way in no time," said Williams. His lies were getting better and better.

"Good," said Garrad, "because otherwise we will have to find an alternative form of transportation."

Morgan, who had been listening to this exchange from his bedroom window, froze—he hadn't anticipated that they would be prepared to leave without their precious car. There was another, very easy way to leave Ffynnon Garw—from the railway station. In a flash Morgan was off, hightailing it down the back lane to see Thomas The Trains.

"So," concluded Williams, "if you gentlemen would like to remove your luggage and then push me down to the garage."

"Push?" Garrad had never engaged in such manual labour.

"I'm afraid so," said Williams.

Garrad looked to Anson for backing, but Anson let him down. "Push," he said simply, as if it were a natural thing for an ex-Brigadier like Garrad to do on a warm Welsh summer's day.

Thomas The Trains was watering his tomatoes when Morgan appeared at speed. Ffynnon Garw was a sleepy little station and Thomas had lined the platform with flowers interspersed with the odd vegetable. It gave him something to do between the infrequent passenger trains.

He saw Morgan coming out of the corner of his eye and gauged from Morgan's stride that trouble was afoot.

"Morning, Morgan," he said and picked out a couple of flowering heads from his tomatoes, "fancy some flowers for Blod?"

Morgan had no time for pleasantries, "The English might come along later," he started, "trying to get a train out."

"Yes . . ." Thomas was dreading whatever Morgan had in mind.

"And you must stop them."

"Stop them?" said Thomas incredulously, "How?" It was a reasonable question.

"How? When? Why? What's wrong with this village?" moaned Morgan, "Hasn't anyone get the least bit of initiative?"

"It's all very well saying "Stop them", continued Thomas, "but if they've made up their minds to catch a train . . ."

"You un-make their minds!" roared Morgan. "Look, Thomas, it's very simple; I don't want to be telling people that this all failed because of you."

Thomas felt his whole body droop. Suddenly his tomato plants looked sickly, the sky looked dark, the station looked tawdry. Morgan had ruined his day. Thomas was a simple man, a quiet man, not given to confrontation. He liked a simple life. He sold tickets, he collected tickets. He opened carriage doors, he closed carriage doors. The trains ran on a timetable created by more illustrious men. He wanted a quiet life, a regimented life. And here was Morgan with all his complications. Thomas's chest felt tight.

"So," finished Morgan, "don't let me down. Don't let the whole village down." And with that he strode away.

Thomas sighed, and picked the head from a dead rose.

CHAPTER 7

Motorcars in 1917 were built to exacting standards and were, by today's standards, very, very heavy, so it was with some considerable effort that George Garrad and Reginald Anson pushed the car over the river bridge towards Williams The Petroleum's "garage".

It was just as well that the car was heavy and that both men were bent double in their efforts to push, for had they looked up at that moment they would have seen the whole village gathered on the river-bank, loading every available cart, bucket and barrow with soil.

"We've chosen a hot day for it," said Thomas Twp, to Reverend Jones.

"Better than rain," replied Reverend Jones whose job it was to dispense optimism.

"But it will rain later," said Thomas Twp Too who had

been watching the larks. They were flying too high for his liking.

"Then all the better to refresh us!" said the Reverend, determined to see the best in all of the Lord's creation.

Morgan, who tended to notice the worst things in creation, had taken a detour on his way back from the station, and was now in the garden of a young emaciated miner known to all as Tommy Twostroke, on account of the fact that he had a motor cycle. Tommy was the forerunner of a movement which would spread through the world of young men—as soon as he had seen a motor vehicle he had been intoxicated by the notion of speed. Already in ill health, he further exacerbated his condition by working every hour of voluntary overtime until he could afford a bike of his own.

He didn't regret it for one minute. To ride the bike was the love of his life. In the first days he'd had it he had ridden the length and breadth of the area. He would happily deliver messages from villagers to relatives in distant hamlets. He was always looking for an excuse to ride his bike on his days off.

Morgan had been one of the first to use Tommy's services, but it became so out of hand that Tommy's wife had demanded Morgan at least pay for petrol. Morgan had reluctantly agreed, and now felt that he owned Tommy's services. Today he needed Tommy to make an urgent trip as part of his grand plan concerning the mountain and the English. Unfortunately it wasn't Tommy's day off.

Tommy's formidable wife, Elsie, was sitting in the garden shelling peas when Morgan came racing through the gate.

She merely glanced up before speaking her mind, "He's not going anywhere for you," she said, "He's sleeping, he's on night shift."

"Wake him woman!" demanded Morgan, "This is a matter of life and death!"

"Life and death my arse," said Elsie and popped another pea-pod.

Morgan pushed past her, grabbed the tin bath, pounded it with a coal shovel and yelled up at Tommy's window, "Tommy! Get down here!" Only the dead could sleep through that.

Davies The School was continuing with the history of Llywelyn The Last when, to his surprise, he saw a force of mothers crossing the playground, and making for his classroom door.

Immediately, and without so much as a knock or an "excuse me," a few of them were in his classroom.

"We've come for our children," said Rachel.

"They're needed at home," said Mavis.

"But this is most irregular!" complained Davies. His words were lost to the wind which rushed through his classroom and spirited the kids away.

Within moments only one child was left.

Tommy Twostroke rubbed the sleep from his eyes and scratched at his woollen pyjamas. He couldn't take it all in.

"It's on the road just out of Cardiff, on the way to Newport," said Morgan.

This was farther than Tommy had ever gone before, "Do I have to go through Cardiff?" he asked. He'd never driven in the city, it frightened him, he liked the open, empty, country roads.

"Not if you don't want to," said Morgan, "you can skirt around it, can't you?"

"We-ell . . ." Tommy wasn't sure. "What if I get lost?"

"Look, it's on the main road from Cardiff to Newport, a bloody big house, proper driveway, very posh, you can't miss it. Just ask for Miss Elizabeth." Morgan was drawing a crude map.

"But Morgan," said Tommy, "This will take me all day and I'm working nights!"

Morgan had no sympathy, "There's some of us working day and night," he countered.

"But all the way to Cardiff and back . . ."

Morgan brought his face close to Tommy's, "I don't want to be telling people it all failed because of Tommy Twostroke." He said it with steel in his voice and menace in his eyes. Tommy shivered, and it wasn't from the cold.

With a final sweaty heave Anson and Garrad pushed the car into Williams's "garage". Garrad immediately collapsed on the running-board and tried to catch his breath. He hadn't felt like this since being chased by a native through the bazaar in Cairo. Would his heart ever settle down again?

Williams disappeared into his back room, "Capital", he said, "I'll just get my tools."

Anson looked around him. Cart wheels, ploughs, an anvil, nothing in sight inspired much confidence. He couldn't help grinning.

Just then Tommy Twostroke appeared, pushing his motorbike to the petrol pump. With the obsessive, methodical concentration of a true fanatic, he carefully unscrewed the petrol cap and wiped it before inserting the hose and hand-pumping a whole half-gallon into his petrol tank.

"I've taken half a gallon on Morgan The Goat's account!" he yelled to Williams, before nodding at the English and getting on his way.

Morgan The Goat's account? Anson and Garrad glanced at each other. How odd.

Williams returned to the car. He was carrying his only suitable tools—a very large hammer and a contrastingly diminutive screwdriver. "Right then, to work!" he said with false confidence.

"Excuse me," inquired Anson, "but did I hear that fellow correctly: Mr. Morgan has an account?"

"Ye-es," said Williams, worried where this was leading.

"So does he have a car?"

"No," replied Williams truthfully, "he just has an account."

Garrad's tiny mind spun like a top—it was now that he decided that he would never, ever understand the Welsh, and there was little point in trying.

Down at the meadow the horses were bridled, the carts were ready, the buckets were full, but all were loathe to begin. It was as if they were waiting for a sign from God. Since Reverend Jones was the next best thing he took it upon himself to relieve a child of a bucket and march from the meadow. "Follow me!" he cried, and the village fell in after him, on their way to the top of Ffynnon Garw with several tons of soil.

—⚂—

Anson and Garrad sat in the shade. Anson was idly reading an out of date newspaper. Garrad was staring at the parts of his car which were beginning to litter the ground around them. Williams was still under the bonnet, making frightful noises with his hammer.

"Do you think," asked Garrad, "that he has the foggiest idea of what he's doing?"

Anson looked up, he was enjoying the show, "He's certainly stripping it with great confidence," he observed.

"I know," said Garrad, "but . . ."

"I'm afraid I don't know the first thing about motor cars and their petroleum engines," admitted Anson.

"Unfortunately, neither do I," said Garrad.

Williams could easily hear their conversation and looked around the remains of the engine. He had to think of something quickly.

Anson returned to reading the paper. Garrad twiddled his moustache. They'd been sitting here for over an hour and he hadn't seen a soul walk down the village street. It was making him very uncomfortable.

"I'm not sure that I like this village," Garrad continued to disturb Anson's reading and further worry Williams, "it's altogether much too quiet."

"I've noticed," agreed Anson, "but I rather like it."

"You like it?" said Garrad, "Good God, Anson, you do sometimes say the oddest things."

At that moment Williams freed a small rod and snapped it in his hands, "Aha!" he exclaimed, "I think, gentlemen, that I have found the problem!"

Anson and Garrad were immediately on their feet. Williams showed them the snapped rod.

"And how do you think that happened?" asked Garrad.

"Wear and tear," replied Williams.

"Wear and tear? It's practically new!" complained Garrad.

"Well in that case I'd say that it was probably defective to begin with. You'd best be having a word with the manufac-

turers when you return to London." Williams was pleased
with that, it sounded very knowledgeable.

"And what is that part, exactly?" asked Garrad who was
going to make a note of it for his letter of complaint.

"We-ell, I don't know the English word," said Williams,
"but in Welsh we call it a *bethyngalw*." He wasn't lying when
he said he didn't know the English word, but he didn't know
the Welsh either. *Bethyngalw* means thingamajig, or what-
d'you-call-it.

"A what?" demanded Garrad.

"A berthaingalloose," replied Anson as if he understood
completely.

"Close enough," said Williams.

"And where," asked Garrad, "can we find a replace-
ment?"

"Ooo," said Williams, as if confronted with one of the
greater mysteries of life, "we'll have to send Tommy Twostroke when he gets back. He'll probably have to go as far as
Cardiff."

"Cardiff?" moaned Garrad, seeing his escape disappear.

"Not to worry, George," said Anson, "it just means we'll
have to stay here for a couple of days."

Garrad shot him a look that Anson did not want to receive again. It was a look which had inspired many an upris-
ing in the Far and Middle East.

"So, Mr. Williams," Anson quickly asked, "is there any
other transport for hire?"

"No," said Williams, "it's all being used for . . ." He
stopped himself just in time. He was going to say for the
mountain. He took a deep breath and tried to compose himself.

"Yes?" pried Anson, "Do finish—used for what?"

Anson now knew exactly what the transport was being used for! They were building the hill into a mountain.

"We-ell," Williams's mind raced and quickly seized on something, "It's all being used for the War!" It was brilliant! Something that Garrad would respect. However Garrad's mind had moved on.

"I thought I heard a train last night," he said, "so is there a railway station?"

Williams didn't know what to say. If he told them where the station was they could leave on the evening train. He stared at Garrad in mute confusion.

"It's not a difficult question," said Garrad, "Is there—or is there not—a railway station?"

"Well, not really . . ." said Williams. It was the best he could do in the circumstances.

"Not really?" said Garrad tapping his foot . . .

Unlike its rather larger brothers, Everest and the Eiger, there are as many ways to climb Ffynnon Garw as there are to skin a cat. It is possible to hike up even its steepest incline in just a pair of sturdy boots, and for those who don't mind a longer excursion, there are several farm tracks and sheep paths which lazily zig-zag from the valley to the summit.

If, however one was to take a large horse and cart—as many of the villagers were now doing—there was only one tenable route.

Starting from the meadow the villagers had passed the pub and the chapel and continued up the main road to a gate which opened onto a slightly inclined field. At the far end of the field an ancient, tree-lined track traversed the lower slopes

of Ffynnon Garw. After a mile it turned almost back on itself
before ending, quite abruptly at a large outcrop of rocks. This
was the highest place that a horse and cart could easily reach,
and had, as such, been recognized by Morgan as the place
where the village was most likely to pause before transferring
all the soil to buckets—the rest of the journey would involve
carrying the earth by hand.

It was at this spot—which to this day is known as "The
Lemonade Stand"—that Morgan had stopped and pitched a
rudimentary canvas tent over a scrubbed table. On the table
he had two large barrels of beer, complete with taps; several
dozen pint bottles of lemonade and saspirilla; not to mention
an array of summer fruits including apples, pears, peaches
and damsons.

As the column came into sight, led by Reverend Jones,
Morgan rang a bell and called out to the labouring hordes,
"Beer! Lemonade! Refreshments!" He thought that he would
be a welcoming sight, and to many he was—excepting, of
course, Reverend Jones.

The good Reverend put down his bucket and pounced
on Morgan. "This is typical!" roared the Reverend, "While
the entire village—with the notable exception of Davies The
School—labour in this heroic task, you have applied your labour to making a profit and . . ." his voice grew louder as his
temper flared to white-hot, ". . . further disseminating the evil
of alcohol!"

"Now, now, Reverend," smiled Morgan, "I think the
heat is getting to your good temper. I'm providing a service."

"Ha!" growled Reverend Jones, "A true service would
be *free*!"

"Trust me," replied Morgan, "I'm making no profit
from this."

Reverend Jones fixed him with a vicious, steady glare, "Trust you? Trust *you*? The day has yet to dawn when I will trust you!"

Morgan, as usual, was and wasn't telling the truth. He was of course making a profit, but he intended to use it to help pay off his debt to Betty, and thus sweeten her for the task he had in mind.

Though the Reverend Jones didn't avail himself of refreshment, many villagers did. But firstly the large and small carts were emptied at the last place where they could safely turn before returning to the village. One by one the carts deposited their loads and when all were empty the villagers were appalled to find that the resulting heap was hardly taller than a man. This volume, which represented a morning's digging, still had to be man and womanhandled to the summit. It was going to be a longer day than anyone had anticipated.

As people paused for a drink they organized themselves into those who would return with the carts and wheelbarrows to the meadow and those who would press on with buckets to the top. Neither job was thought easier or harder and people did not cast themselves by sex or age. All were united in what was turning into an epic undertaking.

Davies The School sat at his desk, silently staring out of the window at the column of figures who were climbing the mountain. What did they think they were going to achieve?

He found himself lazily drawing a conical shaped mound and speculating the mathematics. The volume of a cone, yes, how did one calculate the volume of a cone? $\frac{1}{3} \times \pi r^2 \times$ height? Yes, that was it . . . And if the height were twenty feet? He made a rough drawing. The base would be wider than twenty feet. They'd be lucky to contain it to thirty feet, for that would still produce quite a steep angle. And if the base were thirty feet? That would give a radius of fifteen feet . . .

$$\frac{1}{3} \times \frac{22}{7} \times 15^2 \times 20 = ?$$

He idly pulled a slide rule from his desk. In moments he had the answer: it would take four thousand, seven hundred and fourteen cubic feet of soil. A good size bucket probably contained just less than a cubic foot! Five thousand bucketsful! He was sure that none of them had made this calculation. That was the difference, he prided himself, between the educated and the uneducated. There they were struggling, blissfully unaware that their task was well nigh impossible. Five thousand bucketsful! Davies The School let out a chortle.

His chortle was echoed by a small cough. He had completely forgotten in his speculations that there was one small girl left in his classroom.

She had her hand raised, hoping to ask a question, and Davies knew exactly what the question would be.

"Go on," he said wearily, "go on home. Join the rest of the mad buggers." It should be noted that this was the one and only recorded time when Davies The School swore in front of a pupil.

The child was up and out of the classroom before Davies had the time to change his mind.

Having left Morgan without availing himself of any refreshment, and fuelled now by anger, Reverend Jones continued up Ffynnon Garw. The path grew steeper and adrenaline surged through his old veins.

Within forty minutes he had reached the summit. With great ceremony, and a certain amount of wheezing, he emptied his bucket at the foot of the flagpole and sank down onto his haunches for a well earned rest.

When he had recovered his breath he looked at his bucketful, and the bucketful of those who had followed him. It was a pathetic molehill of soil. This was going to be harder than he had imagined.

It had been easy to think that a twenty foot tump was nothing at all, and it was certainly inconsequential to most mountains. But, while not indulging in the precision of Davies' calculations the Reverend found himself thinking of three men, balanced on each other's shoulders, and the pyramid of earth that it would take to cover them—yes, it was a daunting task.

—ɷ—

The best that Williams could come up with by way of delaying Anson and Garrad's escape by train was to send them off in the wrong direction. This ruse, clever as it was, did not frustrate the Englishmen for long, since most paths through the narrow valley of Ffynnon Garw inevitably crossed the railway tracks, and the tracks inevitably pointed towards the station.

After a series of circumnavigations Anson and Garrad finally approached Ffynnon Garw railway station and as they did they distinctly heard the whistle of a departing train and observed the boiling clouds of white smoke which it left in its wake.

The only passengers for Ffynnon Garw Halt on this particular train had been three baskets of homing pigeons and when Anson and Garrad entered the ticket office they discovered Thomas The Trains talking to the pigeons through the mesh of their baskets.

"Coo-de-coo," he said, "Coo-coo-dee-coo."

"Excuse me," said George Garrad and Thomas The Trains spun around in shock to find his worst fears come true. It was the English.

"Yes?" he stammered.

"Do you have a train timetable?" asked Garrad. It seemed a logical question to ask in a railway station's ticket office.

Thomas furrowed his brows and looked somewhat mystified, "Trains?" he asked, as if they were talking about sequinned pantaloons from the court of Louis XIV.

"Yes," said Garrad, already losing his patience, "Trains. Choo-choo . . ." he added in case Thomas couldn't quite understand English.

"You're English are you?" asked Thomas. He was pretty sure from their accents and dress, but he wanted to be certain.

Garrad rolled his eyes and motioned for Reginald to take over, "Anson," he barked.

"Yes actually," said Anson with a smile. He didn't know which he was enjoying more: watching the station master pretend that there were no trains, or George's irritation. It was frightfully entertaining. "And we'd like to catch a train."

Thomas smiled as innocent a smile as he could muster, "No trains," he replied. After all, Morgan had told him to lie, and this was the sort of lie that he assumed Morgan would want.

"Good God, man! I just heard a train! I heard the whistle, I saw the steam! This is a railway station isn't it?" snarled Garrad.

Thomas's heart sank, what on earth could he say now? He swallowed, took a deep breath, and sure enough he had a moment of divine inspiration, "That was a coal train," he replied blithely, adding, "There's coal trains all day, coal trains all night, but no passenger trains. You don't see any passengers do you?"

And the pigeons cooed.

—◊—

Albert Evans, or Evans Thirty-To-One as he would always be known after winning a sizeable bet in his younger days, rushed down to the meadow as fast as he could. "The English are on their way back to the pub!" he called.

Immediately all work stopped, and the continuous procession from the meadow, past the pub and onward up the mountain was halted. Ivor's youngest was sent racing up the road to warn those returning to refill their buckets and carts.

Consequently when Anson and Garrad arrived back at Morgan's pub they found an empty square and a quiet street. Only Evans Thirty-To-One was sitting there, idly gazing into space. Anson smiled at him, but Garrad gave him a cool stare. For though Garrad had no inkling of what was taking place, he had a keen instinct for difference, and this village was different today. Nevertheless Garrad entered the pub and within minutes was lying on his bed, snoring. The day had exhausted him.

And as soon as Garrad and Anson were out of sight Evans Thirty-To-One gave a low whistle and the procession began again. Cart-load after cart-load, wheelbarrow upon wheelbarrow, bucket after bucket, tin bath on tin bath. Minute by minute, hour by hour, the river bank was relocating to the top of Ffynnon Garw.

—ᴍ—

Tommy Twostroke had not had a good day. He had left Ffynnon Garw with Morgan's cursory map clasped in his hand. It
wasn't long, however, before he realized that Morgan had
omitted the most elementary details, like approximate distances. It's all very well to tell someone to take the last left
before you get into the city proper, when you know where the
city proper starts. Consequently, Tommy had taken a left
when he'd seen the first thing that looked to him like a metro-
politan area. Unfortunately it hadn't been anywhere near
Cardiff.

Luckily he had a fair sense of direction, and aided by the
sun, he had continued to travel in a south-easterly direction
until he found himself, with some surprise, staring at the sea.
He'd never seen the sea before and wished that the circumstances were different. He would quite liked to have stopped
for a paddle.

Though the sight of the sea stumped him, he had to
admit that the presence of an expanse of water made his
choices simpler, since there was one less direction in which to
travel.

Better still, he found himself on a fairly well populated
road. This, it turned out, was the road from Cardiff to Newport—the very road he wanted. Unfortunately, he had rather
overshot his mark and was now nearer Newport than
Cardiff. Still, he was at least on the right road at last, and
travelling in the correct direction. All that he had to do was
look out for a large building on the right of the road, rather
than the left that Morgan had indicated.

He finally rounded a bend and discovered a long wall
running alongside the road. It was the kind of wall which
encloses a large house and Tommy started to look for a sign.

Sure enough, after a quarter of a mile, and at the opening of a drive, the place announced itself as Assam House.

Tommy turned into a gravel drive lined by majestic elm trees. The house was still hidden and Tommy began to wonder if he was up to the task. He had never seen anything like it, outside of illustrations and photographs. He was made even more nervous when he eventually saw the house proper. Built in Elizabethan times, it was a stern palace of a place. Tommy wasn't even sure where the front entrance was, it all looked so grand. The drive led through a manicured garden before turning between hedgerows into a swath of lawns which were dotted with fountains. Tommy felt very small.

Parking his cycle at an imposing set of polished doors he rapped loudly and reminded himself that he was here on official business, Morgan's business, and—most importantly—the lady in question was a friend of Morgan's. Tommy had seen her in the pub once and had been struck by her fine features and her expensive clothes. Yes, she was intimidating, and her house was imposing, but he was Morgan's envoy.

"Yes?" An elderly butler looked him up and down and then stared contemptuously at Tommy's motor cycle and the trail it had made across the gravel.

Damn this, thought Tommy, I'm not going to be intimidated by her butler. He put on his poshest accent, "I've got a message for Miss Elizabeth," he announced.

He expected this to cause some excitement but instead the butler looked genuinely puzzled, "Miss Elizabeth?" he asked.

"Yes," replied Tommy, "Miss Elizabeth!"

"I'm afraid," moaned the butler, "that there is no Miss Elizabeth in residence."

"Don't be daft!" blurted Tommy, "Morgan says she lives

here." Then an awful thought struck him, "This is Assam House isn't it?"

"I can confirm that yes, this is Assam House and that there is not, quite definitively, a Miss Elizabeth." The butler started to close the door, but stopped as he remembered something. "Ah," he said with even more contempt, "You might try Betty—at the rear entrance." And with that he slammed the door.

Tommy trudged around the corner, this house seemed to go on for ever, and found himself near an area of stables. One had been converted to a garage, and outside was a large car which Tommy had seen in Ffynnon Garw. This surely was Miss Elizabeth's car, and that surely was her chauffeur cleaning it. He strolled over and was about to ask the man a question when Miss Elizabeth appeared from a doorway.

Tommy's face dropped—she was dressed as a maid.

Since George Garrad's room at the inn looked out over the square, it should have been quite easy for him to see the shenanigans which were taking place. However, the gins before lunch coupled with the extreme exertion of pushing a car two hundred yards—not to mention the frustration of talking with imbeciles like Williams The Petroleum and Thomas The Trains—had taken their toll. George was sleeping like a baby fed on opium.

However, Reginald Anson's room ran from front to back and he was watching in amazement. Not only had he noticed the procession through the square, but he had also looked out of the rear window and seen the trail of figures ascending the ridge to the flagpole in the distance around whose base a decent pile of earth was emerging. Anson couldn't help but smile.

In his mind he was merely an observer. He belonged to neither the village's team, nor, more importantly, to Garrad's. He felt that he was outside it all, and as such he was able to see it in a humorous light. It didn't strike him as unusual that he had, in effect, deserted his post, by not informing his superior.

—⁂—

Back at Assam House Tommy was trying to get over his confusion, "But I thought . . ."

Miss Elizabeth, or was it Betty? cut him off, "Never mind what you thought, what are you doing here?" She had recognized him from the village: it wasn't that hard, there weren't many men who drove motor cycles while wearing a couple of shawls tied around their shoulders for warmth.

"Morgan sent me."

"Morgan? What does Morgan want?"

"Morgan says you have to come right away."

"And lose my job?" asked Betty. What was wrong with Morgan? Couldn't he understand that other people had their own lives, their own responsibilities?

"It's an emergency," relayed Tommy, "He said 'Tell her I can't do it without her.'"

"He can't do without me?" said Betty.

"Well, he said something like that," said Tommy, but Betty wasn't really listening. She was surprised. This was very unlike Morgan! Was he making a declaration of love? If so, it was rather odd to send Tommy Twostroke with the message.

"And how am I supposed to get there?" she asked, becoming more practical, "They'd miss the car on a weekday."

"I've got my motor cycle outside," said Tommy.

"Morgan expects me to run away on a motor cycle!" said Betty.

Tommy didn't know what to say to that.

Betty thought for a moment. She hated being a maid, but she valued having a job. She liked being given the nice clothes that her mistress had finished with, but she hated living in a draughty box room at the top of the house.

She liked the little bit of money the job paid, but resented the long hours . . .

"Wait here," she said to Tommy, "I'm going to pack."

"There's not room on the bike for you *and* luggage," said Tommy, but she'd already gone.

—⚬—

In my grandfather's coal shed was a very ordinary object, the significance of which escaped me until I had been told the story which I am now telling you. It was a bucket. A simple, old, battered bucket. What made it different, of course, was that it was the bucket he used in the assault on Ffynnon Garw. When he first told me this, I laughed, thinking that he was further embellishing this story by producing any old bucket which happened to be lying around in the garden shed.

My Grandfather looked hurt, and made me look closer, "What's different about this bucket?" he asked. The only thing that I could see that separated it from a hundred other buckets was that its metal handle was wrapped with a length of very dirty, sweaty, old shirt, forming a cushion for the holder.

"The handle?" I asked.

"Exactly!" said my grandfather and went on to explain that by the two o'clock on the day of the hill build, everyone had started to pad the handles of their buckets.

"You ask around the village," said my grandfather, "and see if I'm not right; you'll find buckets like these in every old person's home."

I can't honestly say that I've checked with every old person in the village of Ffynnon Garw but I have seen several more wrapped handles.

It's a digression I know, but it makes a simple point. It was work—hard, blister-forming, back-aching, knee-swelling, finger cramping work.

In the morning the villagers had dug the meadow, turning an expanse of green grass into a series of loamy hillocks. By midday most of that soil had been transferred to horses and carts, wheelbarrows and buckets. By lunch-time a mound of earth had been deposited near Morgan's lemonade stand.

For the rest of the day the village was split into three main groups. One group remained in the meadow, supplying more earth. The second group shuttled this earth to the lemonade stand, whipping their horses into a lather, turning a quiet track into a rutted, muddied highway. The third group carried the soil—every last spoonful of it—by hand from the lemonade stand to the summit.

Similarly the day broke into three parts. The first was filled with initial optimism as the crowd gathered and the excitement of a collective endeavour fired everyone's imaginations. It all seemed to have a wonderful inevitability to it. People gathered, horses and carts appeared, the meadow was ploughed and dug and it seemed that in no time at all the Reverend, with the first bucket of soil, had reached the top.

But then there was a very definite decline in spirits. It seemed to take a very long time, and a gargantuan effort, before anything even approaching a mound started to appear. The first wave of bucket carriers climbed their way to the top, emptied their buckets—and were disgusted to find that instead of a mound it just looked like several bucketsful of earth. The twenty-foot flagpole ceased to be inspirational, indeed it appeared to take on an ironic, mocking aspect.

There is no doubt that many would have given up early that afternoon had it not been for the indefatigable Reverend Jones. No, he didn't carry as much as many, but wherever he was he worked the crowd, offering encouragement, urging the tired on, congratulating the weary. If there was a single doubt in his mind he never showed it. Again and again he quoted Johnny, "It's possible! It's just hard work!"

Finally that day, and starting late in the afternoon, there was a second wind. Many people said that the psychological barrier was just above the six-feet mark—the point at which the mound was higher than any man—and that once it was attained there was a magical sense of doing something purposeful. It was the point when many individual bucketsful coalesced into a solid thing in its own right.

Suddenly their efforts could be viewed from a distance— and most importantly, viewed from the meadow down in the valley.

Thomas Twp Too was the first to notice it, but didn't even realize what he was looking at. "What the devil is that?" he asked his brother.

Thomas Twp started to laugh, "What are you doing here?" he asked.

"Why I'm digging for the tump," said Thomas Twp Too.

"So what might that be up there then?" laughed his brother.

"Bloody hell!" said Thomas Twp Too, "It's working!"

All the work stopped in the meadow as a cheer went up. That cheer was carried by the updrafts and those at the top could hear the appreciation of those below. Since it was the middle of the summer there were still many hours of daylight left, and in the final hours of dusk something like a frenzy took hold of the villagers. The work became faster instead of slower, people carried heavier buckets rather than lighter ones, and took less time to rest at the top or at the lemonade stand.

Still, as dark approached and people started to wander home, the tump had barely reached fourteen feet. Reverend Jones stood on the mound with the Twp Twins, Ivor and Johnny. They seemed glum. They had hoped to do better.

"Now, now," cajoled Reverend Jones, "the good Lord took a day to divide heaven and earth! We can't expect to do better, and look, we've broken the back of it—we're almost up to fourteen feet!"

Johnny sniffed, "We haven't broken the back of it," he said softly.

The Reverend would hear none of it, "Yes, we have *bach*, we're two thirds of the way there!"

"But it doesn't work like that," replied Johnny, "We'll need a lot more earth as the base grows wider."

"Pshaw!" snorted the Reverend.

"He's right," said Thomas Twp. He may have been a simple hill farmer but he intuitively understood the physical laws governing the relationship between height, width and volume.

"Pessimists all of you!" said Reverend Jones, "and you,"

he pointed at Thomas Twp, then changed his mind and pointed at Thomas Twp Too—even Reverend Jones mixed them up sometimes, "You said it would rain."

Thomas Twp Too looked towards the west and saw nothing to change his mind, "And it will," he replied.

The Reverend waved him away and clambered down the soft earth, making his way home for a well-earned rest.

—⚋—

It had been a long day for Tommy Twostroke and it wasn't over yet. As he covered the last miles to Ffynnon Garw he was racing to get back for his night shift. The poor man hadn't had a moment's rest since Morgan had woken him.

They hadn't got lost on the return journey because Betty knew the way, but his motorbike hadn't been made to transport him, Betty and her luggage. It laboured up the most gradual inclines and simply refused most hills. They had to get off and push the bike, laden with Betty's luggage, up a variety of slopes.

"I'm not dressed for this" said Betty, who was all got up in her finery.

"And I'm not getting paid for it," moaned Tommy.

"More fool you," replied Betty, and then saw herself, shoving a motorbike up another hill, in her petticoats. "And more fool me."

As dusk drew in, it was a relief to see Ffynnon Garw appear before them. It had been an epic journey and in earlier times the court bard would, no doubt, have been stirred to write a poem on "The Journey Of Tommy, Almost To Newport, Cardiff, and Back."

On the downhill run into Ffynnon Garw, Betty, perched

on the back with all her worldly belongings, clung on for dear life. She was amazed as they entered the village to find the street thronged with people returning from the mountain. Many were sunburned, most carried buckets, and all were filthy. She thought it was a very odd sight. She didn't have the faintest idea that she was soon to play a part in this great crusade.

Tommy dropped her off unceremoniously at the pub and made his way quickly home to change into his work clothes and report for the night shift.

Betty entered the pub quietly, she wanted to surprise Morgan. She quickly pinched her cheeks to get some colour into them and then called out in her most seductive voice, "Morgan!"

The pub was absolutely silent.

"Morgan!" she called out again with a rich huskiness.

Nothing.

"MORGAN!" she shrieked.

CHAPTER

8

Morgan, who was well aware of Betty's arrival, was hiding in the corridor off the bar. He didn't want to be the first to see her. He wanted that privilege to go to Anson, or preferably Garrad.

Betty took off her hat and plonked it on the bar. How bloody typical! She'd come all this way and Morgan hadn't the common decency to be here to meet her! Immediately she regretted coming and knew that this visit would end badly. She walked behind the bar and poured herself a sherry.

While George Garrad was still asleep, Anson was very much awake, and thirsty. Only ten minutes earlier he'd popped down to the bar to try and get a drink but Morgan had been perfectly absent. Hearing Betty's voice, he thought there was a good chance that Morgan had returned. He hurried downstairs and found Betty standing behind the bar with her back to him, fiddling with a bottle and thus looking, to all intents and purposes, like a barmaid.

"Excuse me," said Anson chirpily, "but could I have a pint of beer?"

Betty turned to face him. He was grinning from ear to ear. He reminded her of the people she continually waited upon: smug, self-satisfied, handsome, English and probably rich. Well, she wasn't here as a maid, and especially not a barmaid, how dare he?

"Do I look like a barmaid?" she snarled and to her surprise Morgan appeared like something out of a magician's hat.

"Barmaid? Never!" exclaimed Morgan, and stopped both of them in their tracks.

Morgan had been hoping that when Anson or Garrad met Betty they would be beguiled by her beauty. He had been waiting, in the wings as it were, to help only if necessary. He hadn't expected Betty to be in such a bad mood, and to snap at the English without so much as a hello, how are you, delighted to meet you.

"I'm surprised at you, Mr. Anson," continued Morgan, before either of them had time to interject, "mistaking this fine lady for a barmaid, this is our honoured guest, Miss Elizabeth."

Honoured guest? Thought Betty. What is Morgan talking about?

"I'm sorry," stammered Anson, "but I saw you behind the bar and just assumed . . ."

Betty was about to tell this stranger that he shouldn't assume anything and, further, to ask what the hell Morgan was babbling about when Morgan raced on, explaining to Anson, "A natural assumption I'm sure, but the fact is that I like my guests to feel at home, anytime Miss Elizabeth wants anything I tell her 'My home is your home!' "

What the devil was Morgan blathering about? My home is your home?

Now he spun to face Betty and winked broadly, "Back again so soon?" he asked her, but again didn't give her time to reply, "I told you not to return to Cardiff too soon," he winked at her again before spinning to tell Mr. Anson, "she has terrible trouble with her chest—now if I can just get you a drink, sir."

And with that he physically picked up Betty and dropped her within inches of Reginald Anson.

Miss Elizabeth? Honoured guest? Trouble with her chest? Betty was smart, it wasn't difficult to see that Morgan was introducing her as someone else, but why?

Anson, who now found himself face to face with an extremely pretty and curvaceous young woman, stammered and started to blush.

"What was it you wanted again?" asked Morgan.

"Oh, yes, quite, well a pint of bitter, please, thank you," said Anson.

"And put it on my account," added Betty and gave Morgan a smile which would have melted a glacier. Two can play at this, she thought.

"Your account?" said Morgan, before realizing that he'd have to go along with her lie. He returned her wide grin. What else could he do?

"Oh, no really," blathered Anson.

"I insist," said Betty, "to show there's no hard feelings. I don't know what came over me, but I must have appeared a thoroughly impatient and not very nice person." She was trying her best with a posh accent and convoluted grammar, but it wasn't quite emerging as she hoped.

Anson was still standing too close for comfort. He took a half pace back to introduce himself, "Well, very pleased to meet you. I'm Reginald Anson."

"Elizabeth, Miss," said Betty and cursed herself. She had never heard anyone introduce themselves that way. She was making a perfect mess of things, bloody Morgan!

Now that Anson was an extra pace away from her he realized that he recognized her. "Actually," he said, "I think we've met once before."

"Have I?" asked Betty and wondered why she hadn't said "Have we?" Changing her accent was making her say the most absurd things.

"Yes," Anson continued as if she were talking quite normally, "I think you were leaving when we first arrived."

"Was we now?" asked Betty, and wished that the ground would open and swallow her up.

Luckily Morgan barged in between them with Anson's pint, "Well," grinned Morgan like a Cheshire cat, "I'm sure you two have a lot to talk about." And with that he disappeared leaving them alone.

Betty was ready to strangle Morgan.

She took a gulp and tried to speak almost normally, "If you'd excuse me," she enunciated perfectly, "I've just remembered that there are several many matters with which I have to talk to our innkeeper about, thank you." And with that she strode from the room leaving Anson wondering quite what had hit him.

Morgan was holed up in his kitchen when Betty found him.

"Morgan!" she stormed, "What the bloody hell is going

on? I have Tommy Twostroke coming with a desperate message and now that I'm here . . ."

"That's it, Betty!" interrupted Morgan, "Desperate times, calling for desperate messages!" He lowered his voice, and winked again, "Desperate Englishmen!"

"Desperate?" asked Betty, "That stuffed shirt!" She could have found many adjectives for Reginald Anson but desperate was not among them. The truth was that Betty had already developed an attitude towards Anson, and it was the kind of attitude that very young girls have to very young boys, and vice versa. In short, she was so attracted to him that the attraction could only find public expression in feigned repulsion. Moreover, since it was obvious that Morgan was throwing her at him, the last thing she wanted to do was satisfy Morgan and whatever fiendish machinations he had in mind.

"Oh, don't bother with that one, he hasn't got the power," said Morgan, "but the other one, he's much more pukka, a real man of the world—and much more "Miss Elizabeth's 'type.' ""

Much more Miss Elizabeth's type? What was he talking about?

Before she could say anything her worse fears were confirmed as Morgan held up the large satchel containing the money he had made on the mountain, and gave it to her.

Again he winked a very lewd wink, "There's more where that came from!"

Betty felt her eyes closing to slits, "You had better not be suggesting what I think you're suggesting!" she snarled.

"I don't know what you're talking about," said Morgan, "it's just some of the money I owe you."

"And I suppose it's just a coincidence that you happen to be paying me now?" said Betty.

Reverend Jones slowly made his way home. Every bone in his body ached. His knees were sore. His boots had rubbed his heels and arches raw. His hands were blistered. But, he had a beatific smile on his face.

Fourteen feet today, a mountain tomorrow! Johnny had been right, it was possible, better than that, it was now probable. Tonight he would soak his feet in salts and tomorrow, despite the blisters, despite the bruises, despite the aches and pains, he would be back there, he would be at the top when the last, historic, heroic bucket was emptied on the . . .

Drip.

Reverend Jones's thoughts were interrupted and he stopped in mid-step. Had he seen what he thought he had seen?

Drop.

He held out his hand, no it couldn't be rain, not tonight, not now, not on their fresh earth, not when they needed another fine day . . .

For a moment his hand remained dry and the stiffness went from his body, but just as he relaxed, splish, splash, two drops fell, smack in the palm of his hand.

These weren't small drops, these were thunder splashes, the first huge drops of a mighty, gathering storm. The Reverend's heart sank, and even though he was standing on the consecrated ground of the Chapel approach, he found himself swearing out loud, "Damn and blast!"

A gust of air stirred the length of the valley and fell upon George Garrad's neck. He awoke slowly, dimly aware that he was in an unfamiliar bed, but with a very familiar feeling: he was hungover and hungry.

Down in the kitchen Morgan had been trying to explain to Betty what had happened since she'd been away. That was easy, but conveying the full import was proving much more difficult. Betty couldn't believe what he was telling her. Worse than that, she was mad as hell: Morgan was building a mountain and wanted to enlist *her* to keep two English map-makers "entertained" while he did it?

Dispensing with words, she expressed her precise feelings by wrapping her hands around Morgan's neck, and tightening them into a stranglehold. With his head thus secured she used all her strength in an attempt to beat Morgan's brains out against the kitchen wall. She was a fiery young thing.

"To think I've probably lost my bloody job over this . . ." She said as she methodically dented the plaster with the base of his thick skull.

"Ahem . . ."

Betty was stopped by Garrad's voice coming from the corridor. She spun to look, and he slowly came into the dim light. This corpulent figure was more Miss Elizabeth's type? Betty's hands fell to her sides, exhausted by the sheer absurdity of it all.

"Mr. Garrad, sir," said Morgan chirpily, as if he was to be found with a woman trying to strangle him on most afternoons, "What can I do you for?"

"Sorry to interrupt," said Garrad with his usual lack of tact, "but I was feeling rather peckish and wondered whether you could rustle me up a sandwich or some such."

"Delighted, sir, delighted." He turned to Betty, "If you'll excuse me, Madam," he said, and scuttled off to the pantry.

Garrad half-smiled at her but she didn't notice as she strode out into the garden to calm down.

It was starting to rain and she stood under the back porch reviewing her situation. She had possibly lost her job and was stranded here without transport. First thing in the morning she would have to invent a plausible excuse to telegram to her employers in the hope that they would take her back. Better still, she hoped they'd send a car for her. But until then she had no option, she was stuck in Ffynnon Garw.

Anson was sitting in the main bar, reviewing his notes when Garrad entered from the kitchen with a couple of large cheese sandwiches.

He looked around furtively before speaking, "Anson," he hissed, "there's dirty work at the crossroads."

"Really?" Anson wondered what he knew.

"I've just been speaking to Mr. Morgan," continued Garrad, "and he wasn't the least bit surprised that we were staying another night."

Anson thought quickly, "Oh, not to worry, George, I think it's quite simple, you see Williams The Petroleum had already told him about our troubles."

"He had?"

"Yes, he had."

Garrad was quite deflated, "Oh . . ." He thought about it for a minute and couldn't resist a homily, "Can't be too careful in foreign climes, you know."

Anson pointed out "It's only Wales, George."

"Still foreign!" snapped Garrad.

Betty came in from the garden and leaned—or rather collapsed—against the table. She felt drained. Morgan snuggled up next to her, trying to better her evil humour.

"Don't try anything," warned Betty.

"Now, now," said Morgan, "it's all for a good cause." She turned to face him and shook her head, "Morgan, you're mad! All this for just a map?"

"Just a map?" sneered Morgan. "Is that what you think? Just a map?" He cwched closer and stared at her jutting breasts.

"Maps my dear, Betty . . ." Morgan couldn't help himself, his hands were nearing her bosom, "are the undergarments of a country." Betty hadn't noticed his open palms approaching, "they give shape to continents!" Morgan gave her breasts a sensuous squeeze.

That was the last straw! Betty picked up a metal tea tray and would have knocked him senseless had he not rushed from the room. She threw down the tray and chased after him, determined to rip him limb from limb before boiling him in oil and peppering the pieces.

Morgan raced out into the bar with Betty hard on his heels, only to find Anson and Garrad sitting there, staring at his approach. He slowed and smiled, just as Betty emerged and skidded to a halt too. At least she was good-mannered enough not to kill him in front of strangers.

Anson turned to Garrad, "Have you met Miss Elizabeth?" he asked laconically.

"Yes, a moment ago," replied Garrad, standing in deference to her sex. "And how long will you be staying here at the inn?" he asked her.

"Oh, I don't know," Betty tried to smile, "just as soon as my head clears . . ."

At the Twp farmhouse Thomas Twp was putting a kettle on the range when he heard the first heavy lashings of rain on the window. He turned to his brother, "You were right," he said.

"I'm never wrong about the weather," replied Thomas Twp Too.

Together they both stared at the rain.

"This is set for a few days," continued Thomas Twp Too after due consideration.

"And thunder?" asked Thomas Twp.

"Oh, yes," replied his brother, "plenty of thunder."

Morgan poured drinks all round and moved to unlock the main pub door. He was shocked to find a curtain of rain.

"Bloody hell!" he exclaimed, "it's a deluge!"

He was right, the rain was falling like stair-rods and tamping up from the ground like tennis balls.

Anson, Garrad and Betty came to see what he was talking about.

"Good God," said Garrad, "it reminds me of the monsoons in India. One was apt to get terrible mud slides on nights like these. Whole villages swept away, roads, temples!"

Garrad continued with his boring litany but Morgan's mind had seized on one phrase.

Mud slides!

His eyes darted towards the mountain—the mound, the fresh earth . . .

Morgan had every reason to worry since at that very moment his precious mound was washing away. With nothing to hold the earth together it was turning to slurry and spreading across the summit in a large, brown pool.

Morgan returned to the bar and poured a round of drinks, including a stiff one for himself. Garrad was jabbering away but Morgan couldn't hear him, his mind was racing.

Mud slides, mud slides, mud slides . . .

In his mind's eye Morgan saw all their work obliterated. He knew that today's work could not be jeopardized—he had seen the villagers at the end of the day and knew that they were exhausted. Yes, they would work another day and complete the work, but there would be no getting the villagers back up there to start again if it had washed away to nothing. But what could he do about it?

Perhaps it was just a shower, perhaps it would stop soon. Excusing himself, Morgan went to his kitchen and then out into the garden. If anything the rain was heavier and it was swirling so wildly that he could hardly see beyond the stable mere yards away.

This, Morgan realized, is not going to let up soon.

With a heavy heart and a feeling of impotence he returned to the bar.

Garrad was still droning on. Morgan poured himself another stiff drink.

"I hope your Mr. Williams will have the sense to cover it up," said Garrad.

"Excuse me?" said Morgan, "My mind was somewhere else."

"My car. Parts were all over the place. I just hope Williams has the good sense to get them covered them up."

"Now there's a thought," said Morgan. He grabbed his coat. "I'll just go and check that for you, be back in a minute." He rushed off in the rain towards Williams The Petroleum's garage.

"Fine chap," observed Garrad, who was duly impressed, "nothing's too much trouble."

Betty agreed, "Yes," she smiled, "you don't know the half of it."

—∞—

Morgan raced through the village, running faster than he'd run for several years—he hadn't run this fast since an angry husband had caught him in a compromising position, and that had been before the war.

He cussed as he stepped in puddles which splashed him clean up to his waist. He jumped a stream which had formed in the middle of the street and raced into Williams' garage, "Williams!" he yelled like a banshee, "Williams?"

Williams The Petroleum had just sat down to a hard-earned supper. He had been delayed by the onset of rain. As soon as he'd heard it he'd searched for his large tarpaulin and covered the Englishman's open-topped car. That accomplished he had just settled down to some tea and bara brith when here was Morgan, yelling through the rain. Williams went out to see what the devil was the matter.

"Morgan?"

"We need tarpaulins up the mountain!" yelled Morgan through the rain which was getting even heavier by the minute, "Or all our work will be washed away!"

"I've only got the one," said Williams, pointing to the canvas that was covering the car.

"That'll do," said Morgan and started to remove it.

"But Morgan . . . !" Williams tried to stop him.

"I don't want to be telling people it failed because of you," said Morgan and ripped the tarpaulin from the car, "Now get Johnny Shellshocked and get up that mountain, quick!"

"But the car!" complained Williams.

"This car was made for all weathers," lied Morgan, "Mr. Garrad told me so himself."

"But Morgan!" Williams was yelling.

"I can't do it all myself!" moaned Morgan and disappeared into the night, back to his warm, dry pub.

Williams looked at the car and thought of the mound. His mind raced for another solution, but couldn't find one. Bloody Morgan! He pulled the tarpaulin from the car and folded it. Already sodden it had doubled, if not tripled, in weight. Yes, he'd need Johnny to help him.

The events of that night, and indeed the following days, might have been very different had Johnny's sister Blod not been visiting a friend. As it was, Williams found Johnny alone at home. There is no doubt that Blod would have stopped Johnny from ascending Ffynnon Garw on such a foul night— but, as I said, her voice, the voice of reason, was not there to protect him. And so Williams and Johnny, labouring under the growing weight of a tarpaulin, set off up Ffynnon Garw.

It's shocking how weather can change a landscape. Look out across many of the Welsh hills and mountains on a fine day and you will find it hard to imagine that these sunny, fern and heather covered stretches could hold danger for anyone. But go closer, walk those ridges and there you will find cairns, crosses, small memorial stones, all left to commemorate poor souls who, on a bad night, lost their way in the most familiar of landscapes and withered away into the mist and cold.

"Here lies Thomas Jones, farmer!"

"Buried here the remains of Trevor Hopkins, boy of this Parish . . ."

". . . discovered here in the snow of 1895 and laid to rest."

The track that the horses and carts—not to mention the trudging boots—had followed was becoming a quagmire. Johnny and Williams struggled up for a quarter of a mile, making very slow progress, before they were forced to leave this trail and take a more direct, yet much steeper route.

Williams cursed Morgan with every step and yet he continued, since he knew Morgan was right—If the mound wasn't covered, and covered soon, it would be entirely washed away.

Not even a third of the way up they stopped to get a breather next to a drystone wall. It offered a modicum of shelter from the driving rain.

"All right?" Williams asked Johnny.

Johnny returned a nod.

"You're wishing you'd been out visiting with Blod, aren't you?" joked Williams.

Johnny gave him a wan smile.

"Don't worry," said Williams, "I reckon Morgan owes us one after this. I'd say free drinks for a week, what d'you say to that?"

Johnny smiled again.

"All right," said Williams, rising, ready to struggle farther, "onwards and upwards—and then home to a nice hot bath."

Down in the valley many villagers watched the rain lashing against their windows, or lay in bed listening to it drum upon their roofs.

Reverend Jones sat in his spartan study and stared at the patterns that the rivulets made as they cascaded down his window. With every rivulet he imagined another shovelful of soil turning to mud, and rushing down the slopes of the mountain, back to the river bank from which it had come. He was not a superstitious man, but he found that his faith was being tested. The classical image of Sisyphus filled his mind: a soul destined to labour each and every day, pushing a boulder up a hill, only to see it descend . . . He shook himself from his mournful reverie and turned to the Bible for succour.

Ivor and Rachel looked out from their kitchen window, and while they both had the same thoughts, they said nothing in front of their children. This, they imagined, was a worry to be borne by adults.

Davies The School, derisive of the intent and unabashedly cynical of the whole operation, was the only one to smile that night. In Davies's mind the villagers had sacrificed their labour to the great god of vanity, in much the same way that the ancients had sacrificed virgins to appease their gods. He looked forward to hearing their apologies when a sobered village would have to face their ludicrous mistakes.

"Fight nature at one's peril!" he said aloud, just to himself. Yes, he liked that—these foolish villagers thought that hills could be redefined by a few bucketsful of earth! Ha! If they had only been educated, as he had, they would know that these mountains were the product of *erosion*—they were what was left when the rest had been washed away. Did they really think that their paltry efforts would stand up to the wind and rain?

And while Davies smiled happily, Morgan attempted the smallest of grins, since he was being regaled with long, torturous stories by George Garrad. No villagers had come out to drink on such a filthy night and Morgan found himself alone with Anson, Garrad and Betty. However, Betty, damn her, had seated herself at a table with the shy Anson, leaving Morgan alone at the bar with Garrad who was holding court on his favourite subject: India.

"So this native entered to with a large basket, about so big," Garrad demonstrated the size with a grand wave of his arms, "and assuming that it contained fruit or some such I ordered him to go ahead and open it."

Morgan nodded, and tried to smile. Would these stories never end?

"So!" said Garrad, "You can imagine my complete, and utterly horrified surprise when he opened it to reveal, well, what do you think it contained, Mr. Morgan?"

Morgan couldn't have cared less if it had contained the Blackpool Tower, festooned with dancing girls, "No idea, Mr. Garrad."

"Go on, have a guess!"

What the hell could be in the basket? Morgan took an idle, uninterested guess, "A viper?"

Garrad's face fell a furlong, "Yes, actually, you're right, a viper, as thick as my arm."

"Well, well a viper." Morgan tried to sound interested.

Betty twisted in her chair, having heard every word, "A viper!" she repeated, "We have those in Wales," she fixed Morgan with a pointed stare before taking her gaze back to Mr. Anson. "I tell my gardeners to stamp them out whenever they see them."

Tommy Twostroke and all of the night shift were unaware of the rain, since they were half a mile underground, sweating in narrow tunnels, mining tough seams.

Tommy dragged himself about, he'd been awake now for a day and a half. It made it worse to be in the half-light, working only by the illumination from their Davy lamps.

Tommy felt as if he'd stumbled into an odd world, somewhere between waking and sleep. He was almost dreaming with his eyes open. One minute he'd be hacking at a seam, the next he was still on his motor cycle reliving a sharp bend, or a steep hill. For most of the morning he had driven about South Wales, lost. He still felt lost. All he wanted to do was to curl up in a dark corner and sleep.

It was very slow going up the mountain with a very heavy tarpaulin and having only made it to the halfway point, Williams and Johnny were feeling much the same. All Williams could think about was getting home and sitting himself in front of a blazing fire before curling up in a comfortable bed.

Worse, Johnny was beginning to feel a different discomfort. The rain and the mud were horribly reminiscent of his time in the trenches. Try as he might to calm himself, he found that he was increasingly nervous, as if expecting German soldiers to appear over the next ridge, as though a shell would fly out of the rain and explode near them. He was not enjoying his trek up Ffynnon Garw.

At the top the mound was eroding swiftly. Almost three feet of soil had gone. The ten-foot mark was becoming visible, disappearing as easily as a child's sandcastle on the beach faced with an incoming tide.

Down in the pub Morgan was trying to bring George Garrad's monologue to an end, "Well, it must be nice to have travelled to a place like India," he offered.

"Been everywhere," said Garrad, "Did I tell you that I spent some months in Palestine?"

"Really?" said Morgan with a sinking heart.

"Absolutely," said Garrad and proceeded with another chapter in his damnably boring life.

At their table Betty was having difficulty drawing Anson into conversation. Not that she really wanted to talk to him, you understand, but in keeping him to herself she was forcing Garrad upon Morgan, and that was giving her great pleasure.

"Have you travelled much, Mr. Anson?" she asked.

"No, no hardly at all, and nothing compared to George," he smiled, and returned to polishing an instrument.

He was an enigma to Betty. She was used to men fawning over her, of men boasting to her, or men bossing her around. Anson seemed shy, nervous, almost timid. He didn't seem to have the self-confidence of his class. So many men of his age found it necessary to dominate a room. Put two of them together with a single woman and they traded stories, jokes, and what passed for repartee, in a dogged contest to show themselves the most witty. Most of them would have considered Anson vapid. But Betty sensed that he was quite self-contained, that he cared little for what people thought of him.

Was he inexperienced with women, she wondered? Perhaps he was married, or affianced. Yes, that was it, she decided. This man had a sweetheart and was constant and true. And having decided that, she found it even easier to like him.

Up at the mound the nine-foot mark was visible—almost five foot of earth had washed away before Williams and Johnny crested the ridge, hauling the sodden tarpaulin between them.

"Almost there, Johnny, boy," said Williams and quickened his pace.

However, in the very next instant they were stopped in their tracks by a crash as a lightning bolt seared through the rain, earthing within yards of where they walked.

Williams immediately threw himself to the ground but was horrified to see that Johnny stayed standing, rigid—and screaming. The sound that came from his body was like nothing that Williams had ever heard before. It was like an animal at slaughter, a piercing whine, a dreadful shriek that seemed to come from the very depths of hell.

Johnny's body had turned to stone, even his eyelids were fixed open. His mouth was contorted by his long, howling, yowling scream. The thunder rolled and broiled about him, the lightning crashed into the ridge, but Johnny saw none of it. Johnny saw a muddy bank in France, heard the shells, the mines, the screams of his comrades. The rain was blood, splashed as a friend was eviscerated before his very eyes. He couldn't hear Williams, he couldn't see where he was, and though he was frightened—beyond frightened—he could not fear the lightning, because for Johnny it wasn't there.

"Get down!" yelled Williams, "Johnny! The lightning!" Johnny didn't hear him, Johnny didn't budge and Williams watched in horror as forked lightning sparked all around them. It was so close that Williams felt the hair on his head and arms rise with the static in the air.

Williams pulled himself into a low crouch and rushing across the few yards that separated them, he brought Johnny to the ground with a hard crunching tackle.

Still Johnny continued to scream.

"Stop it, Johnny! Stop it!" he yelled and then instinctively slapped him, hard.

Johnny's screams turned to a whimper. His teeth were chattering, his whole body seemed consumed with terrible shaking convulsions. He stared ahead, as if Williams were invisible, as if the rain weren't pouring into his open eyes. His hands were clenched on the tarpaulin with the strength of a drowning man hanging onto a line.

"Let go, Johnny bach," said Williams and tried to release his grasp. "Come on," repeated Williams, "let go, so we can get the hell out of here."

Still Johnny's fingers cramped tight.

With one hand Williams gradually loosened them, while his other hand softly stroked Johnny's face, as if he were a child. Slowly but surely Williams released Johnny's grasp. "I'll be back in just a minute," he said, and rushed off to the tump, to finish his night's work.

Clambering up the mound was nightmarish. The rain was flooding down, the thunder cracked above, the lightning swirled around him. The whole mound had turned into a slimy, moving, hideous creature. Williams crawled, slipping and sliding, dragging the tarpaulin behind him. The erosion was worse than he had dared to imagine and he was shocked to see the nine-foot mark. He quickly tried to cover as much as he could with the tarpaulin, but it was hard to manoeuvre. It now weighed many times more from the water it had absorbed, and with each tug it became even heavier with mud. Williams slid and slipped, grabbed and tugged, kicked and pulled it into position. The wind and rain whipped at his clothes and tore at his flesh. The rain lashed so hard that he felt it might take the skin off his face and the hair from his head. It ran in rivulets down his face, like a burst dam of tears. He could hear Johnny's whimpering in the distance as the wind changed and carried his cries. The lightning continued to crackle all around them as the thunder rolled above, and the storm turned this sedate hill into a lashed rock in a watery sea from hell. With one last mighty wrench—a wrench that broke a nail clean from his forefinger—Williams secured the tarpaulin and with his work completed he rushed back to Johnny.

Despite the continued lightning he hauled Johnny across his shoulders, "Come on, bach," he whispered, "we're going home."

With a draughts board, some tumblers, a few pipe cleaners and several matches George Garrad had assembled a schematic of his most important battle on the counter of Morgan's bar. In truth it was a plagiarized version of a battle fought by General Gordon, but in Garrad's gin-sodden mind, he and the great warrior had become one. Somehow Gordon's warring exploits had become fused with his own inept map-making journeys through the middle east.

"So," Garrad paused to make sense in his own mind before further explaining this fiction to Morgan, "my forces were arranged here, here and here. The most important strategic place being, of course, Cairo."

"Of course," echoed Morgan. God he was tired of being Garrad's only audience. For the umpteenth time he tried to drag Betty and Anson into the conversation. "Did you hear that, Miss Elizabeth," he asked, "Mr. Garrad's been to Cairo."

Garrad looked up, miffed that Morgan had spoilt his flow. Didn't this publican realize that it was hard to concentrate?

"Cairo, eh?" Betty gave Morgan a withering smile and pointedly turned her attention back to the shy Mr. Anson.

"Have you ever been to Cairo, Mr. Anson?" she asked in a seductive manner more designed to annoy Morgan than excite Anson.

"No, 'fraid not," demurred Anson, "though of course I'd like to, one day."

"Hellhole," interrupted Garrad who needed to regain the floor, "and not a place to be described in mixed company. Now, as I was saying, our forces were arranged here, here, and here. Now did I mention that this tumbler represents Cairo?"

And so he droned on.

Williams slipped, Johnny tumbled, Williams picked him back up and carried on, racing as quickly down the mountain as was possible. Williams didn't know what exactly was wrong with Johnny but instinctively he knew it was bad, very, very bad. He had seen the Johnny who had returned from the trenches, a figure of skin and bone who hid in his room for several months, a shadow of a man who gasped at the slightest sound and jumped if a small bird flew up to his window. He didn't want Johnny to return to that state. And while he was rushing to get Johnny home, he was not looking forward to seeing Blod. Johnny's sister had a formidable temper and was as close as a sister could be. If she were to blame Williams for tonight's disaster . . .

They reached the village and Williams rushed down the main street as fast as his weary legs would carry him. Charlie Evans' son was coming back from his Gran's. "Mr. Williams?" he said, surprised to see this muddy figure coming down the middle of the road. "Are you all right?"

Williams leaned against a lamppost to get his breath, "Yeah, I'm OK."

Charlie Evans' son looked at the body across Williams' shoulders. "Anything I can do?" he asked.

That gave Williams an idea, "Go to Blod's," he said, "tell her to come to the pub, quick."

"It's Johnny?" said Charlie Evans's son, trying to make out the gibbering face under the mud.

"Yes," Williams nodded sadly, "it's Johnny."

The child ran off in the rain and Williams continued on to the pub.

Yes, let Morgan take the justified blame for this, thought Williams.

Garrad paused for a moment. Were his forces in Palestine or Cairo? It wasn't easy to remember, especially since he'd never commanded a force of soldiers in his life and was fabricating his story piecemeal from several exploits in the lives of Britain's greatest Generals.

"Another for you, Mr. Garrad?" asked Morgan, hoping that one more large gin would send him into a silent stupor.

"No thank you," slurred Garrad.

"And you Mr. Anson?" asked Morgan.

"No, I'm fine thanks," replied Reginald.

"I'll have another." This was Betty, beaming at Morgan like a long lost relative, "and one for the gentlemen—and put them on my account."

That bloody woman, thought Morgan. I've created a damned monster.

"How very kind," smiled Garrad, who found that his thirst had magically returned now that someone else was buying the drinks "I'll have a double."

"Oh, Miss Elizabeth's benevolence knows no bounds," said Morgan between gritted teeth.

He was about to pour the drinks when there was a re-

sounding crash and through the doorway fell two unrecognizable figures, covered in mud.

"Bloody hell!" said Morgan and was about to throw
these two filthy tramps out when he realized it was Johnny
and Williams.

"There was only thunder and sodding lightning wasn't
there!" said Williams. He unceremoniously laid Johnny out
on the flagstone floor. Johnny continued to stare straight
ahead, his eyes unblinking. His whines had changed to a soft,
repetitive, pathetic chattering, as if he'd been reduced to a
child trying to speak. His body shook continually and the
shaking was only broken by irregular pulses that swept from
his scalp to his toes, momentarily contracting every muscle in
his body.

Anson quickly rose to his feet and stared at this poor
creature. Unfortunately it wasn't the first time in his short life
that he'd seen such a vivid, gibbering wretch.

Morgan rushed around the bar and huddling close to
Williams whispered "But what about the mound?"

Williams' eyes narrowed, could Morgan think about
nothing else? "Oh we saved your bloody mound all right,"
he hissed back and then rose to his feet and started to leave.

Morgan was horrified—what was he going to do with
Johnny? "You can't leave him here," he exhorted Williams,
"you should take him to Blod's."

"I've done enough for one sodding night," said Williams
and tramped out.

For a moment there was utter silence. Then Anson
sprang into action, "For God's sake!" he said, "We can't just
stand here, we must help the poor man! Mr. Morgan, towels,
and blankets, quickly! Miss Elizabeth, a brandy!"

This was an Anson that none of them had seen before.

He was commanding, decisive. Immediately he was on his knees, already unclenching Johnny's fingers. The only person who hadn't moved was Garrad. He was still sitting at the bar, viewing it all as if it were a performance from a penny-dreadful, staged for his amusement.

Garrad had, however, been around the edges of His Majesty's various armies long enough to recognize Johnny's shellshocked symptoms. "Poor beggar," he pontificated as he took another swig of gin, "saw a lot of this sort of thing in Sebastopol."

"Bugger Sebastopol!" cursed Anson, "Don't just sit there, give me a hand!"

Garrad almost fell off his barstool—how dare Anson speak to him, a senior officer, like that!? Nevertheless, Anson's voice was so commanding that he was off his stool and on the floor in a trice.

"Give me your jacket," said Anson, "I need something under his head, look, help with his fingers, I have to check if he's swallowed his tongue . . ."

"All right, all right," moaned Garrad as he gave up his favourite smoking-jacket to prop the head of this filthy local Welshman.

Betty was amazed. Anson had taken over the proceedings with the confidence of a doctor. He seemed to know exactly what had to be done, and was doing it with the minimum fuss. She was very, very impressed.

Then, to her surprise, the pub door burst open again and in rushed Blod.

Now while Betty and Blod knew of each other's existence, Morgan had been very careful to ensure that they had never met. If pressed he had always described the other in a very unflattering light. It didn't take Betty more than a moment to realize that this was Blod, and to notice how pretty she was. But Blod, in her concern for Johnny, hardly even registered the well-dressed woman standing at the bar holding a large brandy.

When Morgan rushed back in the room with an armful of towels and blankets his eyes popped—it was his worst fear come true, "Blod!" he sputtered, "What the hell are you doing here?"

"What have you done to him!" she screamed back.

"I haven't done anything!" argued Morgan, "It was the thunder, and the lightning . . ."

Then Morgan made his mistake—he was trying to draw attention from himself when, seeing Betty with the brandy firmly in her hand he accidentally blurted out the one name he should not have spoken, "Betty," he said clearly, "give the man the brandy!"

Blod's eyes flashed, "Betty? So this is Betty! What the hell is she doing here?"

"No, no," stammered Morgan and hoped that the ground would open up now, "this isn't Betty-Betty," he was now improvising wildly, "but another woman called Betty— Miss Elizabeth really—who happens to be with these gentlemen, isn't that right?"

Garrad looked from face to face, what the hell was Morgan talking about?

Anson looked up, distracted by Johnny, and found Betty staring at him with pleading eyes which all but screamed "Help Me!"

"Yes," said Anson to Blod, "she's with us, now can we get on with helping this poor man, he's in deep, deep shock."

"I'm sorry," said Blod to Betty, "I really thought you were somebody else." She gently removed Anson's hands from Johnny and pulled her brother close to her. "It's all right," she said, "I know what to do." She rocked him gently like a baby and smoothed his hair. The awful sobbing slowly stopped. The whole room watched transfixed as she nursed her brother into calmness.

When the tension seemed to be leaving Johnny's body, Blod turned to Morgan. "Come on," she said softly, "help me get him home."

So for the first time that night Morgan found himself doing some serious work as he lifted Johnny onto his shoulders and lugged him home to Blod's, like an old sack of potatoes.

After they left, the pub seemed deathly silent. It was as if a whirlwind had rushed through the place, breaking fragile allegiances, perhaps rearranging new ones. Anson, Garrad and Betty stood silently, avoiding each other's gaze. Garrad was furious. Anson had barked orders at him, treated him like a junior officer and then—and this Garrad couldn't *begin* to understand—had lied about their relationship to this lady. He was, to put it mildly, miffed.

"Well," he said, "I've had quite enough excitement for one evening so I'll say my goodnight."

Anson noticed his smoking-jacket, still lying on the muddy floor. He picked it up, "George . . ."

Garrad viciously cut him off, "Goodnight!" he thundered and marched unsteadily up the stairs.

Anson and Betty stood for a moment in complete silence, and then Betty quietly walked out to the front corridor, closed the front door—and then locked it.

She saw Anson's questioning look, "Oh this isn't the first time I've locked up for Morgan," she said, adding, "he won't be back tonight."

She moved to the table and picked up a few glasses and brought them to the bar. Anson didn't really know what to do, he didn't want to retire yet, so he started to collect dirty glasses too.

He returned to the bar with his hands full and was shocked when Betty insinuated herself between his arms and kissed him, full on the lips.

She stopped, "Thank you," she said, "for helping me with Blod."

Anson really didn't know what to say. He felt such a fool, with his hands full of glasses, being kissed by a woman who was as good as a perfect stranger, "Well," he stammered, "it just seemed the thing to do." He smiled—only to find that she was kissing him again.

Betty expected him to react, to kiss her in return, but he just stood there quivering, almost rustling like poplar leaves in a soft breeze. His lips were warm, she could feel that, and for a moment she thought she could hear his heart, thumping like the hooves of an approaching horse. But, in truth, the kiss was about as exciting as a cold cup of tea from a chipped enamel mug. Betty decided that it was better to let him withdraw before he fainted—or threw up.

"Well then," he continued to stammer badly, "um, er, well . . ." He was making for the stairs, "Thank you for a lovely evening . . ." He started to climb the stairs.

She stopped him in his tracks with a pertinent question, a question which she had been debating all evening. "Are you married?" she asked bravely.

"What?" said Anson, further wrong-footed.

"Are you married?" she repeated.

"Well . . . no . . ." stumbled Anson. The stairs creaked under him in sympathy or pain.

Betty smiled, more to herself, "Not even married!"

Anson stared at her. Who was this woman and what did she want? He was in turn mystified, terrified and utterly excited by her. She was unlike any woman he'd ever met across the border in England. A good, middle-class English gal would never have kissed him like that, would never have spent the evening in the pub, would have died before asking if he were married.

"Goodnight, Mr. Anson," Betty smiled, "you're a gentleman."

Anson paused to consider that and then rushed upstairs.

It was only as he approached his room that he realized his hands were still full of empty glasses.

By the heat and light of the kitchen coal fire, Morgan held Johnny as Blod pulled off his sodden, muddied clothes and gently wiped him down with a flannel.

She softly dried him with slow, graceful strokes. She's just like a cat, cleaning a kitten, thought Morgan as he watched.

All the while Blod hummed quietly. It was a simple child's tune, a bare repeating refrain that was designed to send infants to sleep and seemed to soothe Johnny. His shivering was calming, the look of terror had left his eyes. Now his features softened, his lids lowered, and once they'd got his pyjamas on, Morgan and Blod were able to put him to bed.

Morgan withdrew to the bedroom door as Blod tucked Johnny in. Since he'd been here, Blod hadn't looked at Morgan once and Morgan wasn't completely sure whether she was very angry with him, wrapped up in Johnny, or both. He was about to find out.

Blod crept from the room and softly closed the door.

"Sleeping quietly?" asked Morgan.

"No thanks to you," replied Blod.

"I'll just go back to the pub and lock up, I won't be long," said Morgan and was about to leave when Blod cracked her outstretched palm smack in the middle of his chest. It knocked the breath out of him and stopped him in his tracks.

"Don't think you're sleeping here tonight!" hissed Blod, "After what you did to Johnny!"

"I didn't do anything!" protested Morgan.

"That's the trouble," continued Blod, "you never do anything, you get everyone else to do your dirty work for you."

"Now, now, Blod, don't get upset."

Blod cut him off, "And another thing, Morgan: if this was all for nothing, don't even think about darkening my door ever again."

"But Blod!" started Morgan.

But Blod had her reply. She pressed her nose right up against his, "Bugger off, Morgan," she said, with feeling.

Morgan stepped out into the rain and Blod's door was firmly locked behind him. If anything, the rain was heavier. It was falling by the bathful. He looked down at the river's stepping-stones. The river had risen dramatically and the stones were now underwater. Nevertheless, he thought he could dimly make them out. Should he play safe and take the longer route over the bridge? No, it was pouring down and Morgan wanted to get home quickly. He took a tentative step. Damn! The water was cold! Luckily he found a stepping-stone exactly where he thought it would be. He made sure of his footing and steadied his balance before taking another tentative step. Now with both feet in the river, and almost up to his knees in icy water, he felt the tug of the water. His balance felt precarious, and the stones grew more slippery by the step. Throwing caution to the wind he tried to race across the remaining few yards and inevitably came a cropper as he completely missed his footing, leaving him floundering in the middle of the river. He let out a thesaurus of curses, splashed to the bank, shook himself like a dog and then raced up the back lane and down the main street to the pub. With each step water oozed from his boots and all that kept Morgan going was the dream of his warm dry bed, beckoning to him.

He rushed up to the pub's front door and, expecting it to open, struck it hard with his shoulder. It didn't budge and Morgan crumpled into a sodden heap.

Bloody hell! He muttered to himself. Had Betty locked up? He put his mouth to the letter box and hissed into the darkened pub, "Betty? Betty? Open up! It's me, Morgan!"

It might as well have been the night before Christmas for all the creatures that stirred inside the pub. Morgan called through the door again, louder.

Upstairs Betty, who was snuggled up in Morgan's room directly above the front door, heard him only too clearly. She pulled an extra pillow and a thick woollen blanket over her head so she wouldn't hear him again and drifted off to sleep with a broad smile on her face.

Outside in the slashing rain Morgan thrust his hands deep in his sodden pockets—as if that would keep them dry after falling in the river—and made a dash for the side alley which led through to his stables.

That night at the pub Garrad snored heavily, Anson had a fitful night, Betty slept like a log, and Morgan—in the stable between horse and dog—hardly slept at all.

CHAPTER 9

Dawn comes early in mid-Summer, in Wales, and it was well before six when Reverend Jones left his house to climb Ffynnon Garw. He had hardly slept a wink. With every falling raindrop he had seen, in his vivid imagination, a handful of earth washing away. By midnight he had imagined the whole tump reduced to a single bucket of mud. By two in the morning he was beginning to wonder whether the rain would wash further inches off Ffynnon Garw itself. By four he was pacing his bedroom floor, almost demented with worry. Would this rain never stop?

At five he got dressed, and forgoing even his morning prayers, put on his best walking boots, grabbed his sturdiest umbrella and set off up the mountain.

Thomas Twp was already out with his dogs, checking on

his sheep, when he saw the figure of the Reverend sloshing along the puddled, muddied track.

The Reverend's face was set like a stone bridge, "Morning Thomas," he scowled, with everything arching downwards.

"Reverend . . ?" said Thomas, confused as to why this man should be striding across the wet fields at this time in the morning.

"I'm going to inspect our work," said Reverend Jones, "or what's left of it after this foul night."

"It's still blowing up there," said Thomas by way of warning the Reverend off.

"I know, I know," said the Reverend, "but I must survey the damage."

"We'll come with you," offered Thomas, who was worried about the old man going farther by himself in this wind and rain. "Just wait a moment while I get my brother."

It was still early when Anson rose, finally giving up the battle to sleep in a bed which seemed more and more uncomfortable. The truth was that he was very, very hungry. It didn't seem to bother Garrad, who seemed to be able to live on a diet of gin, that they'd hardly had a square meal since they had arrived. The best Morgan had provided were large chunks of cheese accompanied with larger chunks of bread. Anson needed something more. He dressed quickly and made his way down to the kitchen to see whether Morgan had something more substantial hidden in the bowels of his kitchen.

Up on Ffynnon Garw Reverend Jones and both Twp's stared at the mound and puzzled. The mound had certainly eroded in the night, but the worst had been saved by Williams' tarpaulin and neither the Reverend or the Twps had any idea how it had arrived there. It merely covered the crown of the pile of earth, and it's irregular shape had come to define the mound: The sides had eroded to the size of the tarpaulin. Yesterday it had been a conical tump. Now it looked like a withered soufflé. A mere nine feet of earth remained, rising steeply from a sea of mud.

The Reverend shook his head sadly.

Thomas Twp Too voiced his other worry, "We won't be able to work today," he said, as he looked to the west and saw more and more rain rushing towards them.

"No . . ." said the Reverend and also looked westward. "Today we must pray . . ."

Anson snooped around in the kitchen. He discovered several jars full of various pickled vegetables and dried meats, but didn't really fancy any of them. He found a half gallon of milk, but it was rancid. Surely Morgan must have eggs or bacon hidden somewhere.

He was sniffing the contents of yet another mysterious jar when he was disturbed by the door opening—and Betty. She was dressed in a soft, thin, cotton nightdress barely covered by the silkiest of dressing-gowns. Both items were hand-me-downs from the owner of Assam House, and were an example of one of the few perks of her previous job. Not that Anson wondered about where they came from, he was too busy being embarrassed in the presence of a woman who wasn't properly attired.

"Good morning!" said Betty breezily, and brushed past him. The room swam. Anson had to reach out for a chair to steady himself. He put it down to hunger.

"You're up with the lark," continued Betty.

"Ye-es," was as much as Anson could manage in reply.

"Couldn't you sleep?" she asked with a mischievous grin.

"N-no," he stammered, "I think it must have been the rain, it was fairly hammering against my roof, on and on," now that Anson had started he didn't seem able to stop, "I don't think I've heard rain like this . . ." He dribbled to a an inconclusive halt.

"I slept like a log," volunteered Betty, "it's so quiet without Morgan banging around."

"Hmm, yes," Anson didn't really know what to make of that statement. "So, are you leaving today?" he wondered if that was why she was up and about so early.

"We'll see," said Betty, aware that she would soon have to send a telegram which would decide her fate. "Though you won't catch me rushing around in the rain if I can help it. I'd much rather stay all snuggled up in a warm bed and just stare at it." She glanced out of the window to see Morgan rising from the hay in the stable. She smiled to herself, "Everything looks better when it's wet, don't you think?"

"Yes, well . . ." Anson didn't seem to have an answer. What was wrong with him? Either he was tongue-tied with this woman or blathering on like Garrad after a pint of gin . . .

Betty looked at the jar in Anson's hand, "Are you hungry?" she asked and took a step closer.

"Actually I'm famished," said Anson and took a step away from her.

"Yes," said Betty, coming dangerously close again, "you look hungry. Shall I see what Morgan's got? Maybe we can cook something together . . ."

Anson's throat had become very, very dry. He was saved

by a loud cough and turned to find Garrad standing in the
kitchen door.

Garrad wasn't sure what to think. He'd left these two
alone last night and now here they were, in the kitchen together. And this woman was not properly dressed.

"Morning," said Garrad and made it sound like a call to
attention."

Betty moved away to the stove and put on the kettle.
Anson watched her every movement.

"Right Anson," Garrad continued in his most military
voice, "order of the day: sort out the car."

He realized that Anson hadn't heard a word. The man
was openly staring at this young tart who was trolling around
the kitchen in her night garments!

"Anson!" he barked harder.

Anson spun around to face him, "Yes George?"

God, he hated it when Anson called him George! "We
can't hang about here all day waiting for some joker on a
motorcycle . . ."

Betty's face fell, "Are you off?" she asked, "Back into
England or further into Wales?"

"North," explained Anson, "north-west actually, into
Wales."

"Well if it's raining here," laughed Betty, "it'll be raining
more there! You'd best wait here."

Outside, footsteps splashed across the yard. Morgan was
making a dash from the stables to the kitchen. He hammered
on the back door, "Betty! Let me in! I'm so wet I'm melting!"

Betty moved to the door, "And you don't want to spend
much time in North Wales," she said to Anson and Garrad,
"The inns up there? Ugh! Like sleeping in stables!"

That last part was, of course, for Morgan's benefit who

at this moment collapsed into the kitchen in a very dishevelled state. There was straw everywhere, sticking from the hair on his head and from the socks on his feet. His whole skin had pruned and he was an unpleasant shade of blue-grey.

Anson and Garrad stared as if they'd seen an apparition.

Morgan returned their stares with a big grin, "Morning" he said, and then grabbed Betty and bundled her into the pantry and closed the door behind them.

Anson and Garrad exchanged glances. Were they observing a strange Welsh custom? They said nothing, and did less.

In the pantry Morgan squashed Betty up against a side of smoked bacon.

"So?" he asked with a lascivious grin.

"So what?" hissed Betty.

"You know," said Morgan, "last night, 'Miss Elizabeth' and the English . . ."

Betty grabbed a knife from the bacon and almost sliced off the tip of Morgan's nose. "Firstly," she waved the knife, " 'Miss Elizabeth' died in her sleep, and secondly Morgan, they're not animals like you, they're gentlemen!"

She really wanted to poke the knife in Morgan's ribs, but she restrained herself and stabbed the bacon instead, before pushing Morgan aside and leaving him with the dead flesh.

Morgan pondered her words. So they were gentlemen . . . That was one thing, but more importantly, she had called him *an animal*. It was the biggest compliment she, or any other woman, had ever paid him. He pulled himself to his full height and rolled the word around in his chest, "An animal!"

Williams The Petroleum rolled over in bed and groaned. He felt as if his whole body were one large, blooming bruise and that all his joints had fused in the night. Bloody Morgan, he thought, and cursed himself too for being stupid enough to get caught up in the whole mad enterprise.

He could see the rain lashing against his window and was about to turn over and go back to sleep when he remembered the Englishmen's car which had been sitting, unprotected in the rain all night. Dragging himself from bed he looked out of the window, down at the car in his yard below.

His heart sank. It had filled with water. Within moments he was dressed and rushing through the back lanes to Morgan's pub.

Williams hoped that he could sneak in the back door and have a few words with Morgan, but to his horror he found himself in the kitchen, face to face with the Englishmen who were devouring a hearty breakfast.

"Morning, Williams," said Betty amiably, "Fancy some bacon and eggs?"

Williams would have loved some, but didn't really want to share the company. "No thank you," he managed with a sinking heart.

"Ah, Mr. Williams," started Garrad, "Just the man I wanted to see."

"Yes, I thought you might be on your way," replied Williams.

"Any news?" asked Anson.

"I've just sent Tommy," lied Williams, "he should be back in no time."

" 'In no time'?" said Garrad with arching brow, "Queer expression I've always thought. When exactly might that be, in *my* time?"

"Oh, I'm sure he'll be back before eleven," said Williams

and attempted a smile. He turned to Betty, "Morgan around?"

She nodded her head towards the bar.

Morgan was stoking a large log fire in the back bar and warming himself with a hot toddy.

"Morgan . . !" started Williams.

"Don't you start," said Morgan, "I've had Blod at me, I've had Betty lock me out, I've slept with the bloody horse, now the English have found my best bacon . . ." He left out the fact that he'd fallen in the river. He didn't want to appear stupid.

"Their bloody car is full of water!" whispered Williams.

"So?" said Morgan.

"So? So? So I was supposed to be looking after it!"

"So make up an excuse."

"An excuse? For God's sake Morgan, I've ruined their car!"

"Tell them the tarpaulin blew away in the rain," said Morgan as if it were the most plausible excuse in the world.

"Blew away in the rain?" said Williams with incredulity.

"Well what else are you going to say?" asked Morgan.

Reverend Jones returned from the mound with a sinking heart. It wasn't the fact that they had lost so much earth, though that was bad enough. What worried the Reverend was that they might have lost the initiative. It was one thing to have them all toiling up and down Ffynnon Garw for a couple of days, but now the momentum had been broken. Could the work be completed in just one more day? Johnny's words stung him to the core, "We'll need more as we go higher and the base grows wider." The Reverend tried to calculate: had they taken a third of the soil up? More? Less?

Could the mound be completed with one more day? Or two? Or three? He reached his house and slunk inside.

Blod took Johnny a strong cup of tea. He was already awake and just staring into space. "Morning Johnny," she said and was relieved to see that he acknowledged her with his eyes. But he didn't speak.

"It's still raining," she said.

He took the cup of tea and sipped hungrily, only pausing to stare out at the rain, out at Ffynnon Garw.

"I won't be far away if you need anything," said Blod and went about her business.

As soon as breakfast was over Betty made her way down to the Post Office.

"I need to send a telegram," she said to Hughes The Stamps.

"I see," he replied—he was a man of few words—and passed her a form and a pencil.

Was a family illness enough, or would Betty have to pretend that there had been a death? She wasn't sure. She could hardly tell the truth—"NEEDED TO WOO ENGLISH MAP-MAKERS STOP MOUNTAIN BEING BUILT STOP ALL MORGAN'S FAULT STOP." No, that wouldn't do.

It needed to be something tragic: yes, that was the word, tragedy! "DEEPEST APOLOGIES FOR LEAVING AT SHORT NOTICE STOP FAMILY TRAGEDY STOP RETURNING SHORTLY STOP." She passed the telegram to Hughes The Stamps.

"How much will that be?" she asked.

"First delivery or second?" replied Hughes.

"First, the fastest."

However, Hughes, who had been counting the words,

had stopped, and seemed to be reading the telegram over again.

"I can't send that," he said.

"And why not?" asked Betty.

"Because it's not true, and it's an offence to send lies over the telegraph service."

"And who are you to decide what's a lie and what isn't?" asked Betty, "And to be reading my telegram in the first place? I thought telegrams were private!"

"They are," said Hughes.

"But you just read it!"

"But I'm the Postmaster, it's my job."

"All right, Mister Postmaster," said Betty, "you stick to your job and I'll stick to mine: I'm here, working on these English for Morgan. Do you want to ruin everything?"

Hughes The Stamps sniffed, he didn't want to upset Morgan. "Well why didn't you say so?" he said and returned to counting the words.

Betty returned to the pub and found Anson polishing another instrument.

"You're not going to do that all day, are you?" she laughed.

"Well . . ." Anson didn't have anything better to do.

"Morgan's got a draughts board in the bar," continued Betty, "Fancy a game?"

It was pouring with rain and there was nowhere to go— How could Anson say no?

Morgan lay on his bed, the covers pulled over his face, trying to get some sleep. His night in the barn had been veritable torture. He ached all over. However, try as he might, sleep wouldn't come. His mind was racing: How long could he keep the English here? How long would the rain last? How long to finish the mound? For a moment he thought he heard the rain lessen; quickly he pulled back the covers only to find that it was still pissing down.

He stared at it and sighed.

George Garrad also stared out at the rain—and bristled with anger. He felt that he was losing his authority over Anson and worse, losing control of the whole expedition. They had now been in Wales for four days, during which time they had managed to survey just one, insignificant hill. His car had been disabled and like the car, Anson seemed to have snapped a *bethyngalw* and lost his drive. It was Garrad's opinion that Anson was close to going native, a nasty phenomenon which he'd observed throughout the Empire. He had seen disgusting examples in India and the Far East as well-bred, perfectly sane Englishmen had lost their bearings and started to dress like the locals. Before long they found themselves in drug dens and brothels. This was not going to happen to an officer under Garrad's command.

Unfortunately, however, Anson wasn't strictly under Garrad's command. It was all very perplexing, but while their work was tied to the military, it wasn't strictly a military venture, and they weren't here in the hierarchical relationship which Garrad would have preferred. Instead they were employees, one senior, one junior, and while Garrad was in charge, he wasn't strictly in command.

At the kitchen table behind him, Anson was playing draughts with Betty, and losing. Anson couldn't put his finger on it, but his concentration was shot, and Betty's pieces were romping across the board, devouring his with ease.

"You're not very good at this, are you," laughed Betty,

as she took another three of his pieces, "Come on, concentrate!"

Anson was about to reply when his train of thought was
further ruined by Garrad who spun away from the window
in a twenty-one gun peeve.

"He said he'd be here by eleven o'clock! He said he'd
have the part! Dammit, it's almost sodding noon!" barked
Garrad and grabbed his sou'wester. "C'mon Anson!"

Anson looked up. C'mon? It was still pouring with rain.
What was George talking about? "Where, exactly?" asked
Anson.

Garrad looked at him in exasperation. If only they'd
been in the army he'd have commandeered the man now,
bread and water for thirty days, a stint peeling potatoes for
the officers' mess, a few long marches with a heavy pack.
Unfortunately they were just map-makers and George wasn't
Gordon of Khartoum, but Garrad The Maps. "To get the
bloody car!" He thundered, "Where the hell do you think?
Good God, Anson, I do believe you are losing your mind."

"The car! Right, the car!" said Anson and rose from the
table to follow Garrad.

When he reached the front door he found that Garrad
was striding on ahead, cutting a path through the puddles.
His figure inspired comparison with a tug in a squall. Anson
took one look at the rain and readjusted his hat. It was buck-
eting. Hearing a little knock behind him he turned to see Betty
waving from the window. He was just waving back when he
heard Garrad bark for him, and he rushed off, doing his best
imitation of a well-trained dog.

—⚓—

Now the truth is that unless you've lived in Wales or Ireland, you don't know the meaning of the word "rain." The Inuits of the Arctic have many words for snow, and for similar reasons the Welsh have many ways of describing rain.

In Wales they say it "tamps", it "grizzles" and it "curtain-rods". It "buckets", "dribbles" and "hoses". They say there's rain "like two-bob bits", like "pins and needles". They talk of "sheeting rain", "drowning rain", "stinging rain". They talk of "Noah's rain", of "good rain", "bad rain", "God-given rain" and "evil rain". Of rain "that we need", and rain "that we don't need". They talk of rain that is "staying" and rain that is "due somewhere else". They even talk of rain that was "meant for somewhere else," and that somewhere else is probably also in Wales.

The Welsh talk of "soft" rain and "hard" rain, "warm" rain and "cold" rain. Yes, the Welsh have so much rain that they need to be able to talk about it with some degree of accuracy.

Indeed the sad truth is that while we Welsh like to believe that it was the mountains that beat the successive invaders, it was really *the weather* that comes with the mountains—It was the rain that defeated every invader, yes, simple *rain* . . .

The Romans swept through Europe and only met their first defeat when they came upon Wales, the Welsh, their mountains and their rain. Imagine some poor Roman soldier, straight from the sunshine of Italy. His first day it rained, all day; his next day it rained, all day; his third day it rained, all day. And so it went on, day in day out; Why, there was a time I remember when it rained continually from the beginning of October to the end of March—yes, continually. It's debilitating enough for the locals, so you can imagine what it felt like to a bunch of young men in sandals and togas. Yes, the Romans fled Wales, and having heard that Ireland was even wetter, didn't even bother to cross the Irish sea.

Of course George Garrad didn't consider any of this. George Garrad's view of history was a catalogue of heroic battles—and battles always won and never lost. In his world adversaries were sought, found and dealt with.

However, Gordon of Khartoum had never had to deal with rain—or a character like Williams The Petroleum who was unsurprisingly missing when Garrad knocked and knocked at his door.

"Perhaps he's out fixing someone else's car," volunteered Anson.

Williams heard that but resolutely refused to budge from his hiding place under his kitchen table.

Barging through the doors to the garage yard George Garrad found himself staring at his poor, sad, unprotected car. It was with some great shock to his system that he discovered that the passenger area was brim-full of water. He opened a door and water poured out, cascading like a Niagara around his putteed ankles.

Garrad didn't say a word. He didn't even dare look at Anson. And it was just as well, since Reginald Anson was having some difficulty suppressing a smile. Garrad slammed the door and thought for a moment before making a momentous decision. Then he strode off into the rain with renewed vigour.

—m—

A telegram had arrived at the Post Office in the meanwhile. It was addressed to Betty. It read: "ACCEPT YOUR EXPLANATION STOP BUT MUST RETURN TO DUTY SUNDAY EVENING THE LATEST STOP OR FIND OTHER POSITION STOP."

Hughes The Stamps showed it to his wife.

"So?" she asked.

"Bad news for Morgan," said Hughes.

"Oh, what a shame," replied his wife, who had been present at the birth of several children that Morgan had fathered—most notably one of her own, though her husband didn't know that, of course.

Hughes put on his overcoat.

"Where are you going?" she asked.

"Where do you think?"

With telegram in hand he stalked off into the rain puzzling why his wife was so nasty about Morgan. She'll probably want me to give up the drink again soon, he thought as he trudged to the pub.

Morgan was still languishing in bed, and still shivering. Hughes The Stamps entered the bedroom, much in the way that a courtier would enter the chamber of an ailing king.

"I thought you should see this," he said, and passed Betty's telegram to Morgan.

"Well done, well done," said Morgan and threw it on the fire.

"You can't do that!" said Hughes in horror.

"Sorry," said Morgan, "but I already did."

"That's property of the Crown!"

"I thought it was addressed to Betty," said Morgan.

"Well it was, but it belongs to His Majesty's Telegraph Service until it gets to her!"

"Well I received it by poxy for her," explained Morgan.

"*Proxy*," Hughes corrected him. "And what's going to happen when she doesn't get a reply?"

Morgan sneezed and cogitated. "You're right. We'll have

to send her another one." He thought for a moment while Hughes The Stamps fumed, "Damn," said Morgan, "I wish I knew when this bloody rain will stop."

Hughes The Stamps, who had been too angry to speak, finally calmed down just enough to speak, "If you think that I'm going to send a duplicitous message . . . !"

Morgan looked him up and down, "But I don't see an alternative," he said innocently, "you said yourself that she'll be expecting a reply." He casually jumped out of bed—he was feeling better now that there was something positive to be done, "Come and have a drink while I compose a reply."

They went down to the bar, but rather than take his place at the counter, Morgan rushed outside and banged on Ivor's window before returning to pour Hughes The Stamps a drink.

Ivor popped his head around the inn door, "Morgan?"

"Morning Ivor, need a favour: send that boy of yours up to the Twps will you and find out how long this rain is going to last."

"That's two bloody miles," said Ivor, "and it's raining!"

"I know it's bloody raining!" exploded Morgan, "Or I wouldn't be asking the Twps how long it will take to stop, would I? Come on Ivor, this is important! I have telegrams waiting on this!"

"I'm sorry, Morgan," said Ivor, "but I need him in the shop." Ivor started to leave.

"Just one last thing Ivor," said Morgan with a malicious twinkle, "I don't suppose you'll be needing that friendly neighbour to speak as witness to your ink-spilling, will you . . . ?"

Ivor slowly counted to ten, "What do you want him to ask the Twps, exactly?"

* * *

Reverend Jones sat at his window, staring at the rain, and meditated upon the state of things. What had he, and the village done to deserve this? he wondered. Mentally he stopped himself and gave himself a sharp slap. *What had they done to deserve this?* That was surely superstitious blasphemy! As if the good Lord had time to think about them and their petty problems! As if the good Lord had sent this rain just for them!

He knew it was absurd to think in these terms and was shocked to have caught himself indulging in such superstitious claptrap. Nevertheless it chilled him to the bone, for he knew that his thoughts were quintessentially Welsh, and that if he were indulging in such ideas, his fellow villagers would be too.

Indeed at that very moment, Elsie Twostroke was holding court in the village Post Office to Mrs. Hughes The Stamps.

"The weather was lovely," she said, "until we started messing with that mound. You mark my words, the weather in this valley will never be the same again."

"Shush!" said Mrs. Hughes The Stamps, "The English!"

She pointed towards the door and Elsie turned to find a very wet George Garrad striding in, following closely by an equally soaked Reginald Anson.

Elsie kept talking, but changed from English to Welsh, "It's true," she continued, "and if these two hadn't come . . !" She gave them both a sneer and left.

Garrad shook with cold and wondered whether Elsie's Welsh words had been an ancient witch's curse. He tried to pull himself together, he really wasn't feeling too well.

"I would like," he began, but paused. He was staring at

Mrs. Hughes The Stamps: the Postmaster was a woman. Garrad couldn't bear it. "Anson!" he snapped, and Reginald took over.

"We'd like to send a telegram," said Anson.

"Very good, sir," said Mrs. Hughes.

"To our head office," continued Anson.

"And where might that be, sir?" asked Mrs. Hughes.

"London," said Anson.

Garrad stared wistfully into space and whispered under his breath, "London . . ." He said it with love, with reverence. That simple word expressed a feeling for him—a civilization lost—which he feared would never be re-found. "London . . . !"

The telegram which they sent was simple and to the point: "URGENT STOP CAR DISABLED STOP NO OTHER TRANSPORT AVAILABLE STOP ADVISE AS HOW TO PROCEED STOP IMMEDIATE REPLY REQUESTED STOP REPEAT IMMEDIATE REPLY STOP." As Anson checked it before despatch, he couldn't help smiling that the profusion of "stops" somehow seemed to describe their predicament far better than the message which they served to punctuate.

"That's fine," said Anson, and Mrs. Hughes The Stamps duly tapped out the telegram. Garrad looked around the cramped Post Office, and seeing an old chair, he set himself down.

Mrs. Hughes looked up at him, "Will there be anything else, sir?" she asked.

"No," replied Garrad, "but if it's all the same with you, I shall wait here for my reply."

"Very well, sir," nodded Mrs. Hughes and went on with her business.

"George?" Anson didn't think that waiting in the draughty place was such a good idea.

"I intend to get my reply!" snarled Garrad and shot a look at Mrs. Hughes The Stamps that said volumes about Garrad's trust, or rather mistrust, of the Welsh in general and Mrs. Hughes in particular.

You should think yourselves lucky that my husband isn't sending this, thought Mrs. Hughes.

Ivor's shop boy, a pimply youth too old for school and too young for the army, and to whom nothing as exciting had ever previously happened, fairly galloped all the way to the Twp's and back on Ivor's old nag.

He arrived back in the pub panting and very, very wet.

"So?" demanded Morgan.

"He doesn't know."

"What do you mean, he doesn't know?" asked Morgan. "Thomas Twp always knows about the rain!" Then Morgan thought about it, was it Thomas Twp who was good with the rain, or Thomas Twp Too, he always mixed them up. "Did you ask both brothers?"

"Of course I did!" said Ivor's boy. He wasn't stupid. "And he said it's easy to say when it will start but it's much harder to say when it will stop."

"Bloody marvellous!" groaned Morgan. "Didn't he have any idea?"

"He thought maybe Sunday, but maybe Monday."

Sunday or Monday? Betty's telegram was telling her to return on Sunday, just when he'd need her most.

"Thank you," said Morgan, and gave Ivor's boy a bottle of ginger wine for his trouble.

"So?" asked Hughes The Stamps.

"The telegram must read that she's all right until next Wednesday." Hughes gave him a dirty look, "That's not the exact wording you understand, you're good at how they write these things."

"But . . . ," Hughes The Stamps started but Morgan stopped him.

"I don't want to be telling people that it failed because of you," he threatened, as ever. "Besides, Betty will thank me for this. She hates that job, believe me, she's better off here in Ffynnon Garw."

It had been almost two long hours before Anson and Garrad's reply came, and in those two hours Ivor's boy had been to the Twps' and back and half the village must have found a reason to visit the Post Office to catch a glimpse of the English as they sat, impatiently waiting for a reply.

Naturally everyone who came into the Post Office that morning spoke in Welsh, which only served to further isolate Garrad and Anson and fuel Garrad's fears that the whole place was against him, as of course they were.

"I suppose they get paid for just sitting there," observed one customer.

"You ought to be serving gin," noted another, "you'd make a fine profit."

"Poor thing," said a third, looking at the damp, unhappy Garrad, "maybe we should put some stamps on him and mail him home."

Garrad's mind twisted and turned. While he feared that there was a conspiracy, he also feared for his sanity. Could they *all* be against him? Wasn't that the sort of worry which sent men mad? Wasn't that the sort of delusional fear to which commanders in the fields were prone? One moment he was sure he was right, and that like Gordon of Khartoum he should be on his guard and ready to crush any rebellion: the next moment he checked himself and decided that he really must stop reading the life of the great General.

He was awoken from his meditation by the sound of the telegraph machine clicking into life.

Mrs. Hughes The Stamps read the telegram as it printed. Her face fell.

"I think that's for me," said Garrad before Mrs. Hughes could find a reason to destroy it.

Garrad snatched it and quickly read its contents. It began, "TAKE A TRAIN" . . . and Garrad snorted. "I suspected as much!" he said, and left the Post Office as fast as his frame would allow, "Come on Anson, I think that stationmaster has some explaining to do"!

Mrs. Hughes The Stamps rushed through the back of her shop. No, she didn't like Morgan and was happy to see him in trouble with Betty, but she didn't want to be the one to have ruined everything. Her youngest, Rhiannon, was reading by the fire. "Quick!" said Mrs. Hughes, "Get down to the station and warn Thomas The Trains!" Her daughter sped from the room, "Take the back lane," called Mrs. Hughes, "and run all the way!"

Garrad had just missed his footing and was disappearing up to his ankles in mud when Anson looked around and made a lyrical observation. "Have you noticed," he asked Garrad, "how this village seems both bigger and smaller in the rain?"

Garrad looked at him as if he had lost all his marbles. Bigger and smaller in the rain? Garrad didn't even dignify this stupidity with a reply.

"What I meant," continued Anson regardless, "was that the mist has closed in the views, making it all seem smaller;

but distances are so much harder to navigate, making it seem quite a large place."

"Did I ask what you meant?" asked Garrad, and they continued on in silence.

"It was just an observation," replied Anson quietly, as they turned the final corner to the station approach.

Rhiannon Hughes, who had already been to the station and talked to Thomas The Trains, gave them a cheery wave as she made her way back to the Post Office, "*Bore da!*" What was to her a polite good morning, was as far as Garrad was concerned, yet another gypsy curse.

Thomas The Trains was in a rare state as he watched them descending on his station. His mind was racing for an explanation, for an excuse . . . What on earth would he say to the English? His eyes flew around the room, and then settled on a puddle of water.

"Good morning," groaned Garrad.

"Ye-es," replied Thomas.

"I have been advised by my office," said Garrad with a slow, steady, stabbing rhythm, "that I *can* take a train from here—whatismore, *a passenger train,* to Pontypridd." Garrad held up his telegram, now sodden from the rain, but proof nevertheless of a service which Thomas had neglected to tell him about.

"Ye-es . . . ?" Thomas tried to look innocent, something the Welsh have been practising for years with little result.

"But *you* told *me*," continued Garrad with growing emphasis, "that there were *no* passenger trains . . ."

"Going east . . ." Thomas interrupted him and threw Garrad completely off his stride.

"Going east?" said Garrad.

"Yes, there's no passenger trains, going east. I didn't know you wanted to go north, to Pontypridd."

Garrad slowly counted to ten, "Why, my good man, would you think that I wanted to go east?"

"Because," Thomas smiled broadly, "you're English and well, England's to the east . . ."

For a moment Anson thought that Garrad might reach into the ticket office and rip Thomas The Trains' head from his shoulders. Instead he turned to Reginald, "Anson!"

Anson took over, "Well, we'd like two first class tickets . . ."

Garrad shot him a dirty look.

Anson modified their needs, " . . . two second class tickets to Pontypridd."

"To the north!" added Garrad with venom.

Thomas smiled meekly, "I'm very sorry," he said, "you could have gone yesterday, but you can't today."

"Oh?" said Anson, "And why's that?"

Thomas had a blinding flash. "Flooding on the line."

"Flooding?" said Anson.

Thomas smiled again, "I'm afraid so, terrible flooding with all this rain."

As Anson and Garrad limped back to the inn they couldn't help noticing a large coal train, lumbering through the village.

—⚝—

In the pub Morgan was being harassed by Evans The End Of The World.

"You and that minister have put a curse on this village," said Evans.

"Don't talk daft," said Morgan, "you sound as stupid as Thomas Twp."

"You mark my words," said Evans, "that mound has heralded the second flood."

"Oh I suppose we never had a rain storm before that mound?" said Morgan.

"Not like this," said Evans sagely, "you take heed: we're cursed."

Morgan looked out of the window and caught sight of Blod walking past. She glanced through the window long enough to give Morgan an icy stare.

"I wish it were that easy," said Morgan, wondering whether he'd ever see the inside of Blod's house—or bed— again.

His lascivious fantasies were, however, interrupted by the entrance of Anson and Garrad. Anson looked his normal cheery self, but Garrad looked like a man in pain. And they were both very, very wet.

"Ah, gentlemen," said Morgan buoyantly, "Any success?"

Garrad stopped and stared at Morgan before saying just one word, "Flooding." There was something in his tone that harmonized with Evans The End Of The World's pronouncements. Garrad made it sound like the apocalypse.

"Yes," Anson carried on the conversation with a considerably lighter tone, "and it's rather interesting because while the passenger trains are cancelled the coal trains seem completely unaffected."

Anson smiled at Morgan with a get-out-of-that-one grin, but Morgan was too sharp for him.

"Different lines," he improvised quickly.

"Ah, there you are George!" smiled Anson, "I told you

there would be a very simple explanation, they run on different lines and therefore . . ."

Garrad stopped him dead, "Shut up."

Morgan and Evans exchanged glances; this was significant. For the first time they'd seen the English argue in public. There seemed to be a growing rift in their ranks. Morgan found that very satisfying.

Garrad leaned on the bar heavily. The poor man looked fit to collapse. "I think I'll retire for an hour," he said, "I really must get out of these wet things and lie down."

"Of course," said Morgan, "don't want you to be catching your death now do we."

"Please send some extra blankets to my room," asked Garrad, "and a bottle of pink gin."

"Yes sir," said Morgan, "your very request is my demand."

About an hour later there was a knock at Betty's door.

"Who is it?" asked Betty.

"It's me," said Morgan, as he stepped in.

"Did I ask you to come in?" asked Betty.

"No, but I thought you'd want this," said Morgan and gave her a sealed telegram.

"Thank you." She opened it and read it to herself.

"Good news? Bad news? Anything interesting?" asked Morgan innocently.

"Frankly," said Betty, "it's none of your business." How wrong she was . . .

CHAPTER
10

It started raining on the Thursday night and it rained all Friday morning.

And it rained all Friday afternoon. And it rained all Friday night.

On Saturday morning the dog-racing was cancelled, and on Saturday afternoon even the rugby practice was called off.

In a few short days the village of Ffynnon Garw had been turned into its usual winter quagmire. Streets dissolved into mud, gardens started to yellow. The mould which usually waited until autumn reappeared on indoor walls. Damp patches arrived on bedroom ceilings. The small stream which ran through the village had swelled into a raging torrent and there were fears that the allotments would be flooded.

And up and down the village superstitious talk filled

kitchens and shops and more and more villagers started to doubt the wisdom of their enterprise.

You may laugh, but one must remember that these were people who had been brought up with the Bible. Many had learned to read using the Old Testament as their text and their minds were full of tales of a wrathful God. Some likened their work on the mound to the building of the Tower Of Babel. Had not God cursed those who had attempted to build a structure which would take them closer to heaven, they argued? Others saw the mound as a pagan work, as the worship of a craven image. Wherever Reverend Jones went he was confronted with these questions and while he did his best to allay them he knew that the villagers' deepest fears had been stirred.

While it was difficult to argue that the rain was unusual—as Reverend Jones pointed out, it was something that happened each and every year—many saw divine intervention in the fate of Johnny and Williams. The Lord had sent the rain to wash the mound away, they claimed, and Johnny and Williams had been attacked by lightning for daring to save it. It was nonsense, of course, but it was potent nonsense fuelled by the display of very real thunderbolts from a very turbulent heaven.

Morgan, who like Reverend Jones, had little time for superstition, saw the rain as a mixed blessing. True, it had halted their work, but it was nevertheless helping to keep the English in the village. Garrad was spending more and more time in his room and—much to Morgan's surprise—Anson was spending more time with Betty.

Morgan wasn't sure quite how he felt about this. On the one hand he was more than a little annoyed since now the two women in his life, both Betty and Blod, were completely ignoring him. On the other hand, he had summoned Betty for the express purpose of charming the English while he kept them hostage. In Morgan's grand plan Betty should have flirted wildly with Garrad—and no more. He had imagined that her beauty would have kept the old sot's brain further addled. He hadn't bargained with her using her charms on Anson. Worse, he was severely doubting whether she was acting under his orders. She wouldn't talk to him about it, and whenever he confronted her she pushed him away with a cool, "Bugger off." It was a phrase she seemed to have learnt from Blod.

And if Betty was confusing to Morgan, then Anson had him spinning. He seemed to be like a little schoolboy around the place, reduced to blushes and shy smiles. It was the kind of behaviour, which in a man, disgusted Morgan. Did that sort of thing impress Betty? He didn't think so, how could it? Yet, there they were, always tripping over each other.

On Thursday they had spent the afternoon cleaning Anson's equipment. On Thursday evening he had found them in the kitchen. Betty was cleaning vegetables and Anson was plucking a chicken. They didn't seem to talk to each other— indeed they were working at opposite ends of the room—and their calm silence disturbed Morgan. A silent woman, was, in Morgan's experience, a sign that trouble was coming.

It was all the more galling that they were eating Morgan out of house and home. He wasn't used, or prepared for his guests to expect three good meals a day. But whenever he turned around, there they were, tucking into feasts. Garrad was working his way through Morgan's side of bacon, and Betty and Anson were working through his chickens and ducks.

On Friday Anson and Betty went for a walk in the rain, ostensibly to see the swollen river. Now Morgan thought them *both* mad. Who on earth would walk in torrential rain for no good reason? He could understand an Englishman doing such a foolish thing, but Betty? He was beginning to doubt that she was Welsh, or that he knew her at all.

That evening they were to be found sitting next to the fire, reading books, for all the world like an elderly married couple, bored with the world and themselves, thought Morgan.

However, Saturday brought a change with a long, detailed telegram from London. Hughes The Stamps received it with a heavy heart. It was so complex, businesslike and important that there was no question of showing it to Morgan: Hughes could not let him destroy this one. And there was no way of delaying its delivery.

Hughes strode into the pub. Morgan was behind the bar, and Garrad was sitting at it.

"A telegram for Mr. Garrad," said Hughes loudly and watched as Morgan spilled a pint of beer all over himself.

"Hughes?" said Morgan.

"You heard me," said Hughes who duly delivered the telegram, turned on his heel and left.

"*Traitor!*" hissed Morgan, in Welsh.

The first part of the telegram was an instruction. The second part was a train pass, authorized by His Majesty's Ordinance Survey. Anson and Garrad were to leave by a train "which will be leaving Ffynnon Garw", read the telegram with some authority, "at 0800 Monday morning . . ."

Hughes The Stamps returned to the Post Office and slumped into his chair, emotionally drained.

"Did you deliver it?" asked his wife.

He nodded, and was surprised when she hugged him.

"It's gone on long enough," she said, "we can't be breaking the law for Morgan too. I'm proud of you."

Hughes smiled, but his smile was forced. He was going to have to tell his wife everything; he had been living a lie. "But I already did something terrible," he said and blurted out the story of Betty's telegram.

Mrs. Hughes listened with folded arms and pinched lips. Like most of the women in the village she had little time for Betty From Cardiff whom she regarded as a trumped up, painted tart who probably padded her chest, coloured her hair and corsetted her waist. That, however, did not change the fact that Betty was another woman Morgan was deceiving.

"And what did the original telegram say?" asked Mrs. Hughes.

He told her.

Within moments—and without a coat—Mrs. Hughes The Stamps was marching through the rain. It was evening and the pub was half full. It was not a place where women, except Betty, set foot.

The door crashed open and Mrs. Hughes barged in.

"Betty From Cardiff?" she demanded.

Betty was by the fire in the smaller bar, with Anson, when she heard herself thus paged. "Yes?"

Mrs. Hughes glared at Morgan, "I have a telegram for you," she said loudly, "which cancels all previous telegrams."

And with that, she delivered a facsimile of the original telegram, and left the pub, leaving Morgan gawping like a goldfish. At last Betty knew the truth. She would have to leave on Sunday.

The telegrams changed everything. Suddenly Anson couldn't look at Betty, nor Betty at Anson. However, Morgan had long stopped watching them. He had his eye, and his mind, on one thing, and one thing only: the blasted, bloody weather.

On rising, the first thing that Morgan did was to look out of his window. Just before going to bed Morgan could be found on the back porch of the pub, staring up at the clouds, willing them to part and blow away. All day he listened to its insistent drumming, and if he noticed any variation he would rush outside to see if it was stopping. If it had gone on much longer the villagers would have renamed him Morgan The Rainwatcher.

Of course it had rained like this before, and would again, with monotonous regularity, but just as a watched kettle never boils, so watched rain never seems to stop.

Betty found herself in a hopeless predicament because, against her will, and to her surprise, she had become infatuated with Anson.

The telegram—when she at last received the proper one—had been sharp and to the point: return on Sunday or lose your job. And yet Anson and Garrad would be here until Monday. Would that day make a difference? To her job, certainly; but to her relationship with Anson?

Before she could even think about any of that Betty had to make an escape plan. It was no good asking Morgan, and most of the male village shopkeeper's probably wouldn't help either. Moreover, Betty wasn't popular among the women in the village so she had to walk out and stop the first child she saw.

"Where does Tommy Twostroke live?" she asked and Ethel Davies meekly led her down the back lane.

It was evening and Elsie was in the kitchen boiling nappies, "Come on in, love!" she called, thinking it was her sister. Her face fell when she saw Betty.

"I'm sorry to bother you," said Betty, "but I need to talk to Tommy."

"You missed him," said Elsie with glee, "he's just gone off to work—night shift."

"I need him to take me back to Cardiff on Sunday," said Betty.

"Do you now," said Elsie with no sympathy whatsoever.

"It's important. I'll pay."

"We don't want your money," said Elsie, and managed with just a look to insinuate how it had been earned. "Anyway, it's his one day off," she continued, "and he's good for nothing as it is after gallivanting down to Cardiff for you on Thursday. Missed a night's sleep he did on your account."

"That wasn't my fault," said Betty, "I didn't want to come! That bloody Morgan tricked me, the bugger!" she suddenly realized that she'd sworn, twice, in front of Elsie's two little ones. "I apologize for my language," she said respectfully.

Elsie had always been wary of this woman who she'd hardly seen in the flesh but about whom she'd heard so much. She had expected her to be very posh, full of airs and graces, but she talked just like any other woman in the village, and like *every* other woman in the village she didn't have a good word to say about Morgan.

"Do you want a cup of tea?" asked Elsie, and prepared

to sit down and work something out with a kindred spirit in need.

Betty returned from Tommy and Elsie's more confused than ever. Elsie had promised that yes, Tommy would take her back, but now that Betty had organized a way out she found herself in a panic. What about her last chance with Anson? What about their courtship? She stopped herself short—courtship? Anson wasn't courting her! They were merely two people who happened to have been forced together for a few days by Morgan.

It was true that she had kissed Anson in the confusion of that first evening, but she hadn't kissed him again and he certainly hadn't made a move to kiss her. On the one hand he seemed very happy to be in her company, but on the other he never seemed to instigate a conversation, or suggest that they do anything or go anywhere. Every initiative had been hers and it left her in doubt as to how he felt about her. He'd walked when she had suggested a walk. He'd helped when she had cooked lunch and supper. He'd always been around, hovering like a nervous bird, wherever she had been. He'd found conversation difficult but obviously liked her company. She didn't know what to think.

She remembered a conversation from the previous afternoon. They had been reading in the same room and when she paused, she looked up to find him staring at her. He quickly went back to his book.

"Do you ever feel lonely?" she asked.

"Lonely?" he said, "I suppose so, doesn't everyone get lonely? What I mean is, isn't it quite natural and ordinary to feel lonely from time to time?"

"I suppose so," said Betty.

"It's not something that I think about very much," said Anson.

It wasn't true. He had been profoundly lonely during the war. He had lost so many friends that he couldn't even bring their faces, far less their names, to his mind. He had become an officer so quickly and found that responsibility extraordinarily isolating.

When he had been released from hospital he had found himself in an alien world: London seemed unchanged. People were still going to their clubs, out to dinner, to the ballet and the opera. Life continued as if the war had never started. People paid lip service to it and he was continually congratulated on his 'gallantry' but he felt disassociated from the world that he found himself in. It had only been in this last week, since he'd been to Wales, since he'd found himself in this glorious landscape full of working people—and this young woman— that he had slowly found a way out from his stifling cocoon.

So did he ever feel lonely? How could he answer that question simply? Since he felt she had asked it in a much more naive, and conversational way, it was best to answer with a white lie.

Betty, who had no way of knowing any of this, merely noted that he had not bothered to reciprocate and ask the more interesting question of whether *she* ever felt lonely. If he had asked the question where would that answer lead?

On Saturday night Betty lay restlessly in bed, going over and over the days in her mind. And then, most dangerous and painful of all, she allowed herself to speculate. What if he did like her? What if he were in love with her? Would a man like Anson marry a Betty From Cardiff? Would a man like Anson take Betty back to England, to English life with him? Would a man like Anson stay in a place like Ffynnon Garw for her?

Her heart sank. It was completely unrealistic. He was, she convinced herself, simply being well-mannered. His behaviour, if seen from that perspective, made perfect sense. He probably neither liked her nor disliked her, since, out of his class as she was, she didn't exist as a suitable woman for him. He was charming and polite to her because it was in his nature and breeding to be charming and polite. That was an end to it.

Her station in life was to remain as a maid at Assam House. She thought of her life compared to many other women she knew and decided that she was lucky to have such a post.

Yes, she told herself, she would definitely leave on Sunday morning.

—w—

On Sunday morning, just when it seemed that the rain would never stop, two miracles occurred—it stopped raining and Morgan The Goat talked to Reverend Jones.

Morgan strode to the chapel with purpose and determination. In his mind he rehearsed a very articulate speech. However, as he neared the imposing, haughty, steel-grey building his resolve wavered and his thoughts became confused. He stood at the door for a full minute summoning his concentration and his courage—and then he knocked.

Reverend Jones, who was tidying the chapel hallway, opened the door immediately and found himself face to face with his old adversary.

"Ah!" said Morgan, caught off guard, and unprepared "Reverend Jones!"

Reverend Jones looked him up and down, "Morgan . . ." he replied drily.

"It has stopped raining," said Morgan.

Reverend Jones looked up at the clear blue sky, "Yes, I'm quite aware of that."

"There's no trains today," continued Morgan, stating the obvious.

"Yes," agreed Reverend Jones, "there are no trains on the day of the Lord."

Morgan pulled himself together and gathered speed, "Look, what I'm saying is that today is our last chance to build the mountain, but since it's Sunday everyone will be in Chapel . . ." He dribbled to a halt, he couldn't bear the way the Reverend was staring at him.

Reverend Jones sniffed, "Chapel will start at ten-thirty, as usual, Mister Morgan . . ."

The bloody Reverend, thought Morgan, does he not understand! "No-one will work on a Sunday without your blessing," Morgan was pleading now, "and tomorrow the English will get the morning train out and we'll have missed our chance." He rushed on before the Reverend could interject, "I can't keep them hear any longer! They have telegrams and tickets from head office—don't you understand, man? It's today or never!"

Reverend Jones breathed slowly through his nose and stared deep into Morgan's eyes. Morgan blinked. It seemed like an eternity.

Eventually the Reverend spoke, "Chapel will start at ten-thirty, Mister Morgan," his voice started to rise, "and it would make the good Lord very happy if for once *you* were here!"

And with that he slammed the door in Morgan's face.

What the hell did all that mean, thought Morgan? He

turned slowly on his heel and meandered back to the pub
feeling like a naughty schoolboy.

Betty was in the garden cutting flowers, though her mind was
elsewhere. She hadn't told Morgan, or Anson, but Tommy
was due to collect her straight after chapel. She had packed,
and unpacked, her things twice.

She kept trying to imagine what she would do if Anson
were a young Welshman of her own class. Would she be able
to tell him then that she thought she cared for him? It was an
impossible question to answer. Firstly, Betty had never felt
quite this way about a young Welshman, and secondly, young
Welshmen who felt something for her had made their feelings
very obvious.

When she had met Morgan, for example, he had
whisked her off her feet. She had been shopping in Cardiff on
market day and Morgan had just arrived beside her with a
lascivious grin, "Why, aren't you beautiful!" he'd said to her
without even introducing himself. Morgan was crude, and to
the point, but she had loved his extraordinary energy and
enthusiasm: when Morgan wanted something done, it was
done, and usually without Morgan lifting so much as a finger.
She marvelled at the man. No, there had been no ambiguity
with Morgan, no courtship.

But how did middle-class English people court? She'd
observed English visitors to Assam House and had been
frankly amazed when engagements were announced. The
young couples rarely had any spark for each other, the mar-
riages seemed almost arranged. She had followed one "affair
of the heart" and that seemed to involve months of exchang-
ing letters and tributes. It was all very dry and passionless.

She had thrown itself into Anson's arms and that hadn't

worked. Should she even tell him that she was leaving, or just disappear mysteriously like a character from a melodramatic novel?

She was idly cutting another flower when she heard a footstep behind her and found Anson smiling, and moving from foot to foot as if the wet lawn were hot desert sands.

"Good morning," he smiled shyly.

"Yes," replied Betty, returning his smile with interest, "it's a beautiful morning."

They both looked up at the blue sky, and the last departing clouds.

Anson groped for a way to turn the exchange into a conversation. He pointed at the flowers, "They're very pretty," he said, stating the obvious. God, he felt so tongue-tied around her, what was the matter with him!

Betty grinned, what an inane thing to say, "Yes, they are," she agreed, "but," she added, "not as pretty as me." She turned, looked him straight in the eye, and took a chance, "You're supposed to say that."

Anson gulped and turned as crimson as the rose that she had just picked, "Well . . ." he started but was interrupted by Morgan storming out of the pub.

"Betty!" yelled Morgan and tripped over a bucket.

"What?" asked Betty impatiently. It was typical of Morgan to arrive at the wrong moment.

"Didn't you hear me calling?" asked Morgan, "I need a clean shirt!"

"Don't look at me!" said Betty, "I'm not your housekeeper!"

"But I need one, now!" said Morgan.

"Well you'll just have to borrow one," said Betty, hoping this would send Morgan on his way.

Morgan didn't move. Instead he turned to Anson.

"Well, I'd lend you one," said Anson, "but I'm afraid this is the only clean one I have."

Morgan sniffed, looked at Betty, and looked at Anson again.

"No, truly," said Anson, who was beginning to feel some pressure, "this is the only clean one I have left . . ."

Reverend Jones sat in the chapel vestry and struggled with his conscience. He could hear the congregation gathering in the chapel next door and his mind was blank. He had a hundred sermons to draw on, a lifetime's experience of preaching. He could open the Bible at any page and find a text on which to speak for twenty minutes or more. But . . .

As he sat at his desk he stared out of the window, up at Ffynnon Garw and the small tump that they had added. He knew, unfortunately, that Morgan was right and that the English would be leaving tomorrow. But as Morgan had said, today was a Sunday, a day of rest. No business was conducted on a Sunday in Ffynnon Garw, or for that matter, the rest of Wales. The shops were closed, the pubs were closed. There were no sporting fixtures, there were no entertainments, there was no public transport. Even the coal pits were closed. Sunday was a day when families attended Chapel in the morning and the evening. Children also attended Sunday school in the afternoon. It was a day of peace, a day for families to pray together, eat together, sit together, talk together, rest together. How could they break that covenant and build a mountain on a Sunday?

The Reverend sighed. They had failed. Their mountain would remain a hill. Their tump would last as a sardonic reminder of their foolishness. They would be off the map, and all their work, all their toil would have been for naught. Was this a subject for a sermon? How could he make the village feel better about their failure? It wasn't possible, since he himself could glean nothing positive from the experience.

He stared at the mountain and then closed his eyes and silently prayed to God for inspiration.

Anson's shirt was tight, and Morgan's belly protruded between the buttons. The collar wouldn't fasten and only his badly knotted tie was holding it all together. Over the shirt Morgan was wearing a suit which he hadn't worn since before the war, and that was cutting into him too. Nevertheless, Morgan was dressed in something which approximated the Sunday best as worn by all attending the morning service. He rushed towards the chapel and for the second time that day came to a skidding halt at the door. He didn't want to go in. He *really* didn't want to go in.

Morgan hadn't attended chapel since he was a boy and didn't see why he should change one of his better habits now. Worse, he knew that Reverend Jones often sermonized about him. To enter the chapel and sit through a service seemed like delivering himself up for roasting. Would Reverend Jones come down from his pulpit and breathe hellfire over Morgan? The Reverend's oratory could reach lofty heights—and lowly depths. Perhaps if Morgan could sneak in and sit right at the back .. ? His hand reached for the doorknob, but somehow he wasn't able to go farther.

Inside the chapel the congregation were becoming restless. The Reverend was unusually late and all eyes were fixed on the vestry door, awaiting his entrance. They too, were wondering what the Reverend would preach about. It was, after all, the Reverend who had led them up the mountain, or as some were now saying, up the garden path. It had been his idea to hold the meeting in the village hall. It had been on his insistence that they had carried all that soil from the valley floor.

In the vestry the Reverend was all too aware of their impatience. He could hear the growing murmur and it disturbed his attempts at a silent communion with his God. Exasperated he opened his eyes and stared back at the mountain before idly opening the Bible at random.

His eye glanced at the page. He had opened the Good Book at The Psalms, Psalm ninety-nine, to be exact. The morning sun fell across the open page, illuminating verse nine, and Reverend Jones casually read the words:

"Exalt the Lord Thy God, and Worship at His Holy Hill."

"And worship at His Holy Hill!"

Holy Hill! Reverend Jones mind spun! This was a message, but what did it mean? There was that awful word, *Hill* . . . Did the Good Lord mean that they should be happy with it as a hill? What would it mean to worship at a hill?

The Reverend picked up his Bible and strode from the room. These were questions upon which he could preach, which he could discuss as he preached. He did not know the answers yet but he knew God was with him, working through him and he knew that inspiration—divine inspiration—would come as he preached. That to him—and to his generation of ministers—was what *true preaching* was all about. Oh, yes, they had their prepared sermons of course, but the real thing was to step up into the pulpit and entrust oneself to God's hands, to open oneself up to God's thoughts. When that happened a preacher would speak with authority, with grace, with strength, with extraordinary oratory. They had a word for it, a word that has no English equivalent, they called it the *hwyl*. The *hwyl* could bring tears to the cheeks of the most cynical, smiles to the faces of the most embittered, warmth to the coldest heart. The *hwyl* could bring a congregation to its feet, singing in harmony.

Reverend Jones strode to the pulpit knowing that he would be taken by the *hwyl* today.

As he stepped from the vestry the organist struck up the chords for the opening hymn and the congregation rose. Outside on the doorstep Morgan heard the organ and knew that it was now or never. He took a deep breath, put on his jacket, put out his cigarette, crossed his fingers and entered the Chapel.

The congregation had their hymnals at the ready, and Reverend Jones was climbing into the pulpit when Morgan burst through the doors of the Chapel. All turned to look as he attempted to find an inconspicuous seat near the back. There were none available, the place was filled to the rafters. Seeing a space at the end of a row he rushed towards it only to find that he was next to Blod. With a deft swing of her hips she ousted him from the row, "Don't think you're sitting with me!" whispered Blod.

The whole congregation, and Reverend Jones, watched in utter silence as Morgan made his way down the chapel, getting progressively closer to the front, as he searched for an empty pew. Eventually he found one a mere three rows from the front. He sank into it, hoping that he could disappear. Then he realized that the rest of the congregation were still standing, and he jumped back to his feet. The congregation took their gaze back to the Reverend, expecting him to now lead the opening hymn, but instead he waved at them to sit.

"Please," said Reverend Jones, "be seated. There will be no morning hymn."

Once again all eyes turned to Morgan, the person who had disturbed the start of the service, and all were expecting the Reverend to launch into a tirade against this reprobate who had dared appear in the house of God.

The Reverend paused until the congregation's attention had returned to him. Then he began slowly, in an unsteady voice, "My text today comes from Psalms, Psalm ninety-nine, verse nine . . ." Again he paused, "Exalt the Lord Thy God and Worship at His Holy Hill . . ."

The congregation took in such a sharp breath of air that it almost rattled the windows.

Morgan's brow furrowed, "Hill"?

Again the Reverend waited for his audience to settle and then he started to speak, almost conversationally, "Well, well, well," he smiled, "what a week this has been! We've seen our mountain turned into a hill, and we've used our labour to try and turn it back . . ."

He smiled a fatherly smile before continuing. His voice was still hesitant, he was finding his way. "Did you enjoy the work of digging and carrying?" he asked rhetorically, before adding, "I did—Oh, I know I didn't do very much, I was there more for moral support, but it did my heart good to see the village gathered, working as one, for a common cause," he paused and stared at Morgan, "an *altruistic* cause."

Morgan gulped, he wasn't exactly sure what "altruistic" meant, but he was sure as hell that it didn't include selling beer and lemonade to the sweating crowd. Morgan steeled himself, should he race for the door now? He felt the eyes of the village boring into him. This was like fox-hunting, and

Morgan felt like a lone fox, trapped on a bare moor, surrounded by a very large pack of baying hounds.

However, the Reverend changed tack; he lifted his eyes
to the heavens and with a voice from a music hall melodrama
it quavered with feeling, "And then the rains came!"

Morgan breathed a sigh of relief, but it didn't last long,
as he noticed Reverend Jones coming down from his pulpit to
preach among the congregation.

" 'Oh,' said some, 'it is like the Flood of Noah' " wailed
the Reverend in a perfect imitation of Evans The End Of The
World, " 'Oh,' wailed others," continued the Reverend with
a step nearer to Morgan, " 'we have displeased God!' " The
Reverend paused and rolled his eyes, now just a couple of
paces from Morgan. He smiled, and cajoled his congregation,
"Children!" he said, "Children! When we worship in the
Lord we throw away these childish superstitions! We do not
fear the black cat or the stunted tree, the warty toad or the
hairy crone! We do not fear the Lord without reason, our
God is not like the capricious gods of the heathen worlds."

"He does not judge us for what we build, but for what
is in our hearts when we build it." He moved closer to Morgan, and stood directly in front of him, "He does not chastise
us for celebrating, *but*," and now he thundered, "but for
what we celebrate!"

Morgan shrank in his seat. Once again he waited for the
onslaught, once again he wished that he had not come into
this place which stank of piety and mothballs.

But once again Reverend Jones surprised him as he
turned and addressed himself to other members of the congregation, " 'Exalt The Lord Thy God,' " he quoted again,
" 'and worship at His Holy Hill . . .' "

The Reverend slowly began to return to the pulpit, almost talking to himself in public as he struggled with his own feelings, "I see nothing malevolent in our work, it is honest toil for no profit. I see nothing selfish in our work, it is for all of us. I see it, I see it . . ." his voice dropped almost to a whisper as he paused on the steps of the pulpit, "I see it as a prayer made manifest in soil."

"A prayer made manifest in soil!" The Reverend had said those words as he'd thought them. They had come to him as a gift, and it was the gift that he needed to release himself, and the village, from the sanctity of a Sunday—for if their work was a prayer then it was perfectly in keeping with a Sunday to build the mountain.

Yes, the Reverend had just found his answer.

He paused, and took a series of deep breaths. He looked up out of the windows and then made the announcement which changed the history of Ffynnon Garw, "And therefore," he said with a steady voice, "even though it is a Sunday—but especially *because it is a Sunday*—you will see me, immediately after this sermon, climbing Ffynnon Garw with God's soil in my hand!"

The congregation gasped, people turned to one another in astonishment, hardly believing what they had heard. Morgan sat, transfixed, with a huge smile slowly breaking across his features, hardly daring to imagine that this was really true.

"And I will build that mound," continued the Reverend, "and dedicate it to God! And I will build that mound in memory . . ." His voice faltered, a tear slid down his cheek, "in memory of our loved ones who will not return from war!"

The *hwyl* was with him now, he wasn't preaching, he wasn't speaking, he was singing, it was poetry, it was opera, the words came from him spilling, rising, his body stiffened, he seemed taller, younger, his voice was the voice of God, the voice of Angels, "I will build that mound as a humble echo of the great mountains the Lord has given us, I will build that mountain in celebration of the joy our mountain has given us, and I will build that mound knowing the Lord God is with me! One day our children's children will play where we are piling earth. One day many of you will look up at it from the valley and be reminded of your youth when you were nimble enough to climb there, and with that memory will come a lesson of what was achieved when we were all united as one, in prayer, in joy, in hope, in work, in God!

'Exalt the Lord Our God, and Worship at His Holy Hill!' "

He paused, exhausted, almost spent, but with one last thought, "Here endeth today's sermon—and I expect to see you all up there!" And with that he slammed the Bible shut and strode from the Chapel.

There was a moment of pin-dropping silence and then the congregation stood and began to organize themselves. While most discussed where they would meet after they had been home and changed, Morgan was up and out of his seat in a flash and was just leaving the chapel door when a hand reached out and grabbed him by the lapel of his suit. It was Reverend Jones.

"But don't think for one Satanic minute," he thundered, "that this gives you license to sell beer—or anything else—on the Sabbath!"

—⁂—

In the garden of the pub Betty idly swung in the hammock while Anson circled nervously, like a young, inexperienced butterfly, trying to land on a flower, feeling foolish in just his vest. Like everyone else in the village he found Morgan a very persuasive fellow.

He and Betty had exhausted the change in weather as a topic of conversation, and he didn't know anything about gardening. He had tried to talk about Wales but had become embarrassingly unstuck since he knew as little as George Garrad.

Finally Anson startled Betty by asking her the very question which was most on her mind.

"So," he said casually, "how much longer do you think you'll be staying at the inn?"

Now it was Betty's turn to stammer—it might be mere minutes, "I don't know," she replied honestly, "I can't make up my mind." She smiled, "It's hard to leave once you're here . . ."

He nodded but she had no idea what that nod meant.

"And you're leaving tomorrow?" she asked, and while she tried to sound casual, her throat tightened and her words came out harder than she had intended.

"Yes, I'm afraid so," Anson tried to force a smile, "first train tomorrow . . ." He paused, registering that there was one major problem, "Depending on George's condition, of course."

They had yet to see Garrad this morning, or any recent morning for that matter—George was tending to rise in the early hours of the afternoon.

Betty laughed. "He was frightfully drunk last night, and the night before," she parodied Garrad perfectly, " 'Habit I picked up in Inja, don'cha know.' "

"Yes . . ." Anson almost felt disloyal, laughing at Garrad

like this, "I don't think the poor chap had enough to do out there," he added in his defence.

"Or here," added Betty. She thought about that for a moment, "You wouldn't last either if you lived in a place like this for long. You'd go mad too, wouldn't you?"

"Me? No, I don't think so," smiled Anson, "I think it's splendid here, it's beautiful, quiet, friendly . . ."

"But you'd get bored."

"Bored?" said Anson and laughed—after what he'd seen this week? He'd never seen a village like this, where each and every one of them had been galvanized into action. "No, I don't think I'd be bored in a place like this." He paused for a moment and then something slipped out, a very simple statement, but nevertheless the kind of statement that Reginald Anson rarely made: he shared a feeling, "I've really enjoyed myself . . ."

As soon as he said it, he blushed.

"You have?" smiled Betty and she started to giggle at his discomfort.

Anson stammered on, "But I don't know what I could usefully do in a place like this."

Had he thought about staying? It seemed to Betty that he had. It seemed that in his mind he had turned over many things about village life. Betty was excited, she tried to encourage him, "But you can do anything! You're an educated man."

It didn't seem so simple to him. "I'm not qualified to do much," he said. "I could teach I suppose . . ." He stopped, looked at her and began to say something but then hesitated. He turned and walked across to the barn as if it needed his attention.

"What?" asked Betty. "What were you going to say . . . ?"

"It was nothing . . ."

"Please."

Anson shifted uncomfortably, "It was just . . . Well I was about to say something, to ask you something which was probably indiscreet."

"I don't mind," said Betty disarmingly, and Anson believed her.

"It's just," he stammered a little, "it's just that I know even less about you than I knew about " 'Miss Elizabeth'. . ."

Betty burst into a giggle, " 'Miss Elizabeth!' " she snorted, "I couldn't keep that up for long, could I!"

She thought for a moment, what could she tell him? Her life seemed bland, uncomplicated and trite compared to his. She had little education and had not travelled. There was nothing she could say to impress him or even entertain him. She was reduced to the bare truth.

"There's nothing very special about me—I scuttle in with a tray of tea, bow my head and scuttle out—In other words I'm the kind of girl that men like you usually don't notice."

She was unsure as to how he would react, she hardly dared look at him.

"I'd notice!" said Anson with a beaming smile.

There was something so glib about the way he said it, something so unconsidered that Betty snapped at him, "No you wouldn't!" It was too easy to say things like that, here in this garden, sitting in the morning sunshine as friends, as a man and woman, as social equals who were attracted to each other. But life wasn't like this, not normally, not for Betty. When men of Anson's class looked at her it was either because they or their wives wanted some menial chore to be taken of, or because the man had noticed her beauty and was hoping for a quiet, degrading liaison. No, Reginald Anson would not notice her in ordinary circumstances.

They fell silent as Anson realized that he had been crass. He stared off into the meadow, trying to lose himself in the summer grasses which softly moved with the breeze. A lark burst from cover.

"Can I ask you something?" asked Betty.

Anson shrugged, he had been put firmly in his place, "After that I don't feel able to say no."

"How come you aren't in France?" It was a question that Betty had wanted to ask since they first met. She didn't want to think that he was a coward, or a cheat, he didn't seem the type. Yet nevertheless here he was, a young man in the prime of his life, working as a glorified surveyor while every other able-bodied man was fighting the war.

Anson's face clouded, "Well . . " he began. He stammered hard, he picked at the bark of the tree, "I was . . ." Again he paused. Already Betty was beginning to wish that she hadn't asked.

He took a series of quick breaths, almost as if he were running. "I went out with the first wave in nineteen-fourteen," he said, at speed, "I was at Verdun . . ."

Betty blanched.

"And I came back like Johnny," finished Anson. Then he smiled, as if the episode could be easily forgotten, as if all he needed to do was to tell the story a couple of times, laugh about it, and move on . . .

Betty sat in stunned silence. She didn't know how to look at him. Now she felt as if she'd as good as called him a coward to his face. Suddenly everything about him made sense;

his silence, his insecurity, his shyness. He was, quite simply, a man who was recovering from a terrible trauma. She had totally misjudged every aspect of his personality because she had overlooked the most obvious thing: he wasn't evading the war, he had already been.

He walked around, forcing himself into her field of vision. He was smiling, "It's alright," he said, "I'm alright, really, I am."

Just then they both heard a flurry of activity in the street outside—horses' hooves, and the sound of men driving them.

"What on earth . . . ?" said Anson.

They were both glad of the interruption and hurried through the pub to find Morgan at the front door waving on a shift of miners—and their pit ponies.

"I've got the miners now, too!" grinned Morgan.

"It's like a carnival!" laughed Betty. She had never seen the streets of Ffynnon Garw so full of activity.

The miners and their ponies were making their way to the meadow to load up with earth. Already some villagers with buckets were toiling towards the mountain. One man ran past them in the other direction carrying a half dozen empty buckets, a tin bath and a chamber pot. It was chaos.

"I feel terribly responsible," said Anson, and he did. Some part of him wished that he'd just cheated the first calculation. None of this would have been necessary, these people could have lived in peace, happy with their mountain, their first mountain in Wales.

Morgan slapped him round the shoulders, since surviving chapel he was in a hearty mood, "Don't worry," he said, "you just make sure your Mr. Garrad's ready to measure, because we'll have a mountain for your map by teatime!"

CHAPTER

II

Morgan disappeared into the inn leaving Anson with a most delicate problem: George Garrad.

Betty looked at him searchingly.

Anson pulled himself together, "Right," he said to Betty with some authority, "if you'd just wait here . . . ."

Tommy Twostroke had arrived back from the Saturday night shift and fallen into a deep, wonderful, soothing slumber. His week had been hell, he just hadn't caught up on his sleep since the day that Morgan sent him to Cardiff. Each working night had seemed interminable, while each sleeping day had been too short. His rhythm had been destroyed. Normally on a Sunday morning he returned from the pit, bathed, attended morning Chapel and then had Sunday lunch with his family before falling into an extra-long treat of a sleep, since there was no mining on Sunday night for him.

However, this Sunday morning he had gone straight to bed after a cursory wash. He was going to miss Chapel, he didn't care if he missed lunch, he was just going to sleep until he woke, or until it was time to start work next week— whichever came first. Of course, Elsie hadn't told him that she had made other plans.

Elsie felt terrible about it, but couldn't let Betty down. Also she knew the drive would be much quicker this time. Firstly, Tommy knew the way and secondly, he'd be going downhill with his passenger and her luggage; there would be no need to stop and push today.

"Tommy," crooned Elsie in her sweetest voice when she got home from chapel. He'd been in bed for just a few hours, "Oh, Tommy love . . ."

"Go away," said Tommy from deep under the sheets. He was afraid that she wanted a Sunday morning cuddle.

"Something terrible's happened," said Elsie, "and only you can make it better . . ."

Tommy opened a bleary eye, "Yes?" he demanded cynically.

"The poor girl, she'll lose everything, the roof over her head, her job, her meals, her clothes, can you imagine such a thing?"

"Who are you talking about?" said Tommy, this sounded truly tragic.

"I mean, what has she done to deserve it? I ask? Nothing! It's not her fault, and there she is, set for penury, to sleep in the streets, what can a poor girl do in such a situation?"

Tommy was hooked, "Who are you talking about? What's happened?"

Elsie took a deep breath, "It's Betty . . ."

Tommy's face clouded, he was beginning to see it coming, "Betty From Cardiff . . ." he said dourly.

"Ye-es," said Elsie, "and she has to get back or . . ."

Tommy thrust his head under the sheets, "I'm not going."

"Please Tommy!" pleaded Elsie, "I promised!"

"You promised?" Tommy's head popped back out, "When did you promise?"

Elsie blustered on regardless, "You have to! Think of what Morgan has done to her! You can't say no, I won't let you."

"I just said it," said Tommy, "*No,* I'm not going!"

Elsie took a deep breath and released the biggest weapon in her arsenal. "So I'll be sleeping with the children from now on . . ."

Garrad was asleep, deep in a dream, set somewhere in the British Empire where he was a someone with a rank way above Colonel and just below King. He had been decorated and feted, his exploits provided the stories for schoolboys' magazines, he was a knight among men. Today he was in charge of all of India . . .

Anson paused outside Garrad's room and steaded himself. This was the time to be firm, strong. No messing about, no avoiding the issue, no letting down the village now . . . He rapped on the door with force.

George Garrad came to consciousness with a violent jolt. "Tea wallah!" he yelled, believing it to be his servant. The man probably had news from the border with Kashmir . . .

As he sat up in bed, an empty bottle of gin fell to the floor. Garrad tried, but no matter how much he squinted, his eyes didn't seem to focus. And his servant looked awfully white . . .

"Actually, it's Anson, George," said Reginald and took a gasp. The air in the room was fetid. It was like trying to breathe in a rugby player's sock.

"Anson!" replied Garrad. How unusual for Anson to be in India! Garrad wondered when he'd arrived.

"Just thought I'd take a stroll up the mountain," said Anson matter-of-factly, "it seems that the villagers have made a tiny alteration to the height, thought I'd re-measure."

Garrad stared at him, why couldn't he keep still? And what was he blathering about? Villagers? Alterations? Hmm. Mustn't give the game away, "Splendid," said George for want of anything more sensible.

"You don't want to come do you?" asked Anson.

"Where?" said George. He was having trouble following the conversation. Perhaps it had been something he ate. He made a note to cut down on the curries. Should stick to the mess food.

"Up the mountain," replied Anson.

"Good God no!" said Garrad. Up a mountain? He'd been up mountains once in a place called Wales, and had no intention of doing it again. Terrible bore. All grass, rocks, sheep-shit, absolutely nothing to be gained, "I'll stay here," he continued slowly, "lots of paperwork, scads to catch up on . . ." He couldn't remember when he'd last written home. He must owe London a report.

"Fine," said Anson, "well I'll be off then." He tried to take another breath but it really was impossible. "Would you like me to open a window?" he asked reasonably.

"No, thank you very much," said Garrad who was always careful when it came to pesky mosquitoes: seen many a good man go with malaria. Become blithering idiots, if the Empire was to be lost it wasn't to uprisings and revolts but insects, yes damned insects . . .

Anson quietly withdrew and gently closed the door.

Garrad looked around him and wondered what had disturbed his sleep. Deciding that it was nothing, he slumped back into a torpor.

Betty was downstairs, still watching the procession when Anson returned.

He chose his words tactfully, "I don't think I can rely on Mr. Garrad," he said, "but I will need an assistant."

Betty stared at him blankly.

Anson continued, "I was wondering whether you . . ?"

"Me?" Betty was rather surprised.

"Why not?" said Anson.

"Well, I've never been to Cairo, or Abyssynia, or Sebastopol—and I can't speak with a posh accent for long."

Anson laughed, "All absolutely irrelevant."

"I'm just a maid-servant!" said Betty.

Anson smiled, "I don't think the word 'just' could be applied to you about anything."

"Was that a compliment?" asked Betty with a wicked grin.

"Yes," said Anson, "and now you've made me blush, so please will you be my assistant."

He had turned an extraordinary shade of crimson.

Betty giggled, "Since you said please, and you're blushing, yes, I will."

"Good," said Anson, "let's prepare the transit . . ."

"Prepare what?" asked Betty.

"I'll show you," he said and was about to lead her inside when there was a loud backfire and Tommy Twostroke appeared.

"Are you ready?" asked Tommy.

"Ready for what?" asked Anson.

Betty turned to Anson, "You just go inside and start on the whatsit—I'll be with you in a minute." Anson vacillated for a moment, "Go on!" she said, laughing, "I'll be with you in just a minute!"

"Betty?" Tommy was really confused now.

"I'm sorry, Tommy," said Betty, "but I've changed my mind."

"Changed your mind? I just got out of bed and you changed your mind?" moaned Tommy.

"Well for today, anyway . . ."

"For today, Betty?" moaned Tommy, "I can't do it tomorrow, I won't, not on a weekday again, it buggered me."

"All right," said Betty, "just forget it: I'm definitely not going today."

Tommy switched off his bike, took off his goggles and mumbled several things about the capricious nature of women before wheeling his bike back home. Within ten minutes he was back in bed and Anson and Betty were on their way up Ffynnon Garw, carrying the equipment between them.

If Tommy made one mistake that day it was getting up in the first place. If he made a second mistake it was in believing that he could go back to bed and get some sleep. Within minutes of seeing Tommy wheeling his bike back home there was a small crowd of people outside Tommy's, all clamouring for a favour.

"I need him to get my brother," said Thomas The Trains.

"Don't forget my cousins," said Ivor The Grocer.

The formidable Elsie stood, as always, as the gateway to Tommy. With folded arms she listened as villager after villager gathered with a similar request—all wanted Tommy to go and tell their relatives who lived out of the village. None of these people lived far away, you understand—perhaps just over the mountain, or in the next village up or down the valley—Welsh people don't move too far.

After the Reverend's sermon there was the distinct feeling that this was a day to share with one's nearest and dearest, this was *the* day. Brothers and sisters had to be summoned, cousins called, uncles and aunts, nephews and nieces, even distant relatives mustered—the tribe must be gathered for all to play their part. It was, in part, a call for more labour, for extra help, but even more so there was a sense that this was something not to be missed. This was a day which would not come again.

Elsie wanted to protect Tommy, she wanted to let him sleep, but as she listened, she knew that all of her neighbours had a point: the word must go out.

"I'd take my horse and go round the villages myself," said Ivor who regularly did it anyway with groceries, "but we need the horse and cart on the mountain. But a motorcycle? You can't carry earth with that now can you?"

Elsie was finally convinced.

"Tommy," she said as she woke him, "you don't have to go far, just Upper Boat and Pentyrch and the Gwaelod and Llanharan, not forgetting Tongwynlais, Black Cock, and Caerphilly . . ."

"Let me sleep, women!" he groaned from under a pillow, "Tell Morgan and Blod to bugger off!"

"It isn't Morgan, or Blod," she prodded him again, "it's Ivor, and Davies, and Dai, and Ianto and Mrs. Jones Welsh."

A bleary eye emerged.

She gave him a big kiss, "You'll be a hero, honest you will."

By lunch time that day the roads into Ffynnon Garw were awash with relatives all returning to the village of their birth, all coming to help in the gargantuan task of building a mountain.

The Reverend Jones paused for a breather and looked down the fields into the village. From where he sat a line of bucket carriers stretched to the summit and back to the village. He could see large carts filled with soil on the lower slopes. He could see a clutch of bicycles in the village as more relatives arrived to help.

He fancied that there was something Biblical about it—he was reminded of Mary and Joseph returning to Bethlehem for Caesar's census . . . He caught himself daydreaming, and made himself carry two heavy buckets for having thought such a terrible blasphemy of a thought.

While Anson had known during the week that the villagers were attempting to change the height of the hill, and had been able to see some of their work from his bedroom window at the back of the inn, none of it prepared him for the sheer scale of the undertaking. It was one thing to stare from a distance, but quite another to walk within the throng of bucket-carriers and carts, tin baths and wheelbarrows. Everywhere he looked earth was moving up the slopes of the mountain.

He turned to Betty in astonishment, "This is quite extraordinary!"

Betty gave a wry chuckle, "When Morgan gets a bee in his bonnet . . ."

Anson had seen vast mobilizations in France. He had seen deployments of men and machines which stretched for miles and covered acres. However, all those men had been longing to go home. They had been pushed, pressed, cajoled, ordered, threatened even.

This crowd was different. There was, as Betty had observed, a carnival atmosphere. It was joyous and raucous, good-natured and quite, quite mad.

In the spirit of the Reverend's edict Morgan had set up his stand but had stocked it with non-alcoholic beverages. And even further in keeping with the Sabbath—and shockingly unlike Morgan—he gave it all away for nothing. Ivor was so moved by Morgan's benevolence that he went to his shop and returned to the mountain with a cartload of biscuits, sherbets, breads and pies to be dispensed at lunch time. It seemed that everyone was here, and none would go without.

—⁂—

But not quite everyone was there.

Davies The School wasn't there and neither was Johnny Shellshocked.

Johnny sat on the steps that ran down from his sister's house to the stream. The waters were still swollen from the rain and the stepping-stones were still under a foot of water. Johnny stared as the stream very slowly stripped the moss from a rock.

Blod tried to see what had caught his attention, but the action of the water was so slow that to her he seemed to be staring into space.

Johnny had spent a whole day in bed after the incident
up on Ffynnon Garw. Several times he had called out loudly
in his sleep, just as he had when he first returned from war.
But on Saturday morning he rose as usual. He hardly spoke a
word anyway, so it was hard to tell, but Blod fancied that he
was even quieter. He answered most questions with a simple
nod or shake of his head.

As Blod stared at Johnny she wondered if he was thinking, and if he *was* thinking, what was he thinking. If he wasn't
thinking, what did that feel like? She couldn't imagine not
thinking, not having words, or ideas, or memories in her
mind.

Then, quite abruptly, Johnny moved. He was as unpre-
dictable as a child, or a cat. The mossy rock had suddenly
exhausted his attention and Johnny looked up at the ridge as
if that were, quite logically, the next place to stare. Even from
the river he could clearly see silhouetted figures labouring up
the slopes.

"Johnny . . ." It was Blod gently tapping his shoulder.
She pointed in the opposite direction where there was a flurry
of clouds. Perhaps more rain, even thunder. Johnny's gaze
returned to the river—no he wouldn't be chancing it up Ffynnon Garw again today.

Perhaps the only other person who didn't work that day was
a small boy, Huw Hughes. He was, nominally, the son of
Hughes The Stamps, though his red hair, fiery temper and
entrepreneurial spirit led many to believe (quite rightly) that
he was a hammock child—as they liked the call the results of
Morgan's lazy afternoon liaisons. While all others laboured,
Huw quietly withdrew to a copse of trees near Morgan's lemonade stand and there set to carving a name on a very old

tree. He didn't carve his name, or the name of a sweetheart. Instead he carved the name of the last great Welsh leader, Llywelyn The Last. He took care with his carving, and when he was finished he took moss from around the roots of the tree and pressed it into the carving. It took time and patience but when he had finished it looked convincingly like a carving which had been on the tree for hundreds of years.

He then casually sauntered over to villagers who were taking a break and offered to show them—for a small finder's fee—where Llywelyn The Last had carved his name.

—⚏—

Betty and Anson crested the ridge among an army of villagers, half of them marching to the mound, half of them coming away. Already the mound was back up to almost twelve feet. Anson stopped and shook his head in amazement, "I think they're going to succeed!" he said.

"How could you doubt it?" asked Betty, "With Morgan and the Reverend behind it . . ."

Three men, the Thomas Twp Twins and Williams The Petroleum, were on the mound organizing the loads as they arrived. The buckets were quickly passed up, emptied and returned.

"Keep them coming!" said Williams and then noticed Anson. Damn! Anson was the last man he wanted to see! Williams had been hiding in his house for the last few days. He was so glad to be back out in the fresh air, and now, here was the bane of his life, up on the damned mountain. Williams took his jacket and casually lost himself in a group of miners who were returning to the river bank.

"Hello," said Thomas Twp as Anson approached, "we

lost a lot in the rain, but I think we'll soon have a mountain for your map."

"I think you're right," said Anson and looked at the swirls of drying mud around the base of the mound. "Perhaps you should cover it with turf," he suggested.

"Turf?" said Thomas Twp Too who was unfamiliar with the word.

"He means sod," said Thomas Twp.

"Sod!" Thomas Twp Too looked at the growing mound. "We'd need a lot of sod . . ."

"A lot of good sod," added Thomas Twp who knew that they'd need tightly knitted grass to grow quickly and firm up the structure.

Both men suddenly stopped, stock-still like statues while the hubbub of soil carrying and emptying continued around them.

Anson felt that he'd distracted them, as if he'd cast a spell, "It was just a thought, something for later," he said, hoping that this would wake them back up.

Thomas Twp shook his head slowly, "No, you are right, it needs covering . . ."

"And a lot of covering . . ." That was Thomas Twp Too.

"And if we don't get on with it now . . ." These men, let's not forget, were farmers, who were used to co-ordinating plans over long periods of time.

Presently the light seemed to brighten in Thomas Twp Too's eyes and he led his brother away from Anson and the villagers.

Anson and Betty watched them go.

"Well," said Anson, "better assemble the transit, because I think we will be requiring it later."

"Right," said Betty, who had as much idea of assembling the transit as Anson did of preparing a cream tea.

The Twps strode to the edge of the escarpment and looked down into the valley.

"There you are," said Thomas Twp Too and pointed at an expanse of wonderful turf.

"Perfect, I'd say," said Thomas Twp.

And together they descended Ffynnon Garw, heading for the rugby pitch.

It was a piece of inspiration that led the Twps to the rugby pitch, but someone else would probably have got there, sooner or later that day, because the river-bank was almost exhausted.

The whole area had now been stripped to a depth of almost three feet and the diggers were finding that the soil was soaked through. The clean sound of shovelling had given way to oozing, sucking squeaks. A shovelful was removed, and the surrounding earth seemed to bleed water into the gap. The villagers were working in mud up to their ankles.

Therefore it was quite logical for the whole operation to move to the rugby pitch.

Davies The School had been relaxing in his parlour reading a worthy tome when the first of the villagers tramped past *en route* to the rugby pitch. At first he thought it was a stray, probably an in-law from another village who was hopelessly lost. But then another walked past, and another. Davies was confused and annoyed, his end of the village had been relatively peaceful, but now he could clearly see and hear more and more villagers streaming past his cottage. Where on earth did they think they were going?

The exact same thought struck Johnny Shellshocked. He strolled out of his house to find the procession now walking down his lane. He watched for a moment and was tickled to see Davies The School rushing in amongst them.

"Who is in charge? Will someone tell me that?" demanded Davies.

No-one deigned to answer and the poor man flitted faster and faster, trying to reach the head of the column. Johnny joined on the back, always eager to be there when Davies made a fool of himself.

Having marked out an area of turf that they thought most suitable, the Twps had returned to the summit of Ffynnon Garw. Sergeant Thomas had taken control of the rugby pitch and was organizing two groups of workers: one to strip the sod carefully and neatly roll it into logs, the other to dig the soil beneath the sod.

By the time Davies The School arrived, a goodish area of turf had been removed—not enough to cover the mound, but certainly enough to make the next rugby fixture a difficult match for all concerned.

Davies couldn't believe his eyes. While this pitch was primarily the playing field for the village's adult team, it was also the venue for all matches played by his school-children.

Davies roared across the pitch, waving his arms like a windmill, "Have the council been informed?" he asked, "Does anyone have written permission?"

Many villages paused in their work, suddenly doubting the legality of their actions. All eyes turned to the police sergeant. He coughed.

"Well?!" demanded Davies, "speak up man! This seems to me a bona fide case of outright vandalism, disrespect of public property," he sneered at the sergeant's stripes, "taking the law into one's own hands, and furthermore contravening every article of faith to which you were appointed."

The Sergeant was lost for words. The truth was that he thought Davies had a case—they hadn't asked anyone for permission, they hadn't even put it to a vote. The Twps had suggested it and it seemed like a good idea. He wondered whether he should arrest himself, and had an awful vision of being brought up before Jones The JP.

"And whose idea was it?" Jones The JP would ask. Can you imagine the laughter if he answered "The Twps?"

Johnny arrived in Davies' wake and had been watching from the back of the crowd. He couldn't listen to any more of this nonsense, "Will you stop acting so English?" he asked.

The Sergeant burst into laughter and all the villagers joined in. Only a moment earlier Davies had demanded attention and stature, but now he was revealed as a pompous ass.

"Very good, Johnny!" said Sergeant Thomas, "Back to work everyone!"

And Johnny stayed, happy to help in the valley, but still not daring to venture up Ffynnon Garw while there was a cloud in the sky.

CHAPTER

12

It will be the source of a timeless debate among the villagers
of Ffynnon Garw as to which of the two hill-building days
was the most heroic.

The arguments go like this. On the first attempt the num-
bers were smaller and restricted largely to women, children
and pensioners. Though they only achieved a height of fourteen feet this was a gargantuan effort. The second attempt,
they say, was easier, because so many more people including
relatives—and miners—were involved.

Those who argue for the second day, point out that far
more soil was carried and while the miners were there, their
expertize was largely used transporting soil up to the lemonade stand. After that it was still manual labour to the top.
Moreover, they will tell you that the first day was a long day,

with everyone starting at the crack of dawn, whereas on the Sunday the push didn't start until after chapel.

The addition of the miners was a lucky masterstroke for Morgan as they were not available on any day but a Sunday. Similarly many friends and relatives could come because it was a Sunday.

With the miners came experience. While it sounds simple enough to dump buckets of earth in a pile, it actually becomes quite difficult when the pile is higher than a person, and then higher than two people. The miners were adept at constructing ramps and pulley systems. After they arrived the mound began to resemble a great piece of architecture.

Just as practical, and necessary, they had ways of reinforcing the tracks and paths up and down Ffynnon Garw. The tracks had taken a beating on the first day. Horses, wheels, and feet had ripped the topsoil leaving exposed earth for the following storm. Now an even bigger army was tramping it all into long muddy stretches. The miners laid planks and cut new tracks. It wasn't just the height of Ffynnon Garw that was being altered but her whole physiognomy.

But with the extra people came a strange inertia. Reverend Jones was the first to notice—people were taking longer rests. Because there were so many more of them, it seemed inevitable that the hill would be built, that they would succeed. However, on the Reverend's second trip to the top he saw the truth of Johnny and the Twps words—they would need *so* much more earth as the mound became higher and the base spread and spread. Twenty or thirty bucketfuls could now cascade down the slopes and hardly add an inch to the height, yet the villagers were all assuming that the end was in sight.

The Reverend couldn't order them or berate them: his

only tool was to work by example. He sat with a resting group for a moment and then rose, "Well, back to it!" he'd say and all felt compelled to rise too. After all, if an elderly man was ready for another ascent, how could a younger one stand by and watch?

—⚉—

To my knowledge three photographs exist from the hill build, all taken by a young pharmacist from the next village of Tongwynlais. He had recently acquired a camera and the photographs are among his tentative first shots.

I had seen one of them many times, since my grandfather had a copy in the corner of his study. It looked, to all intents and purposes, like an early landscape study of Ffynnon Garw. The print was fairly faded and only on close inspection—and only after I had been told—did I notice that the photograph dimly captures a row of blurred silhouettes on the ridge. They were moving too quickly for the crude camera to capture them and so they appear almost like ghosts.

A second picture turned up in a cousin's attic and captures a wonderful interlude. It is inscribed simply "Lunch on Ffynnon Garw—late" and shows the entire village sprawled on the grass around Morgan's stand, holding large chunks of bread, and brandishing stoneware bottles of saspirilla or lemonade. To the extreme right one can clearly see Morgan The Goat, Williams The Petroleum and Ivor The Grocer standing slightly apart, as if the three of them are already on to planning something else, not quite legal. On the extreme left of the picture is the figure of Reverend Jones with a bell in his hand, ready to summon all back to work.

It was a late lunch that day—it must have been almost

five o'clock before everyone stopped. Those working at the top came down to the lemonade stand, those working at the rugby pitch came up—except Johnny, who went home to Blod's.

It was immediately obvious to all that there was enough soil at the lemonade stand to complete the mound which was already up to seventeen feet. The pile at the lemonade stand would easily supply the extra three feet. It was decided that immediately after the late lunch the rugby pitch group would return there only to collect the stripped turfs. The work at the base of the mountain was finished. All believed that success was well within their grasp.

During lunch Huw Hughes did a roaring trade charging villagers to see where Llywelyn The Last had carved his name. Good-naturedly all swore that they wouldn't reveal to anyone else where Huw had taken them, and though Llywelyn had lived further north in Mid-Wales, all were pleased to believe that he had ventured this far south.

Reverend Jones had said that it would be historic, a day generations would talk about, and he was right. It was also a day on which one man's name changed.

Thomas Twp and Thomas Twp Too both paid Huw Hughes a farthing to see where Llywelyn The Last had carved his name. Huw duly took them to the copse and showed them the mossy trunk. Thomas Twp Too fell quiet and he and his brother walked back in silence to the crowd. Thomas Twp fell to talking with other villagers but Thomas Twp Too had a long hard think and then cleared this throat and announced to all, "I think the carving is a forgery."

No-one paid him much attention, after all, he was Thomas Twp Too. "I mean," he reasoned, "How did Llywelyn The Last know that he was Llywelyn The Last? He didn't know that there wouldn't be another after him, did he?"

There was a moment of quiet as all thought about this, and then Hughes The Stamps frog-marched his son down to the tree. With a flick of a penknife the moss was removed to reveal that the carving was fresh.

"Well?" demanded Hughes The Stamps but didn't wait for an answer before giving the boy a clip around the ear and the task of returning his ill-gotten gains to each and every villager who had been fooled.

From that day forward the Twp twins were known as Thomas Twp—and Thomas-not-so-Twp.

When the Reverend called them all back to work with a peal of his bell there was a feeling that the real work was over, that all that was left was the mopping up. How wrong they were. It was almost six-thirty before everyone started to walk stiffly back to their stations. After their late lunch many felt very tired—it had been a mistake to relax; muscles were cramping, joints were aching. And suddenly dusk seemed imminent.

Anson stood near the top of the mound with Betty among a throng of people. Two-and-a-half feet of flagpole still poked resolutely from the mound. Anson looked out through his telescope at the summits of Newton Beacon and Whitchurch Hill, the points which he needed to view to make a measurement.

He grimaced, "There's not much light left for a measurement . . ."

"Well stop looking," said Betty, "and help!" She thrust a bucket into his arms.

*　*　*

Down in the rugby field the last wheelbarrows had been filled with turf and the last procession was leaving for the ascent of the mountain.

Johnny stood in the middle of the stripped pitch as the men and women filed past him, "Thanks a lot, Johnny," said one, "See you later, Johnny," said another. Sergeant Thomas paused to give him a slap on the back, "Couldn't have done it without you, Johnny."

All of them appreciated his help—and knew what had happened on the night in the storm. None would try and encourage him up Ffynnon Garw again, not against his will.

Johnny watched them walk away. The squeaking of the wheelbarrow wheels started to fade. Johnny looked up to the ridge, to the row of figures, to the silhouette of the tump they were building. Above Ffynnon Garw was a clear, cloudless sky. He turned and looked north, south and then east—the sky was clear. He took a deep breath, swallowed hard and called out after the Sergeant, "I'll take that!"

While earth was still being delivered to the top of the mound, villagers struggled to turf the lower sections which were being destroyed by the tramping feet.

Williams The Petroleum took a load of sod and carried it to a group of people working the east slope of the tump. "Here's some more for you," he said and then stepped back in horror as he realized that he was face to face with Reginald Anson.

"Mr. Anson!" The words exploded with his surprise.

Anson grinned. He couldn't help but enjoy Williams' discomfort. Anson didn't care one whit about the car, but Williams obviously thought that he did. "Good afternoon, Mr. Williams," he said breezily.

"Look," Williams tried to get an excuse in quick, "I'm

terribly sorry about your motor car, I tried to protect it from the rain, I covered it with a tarpaulin, but I just don't know what happened, I mean the wind must have caught it or something . . ."

Anson's grin broadened and he pointed to the spot where he was kneeling. "You wouldn't mean this tarpaulin by any chance, would you?" smiled Anson. He was kneeling on the tarpaulin.

Williams wanted to put a bucket over his own head and crawl under a gorse bush, "Yes," he stammered, "I'm afraid so . . ." He waited for Anson to explode, he waited for some predictable English reaction, but instead Anson just laughed.

"Don't worry, Mr. Williams," he said, "I wouldn't have missed this for the world."

Just then a ripple of applause came down the wind and Anson and Williams looked along the ridge to see that something had stopped everyone working. One by one people were putting down their buckets and applauding. For a moment neither Anson nor Williams could see what was happening, but then Williams spotted the lone moving figure, with his head down, coming with the last wheelbarrow of turf, "It's Johnny!" yelled Williams, "By God, it's Johnny!"

The whole mountain stopped for Johnny Shellshocked's return. There was much backslapping, and hugging, cheers and applause—and more than a few people admitted to shedding a tear when they saw his diminutive figure back on the higher slopes of Ffynnon Garw.

There was a big enough supply of soil at the lemonade stand, and more than enough turf at the top. Many say the villagers would have succeeded, but, unfortunately fate had one more trick up her sleeve.

—m—

There is much debate as to exactly how many times Reverend
Jones climbed Ffynnon Garw that Sunday. True, he rarely
made it very far without taking a breather and most assumed
that when he wasn't carrying buckets on the upper slopes he
was resting somewhere further down. However, those working the slopes below the lemonade stand had made the same
assumption, thinking that when the Reverend wasn't with
them he was taking a break further up Ffynnon Garw. No-
one will ever know for sure, but when people later talked it
became obvious that the Reverend had worked hard all day
and had rarely—if ever—taken a decent break.

The climbing and carrying that he had done was enough
to make a younger, fitter man stiff. It would be days before
most of the village recovered, and it was definitely too much
for a man of eighty-two years old. Everyone thought that
Reverend Jones was a man in his sixties, but in fact he was
all of eighty-two.

Thomas Not-So-Twp was the first to notice that something was wrong. He looked down from the top of the mound
and noticed that Reverend Jones had stopped, in mid-stride,
and was staring off into space. At first he thought the Reverend was taking a break, but there was something odd about
his posture that held Thomas' attention.

Reverend Jones suddenly didn't know where he was. He
had been walking up and down the same mountain all day
and now . . . What was he doing here with this bucket in his
hand . . . ?

In recent weeks he had caught himself going into his
study or kitchen, and finding that he'd completely forgotten
what he intended to do when he got there. He had laughed at
himself, laughed at the signs of his own senility, but now,

today, he had the same sensation except on a much larger scale. He was totally disoriented, he didn't even know who he was.

He felt nauseous. He tried to focus his thoughts but couldn't hold onto the simplest idea. Memories, facts, even the most mundane pieces of information seemed to have turned into very small, pieces of tissue paper. Almost lighter than air these thoughts and memories defied gathering. The minute his mind moved to pick them up the act of moving—of thinking—would disturb the pieces, sending them all spinning into the air, where they would float for a moment before drifting back to settle in a random pattern. Again, he tried to reach out for them and again they were thrown up. The harder the Reverend thought, the greater chaos he created in these pieces of tissue. They were thrown up and carried on breezes. He chased after them in his mind's eyes but it felt as if they were constantly disappearing around the next corner just before he got to them.

And then, for no apparent reason, certainly not an act of his own will, he was Reverend Jones again, atop Ffynnon Garw. However, while he knew who he was and where he was, he also knew that he felt very, very tired. He began to walk again and found that his legs had lost their co-ordination. He was weaving like a drunk.

I'll just get this last bucket to the mound, he thought, but his legs weren't taking him where he wanted to go. They seemed intent on some dark parody of a dance step . . . and half a pace forward, one to the side, a full pace back and now forward . . .

Now Thomas Not-So-Twp was very worried. He called out, "Reverend Jones," he asked, "are you all right?"

The Reverend didn't reply, he merely raised a hand to

his mouth, as if he were about to vomit, and then slowly sank to his knees, without, it must be said, spilling anything from his bucket.

All work immediately stopped as everyone gathered around. The Twps, Ivor and Williams picked him up and started to carry him back to the village but the Reverend shook his head violently and whispered, "Stop! Stop, put me down . . . I am dying."

Anson and Betty eased their way to the back of the crowd. They stood, set slightly apart from the throng of villagers.

The Twps and Williams gently laid the Reverend onto the ground.

"I am dying," repeated the Reverend.

"Don't say such a thing," said Ivor.

The Reverend took Ivor's arm, and smiled, "But, it's the truth—you needn't pretend it isn't, now get Morgan," whispered the Reverend, "quickly—I must speak with Morgan before I go."

The cry went out along the mountain, "Morgan! Get Morgan! Morgan The Goat!"

Morgan was at the back of the tump, not doing much beyond directing the work in his own inimitable way. He was pushed through the crowd that had gathered around the dying Reverend.

"He wants me?" asked Morgan, both incredulous and a little wary.

Ivor nodded, "Yes, quickly now . . ."

Morgan knelt beside the Reverend.

"Come closer," said Reverend Jones, "take my hand, and listen, because these are my dying wishes . . ."

They had been lifelong enemies but when it came to his

final demand the Reverend knew that there was only one man whom he could trust; only one man with the same passion; only one man with the same fire; only one man with the same drive; only one man with the same authority—Morgan The Goat.

The crowd clustered round but no-one could hear what passed between them.

Morgan gently closed the Reverend's dead eyes and caught his breath. He was surprised to find that his own eyes were filled with tears. He rose to his feet.

"Get Jones The JP!" he thundered and two small boys were sent rushing down the slopes of Ffynnon Garw to find Jones The JP and bring him to the mound.

"Now where's the English?" asked Morgan, looking around the crowd.

Anson was surprised to hear his name called, "Mr. Morgan?" he responded. The crowd parted and then arms tugged at him, pressing him toward Morgan. As he was pushed through the crowd he looked back to look for Betty and was relieved to see that she was following him.

Morgan put a hand on his shoulder. It wasn't a gentle gesture but a very, very firm one, as if he were taking Anson under his control.

"We're going to bury him here, in the mound, on top of a mountain, *a proper mountain,* the first mountain in Wales."

Betty heard Morgan's words and saw Anson look up at the mound and then out at the landscape. She saw his face fall. The mound wasn't finished, and the light was fading fast.

Jones The JP had spent a very pleasant and libatious afternoon officiating at a friend's daughter's wedding. Though he hadn't actually taken the ceremony, he had nevertheless presided over the whole affair, dispensing a certain lugubrious authority. If Jones The JP were there, the middle-class thought, all was well with their world.

He was sitting, rocking, in a large canvas contraption, deep in the garden, wondering where he had mislaid his wife, when he saw two very dirty boys get down from a ragged pony and sprint across the lawn.

Damn gypsies! He thought and was annoyed that he hadn't managed to drive every last one of them out of his borough.

He was rather shocked to find, a few moments later, that a footman was leading these two ragamuffins in his direction.

Three months apiece, he thought as they drew closer and was about to pass sentence when the footman spoke.

"These lads have a message for you, sir."

"For me?"

The boys spoke alternately, in a tumble, "Reverend Jones is dying . . ." "You must come . . ." "Morgan said . . ." "Everybody's there . . ." "The Sergeant too . . ." "He's really dying . . ."

"The Reverend? Dying?" said Jones The JP. He was shocked. Reverend Jones wasn't the kind of person to die. He was built of sterner stuff. He'd expected him to go on for at least another half century. "Dying? Where?"

"Up Ffynnon Garw," the boys said together.

"I can't possibly go up there, at this time of night!" He might have added "in my condition."

But the boys were not to be dissuaded. They had been entrusted with a job. They each grabbed an arm and started to pull him from his chair, "You have to!" they said.

The boys rode in front. Jones the JP's coachman, who had also had a little too much to drink with a young maid-servant at the wedding, followed the boy's lead with equal abandon. They clattered through the country lanes at an extraordinary pace, and if Jones The JP had been less drunk, he'd have had the wherewithal to slow his man down. As it was he was so inebriated that he sat in the back, his mouth wide in astonishment, catching flies.

Things only worsened when he arrived at the lemonade stand. He was met by a group of strong miners who further pushed, pulled and tugged him to the top of Ffynnon Garw. He moaned all the way. One minute he'd been happily lazy, taking in the evening air in a peaceful garden, the next he found himself atop Ffynnon Garw, surrounded by a group of villagers who were covered, from head to foot, in mud.

Eventually he was thrust before Morgan, much as a vassal would have been hurled before a king at a medieval court.

"What's all this nonsense?" he asked as he tried to catch his breath.

"You can consecrate ground can't you?" said Morgan more as a statement than a question.

Jones The JP thought for a moment, consecrate ground? "Yes, of course" he said angrily, "but . . ."

"But nothing," said Morgan, "you'll consecrate this mound as fit to receive the body of Reverend Jones."

"The Reverend is dead?"

Morgan pointed to his body. He was wrapped in a clean sheet. Even as they spoke the village undertaker was dusting down a casket.

"But there must be some proof of death," said Jones The JP, "a person can't just be buried . . ."

"The Sergeant verified death, isn't that so?" said Morgan and Thomas nodded.

"I haven't issued a death certificate yet, but I can do that later," he added.

"Of course you can," said Morgan, "now come on! We're in a hurry! Consecrate the ground man!"

Jones The JP dug in his heels, "Look, Morgan, this is absurd . . ."

Morgan cut him off with a look. He came closer, and looking deep into Jones' eye he threatened him. "If you don't do as the Reverend requested," said Morgan, "he'll come back and haunt you."

Jones The JP shivered, yes, he could imagine Reverend Jones haunting his life. It was a chilling thought.

The last rays of sunlight were dusting the peak of Ffynnon Garw as Jones The JP, in an improvized statement, consecrated the ground. By the time the Reverend's casket was lowered into the mound that he had inspired, on the mountain that he loved, the sun had fallen from the sky. Ivor and the Sergeant looked towards Anson who was surveying the horizon with his telescope. Anson looked back at them and shook his head—it was too late for a measurement.

In the gathering twilight Morgan climbed to the top of the mound.

"I can't really speak for Reverend Jones," he began, "and I'm sure that I'm the last person he would want to give a testimonial at his funeral. However, these are unusual circumstances which we will have to put right at another time, at a proper service . . ." His voice faltered, he was searching for the appropriate phrase.

"However, the fact that I didn't exactly get on with the Reverend Jones, and the fact that Reverend Jones didn't get along with me doesn't mean that I didn't appreciate him. And I'll miss him . . ." He pulled himself together, "So, I think we should all take our hats off," he looked around and saw that all had already taken their hats off, "and pray our own prayers for this man who has given his life—and his very body come to that—to this *mountain*."

He scowled at Anson as he said "mountain." "And then I think the Sergeant should lead you all in a hymn."

The light was falling fast so that a miner quickly improvized torches from spars of timber that had been used earlier to shore up the mound.

And so by the light of flaming torches the Sergeant led the village in a funeral hymn. It could have been a scene from centuries earlier, from Ancient Briton, from the time of their Druidic ancestors. A tribe, gathered around a burial mound, singing a song of thanks and homage to a leader who had fallen.

When it concluded there was a moment of anti-climactic silence, and without a word the villagers slowly began the descent of Ffynnon Garw.

But Morgan, the Twps, Ivor and the Policeman paused to speak to Anson.

"So you're taking the first train out in the morning?" said Morgan.

Anson nodded, he couldn't look Morgan in the eye, "Yes, I'm afraid so . . ."

There was an uncomfortable silence. The wind roared through their torches.

"Well," said Sergeant Thomas, "we gave it a damn good try."

All nodded in agreement. The Sergeant continued, "And if it hadn't been for the Reverend . . ."

Morgan interrupted him, "If it hadn't been for the Reverend it wouldn't have been built in the first place."

"You're right there," agreed the Sergeant.

The villagers started to break away, leaving Anson. Betty hovered in the background.

Anson hated to see the failure in their eyes. Their shoulders had fallen, they all looked stooped and beaten.

"It will be measured again," he called after them, "perhaps we'll even come back here on our return journey . . ."

The villagers nodded, but kept on walking, knowing Anson was being polite.

Betty broke her silence, her voice was angry, hurt, "You won't be back," she said, "this isn't the sort of place that people like you come back to."

"I'll try," said Anson, "I'll really try."

Betty's voice rose, "I'll try? Is that the best you can do?"

Morgan stopped in his tracks, he'd heard Betty use that tone of voice with him. The others stopped with Morgan, all curious to hear what Betty would say next.

She was in full flood now, almost yelling at Anson, "After all they've done?" she said, "After all this work? How would you like them to say it failed because of you?"

Ah, Betty, thought Morgan, I may have lost her affection, but it's good to see that she's taken part of me with her . . .

Anson stammered, he didn't have a solution, he didn't know what could be done, after all it was night! "What am I supposed to do?" he asked, bewildered by her anger, "Wait up here until the first light of dawn, measure, then rush back to the village and pack and . . ."

Thomas Twp interrupted, it was summer, "The sun will be up at five," he pointed out.

Anson looked towards the villagers, and then back to Betty.

Betty gave him a half smile and dropped her voice, "That's only a few hours away," she said, "and I'd keep you company."

She may have dropped her voice, but all the villagers heard her. And there wasn't a man among them who wouldn't have wished for Betty to say that to him.

Anson's torch fluttered, "We-ell," he vacillated but quickly made up his mind, "if it is only a few hours away, and we have come this far, and they have done all this work, I mean it seems a shame, perhaps I should stay . . ."

As one the villagers wished them goodnight and quickly stole away leaving them alone on the mountain . . .

When Morgan arrived back in the village he noticed Blod standing on the other side of the square, staring up into space. His view of the mountain was blocked by the pub, so Morgan couldn't see what Blod was watching: she could see the figures of Anson and Betty, moving closer together. So Betty was out of the way . . . Blod smiled, once again Morgan might be hers.

Morgan thought Blod might have been waiting for him.

"Fancy a drink, Blod?" he asked, even though it was Sunday and way past closing.

Blod gave him such a big smile that he was sure she'd agree. "It had better be a mountain, Morgan," was all she said before drifting off into the dark.

The old bugger can wait one more night for me, she thought.

Morgan stepped dolefully into the pub and was shocked to find George Garrad sitting behind the bar, pouring himself a drink. The old sot was still in his pyjamas. A cigarette dangled from his lip. He hadn't shaved. There were several dirty glasses, an empty bottle of gin and Garrad was working his way through a pint of port.

He hiccupped and cast a bleary eye at Morgan, "It's Sunday, I think," he gasped, "so I imagine they're all in chapel." He waved at the selection of drinks behind him, "And what's yours?" he asked.

—∞—

What happened when a beautiful, fiery young Welsh woman spent a night on Ffynnon Garw with a quiet, well-mannered Englishman? We will never know, but you may remember that the Welsh have strong beliefs about those who spent nights on Holy Mountains, and if Ffynnon Garw wasn't a Holy Mountain before, it most surely was now.

The Welsh say that anyone who spends a night on Cader Idris will return a wise man, a madman or a poet. And for those who spend a night on Ffynnon Garw?

While the whole village was exhausted that night, hardly anyone went to bed. People collapsed fully clothed onto sofas and into armchairs. Some slept fitfully but many whiled away the pre-dawn hours fretting about the result of Anson's measurement.

By half-past five people were drifting into the village square, all asking one another if Anson and Betty had returned, if there was a result. By six o'clock almost all the village had reassembled. Not a miner reported for work that morning. Not a letter or pint of milk was delivered. The baker's oven remained cold, every stable in the village remained closed.

A group of children were despatched to the lower slopes to report if Anson and Betty were in sight and they returned excitedly. Yes, they were returning—the children giggled. And—asked their parents? The children giggled again— Anson and Betty were walking hand in hand . . .

Yes, when Anson and Betty returned that day it was to announce that Ffynnon Garw was a mountain of one thousand and two feet—and that they were engaged to be married.

All day, that day, the silver band played in the square. Elderly men danced with young girls, elderly women flirted with young boys, and everyone danced with Anson and Betty. Morgan passed beer through the front windows of the pub and all celebrated until they passed out. It has been said that if a horse and cart had driven through the square that night it would have killed half of the population who were sleeping—where they had eventually fallen—in the street.

George Garrad did not get the eight o'clock train that morning, but he did manage the five o'clock that afternoon. And instead of travelling north he finally did travel east—as Thomas The Trains had imagined—back to London, in search of a new partner.

He did not return to Wales and thus Garrad's ambition of publishing the definitive map of Wales was never achieved. His one and only contribution to British map making was the inclusion of Ffynnon Garw—on all of His Majesty's maps—as a mountain.

Many rumours have spread about Garrad but none have been substantiated. Some have him back in Africa, others in India or the Sudan. I think it's rather more likely that he never left England again. I've always imagined that he immediately retired to that place that he loved so much: that very flat area called East Anglia.

Anson and Betty were married within the month and

Anson took the post left vacant by Davies The School, who left the village in a fit of pique.

I suppose I must be a bit slow, because I didn't register certain facts when my grandfather related this story. It was only the next day, for example, when I went to school, that it dawned on me that Mrs. Anson—the middle-aged, grey-haired lady who taught me Geography—was Betty From Cardiff.

I was never able to look at her again without blushing.

EPILOGUE

I mentioned that three photographs exist from the hill build, but have only described two. The third photograph was actually taken some years later, yes *years*.

It seems that about five years later Tommy Twostroke, who was now the proud owner of a motorcycle and side-car, became hopelessly lost and was forced to buy a brand new map. He didn't notice, but his eldest son did: there it was in the new edition: Ffynnon Garw—mountain—1002ft.

Before long every villager had a framed copy in their home and on a hot summer Sunday the whole village climbed the mountain in all their finery and posed for a photograph on the tump. I love this photograph, partly because it is a record of some of my family and the parents of my friends, but partly because there is a wonderful naivety about it since the whole village manages, by their presence, to obscure the very tump that they are celebrating.

—∞—

And for those of you who think that this is just a shaggy-dog story, told by a senile old man to his all-too-gullible grandson, I'd ask you to come to South Wales, to the village where I was born.

The area has changed drastically even since my childhood: the railway line has been replaced by a busy road, a motorway skirts the edge of the valley. A housing estate covers the field where the dog-racing was held. Another housing estate covers the small lake that fed the canal. The old rugby pitch has been concreted over for a new school—which would, no doubt, have given Davies some joy. The river bank is now a car park.

In my childhood there was still a coal mine in the village, and one in every other village between here and Merthyr, but the mining has since gone. The landscape is almost unrecognizable as "progress" has eaten into the area.

But one thing remains unchanged and unspoilt: they have failed to build on the mountains. So come to Cardiff and drive north, take the road that winds through Llandaff, and as you do, look out for the first big hill, not just a hill but a mountain.

From even five miles away you can see it—no, I don't mean the mountain, you can see that from much farther—but on a clear day, even from Cardiff you can see a small protuberance, at that distance it looks like a nipple, but as you get closer you'll see that it's the tump, the man-made tump that edged this from a hill into a mountain.

I knew the tump before I knew the story. We accepted it as part of the mountain and every year at Easter the village would trek there on Good Friday to eat their "hot cross buns". And I knew the area of rocks as the "Lemonade Stand" before I ever knew how the place had gained its name.

Walk up the mountain and as you do imagine that you are carrying a heavy bucket. And when you reach the mound imagine a line of people stretching from you to the valley below—each and every one of them with a bucketful of earth. I can assure you that the size of the mound and the distances involved will surprise you, it will all be bigger than you imagined.

Go up, walk on the mound itself, feel the tons of work beneath your feet. But, remember to walk respectfully—for you are walking on sacred ground—on a prayer made manifest in soil.

Not just a mound but a memorial.

And not just a hill, but a mountain.